THE
PARIS
HOURS

ALSO BY ALEX GEORGE

A Good American

Setting Free the Kites

THE
PARIS
HOURS

Alex George

FLATIRON
BOOKS
NEW YORK

THE PARIS HOURS. Copyright © 2020 by Alex George. All rights reserved. Printed in the United States of America. For information, address Flatiron Books, 120 Broadway, New York, NY 10271.

Designed by Michelle McMillian

ISBN 9781250307187

For Hallam

Contents

For, while the tale of how we suffer, and how we are delighted, and how we may triumph is never new, it always must be heard. There isn't any other tale to tell, it's the only light we've got in all this darkness.

—James Baldwin, "Sonny's Blues"

1

Stitches

THE ARMENIAN WORKS BY the light of a single candle. His tools lie in front of him on the table: a spool of cotton, a square of fabric, haberdasher's scissors, a needle.

The flame flickers, and shadows leap across the walls of the tiny room, dancing ghosts. Souren Balakian folds the fabric in half, checks that the edges align exactly, and then he picks up the scissors. He feels the resistance beneath his fingers as the steel blades bite into the material. He always enjoys this momentary show of defiance before he gives the gentlest of squeezes, and the scissors cut through the doubled-up fabric. He eases the blades along familiar contours, working by eye alone. He has done this so many times, on so many nights, there is no need to measure a thing. Torso, arms, neckline—this last cut wide, to accommodate the outsized head.

When he has finished, there are two identical shapes on the table in front of him. He sweeps the unused scraps of cloth onto the floor, and picks up the needle and thread. After the sundering, reconstitution. Holding the two pieces of material in perfect alignment, he pushes the tip of the needle through both layers of fabric, and pulls the thread tight. He works with ferocious deliberation, as if it is his very life that he is stitching back together. He squints, careful to keep the stitches evenly spaced. When he is finished, he breaks the thread with a sharp twist of his fingers and holds the garment up in the half-light. A small grunt of satisfaction.

Night after night Souren sits at this bench and sews a new tunic. By the end of the day it will be gone, a cloud of gray ash blowing in the wind, and then he will sit down and create another.

He lays the completed costume on the work surface and stands up. He surveys the ranks of sightless eyes that stare unblinking into the room. Rows of hooks have been hammered into the wall. A wooden hand puppet hangs from every one. There are portly kings and beautiful princesses. There are brave men with dangerous eyes, and a haggard witch with warts on her ugly chin. There are cherubic children, their eyes too wide and innocent for this motley group. There is a wolf.

This ragtag crowd is Souren's family now.

He unhooks a young boy called Hector and carries him to the table. He pulls the newly sewn tunic over Hector's head. He turns the puppet toward him and examines his handiwork. Hector is a handsome fellow, with a button nose and rosy cheeks. The tunic fits him well. The puppet performs a small bow and waves at him.

"Ah, Hector," whispers Souren sadly. "You are always so happy to see me, even when you know what is to come." He looks up at the clock on the wall. It is a few hours past midnight. The new day has already begun.

Each evening Souren battles sleep for as long as he can. He works long into the night, applying fresh coats of paint to the puppets and sewing new clothes for them by candlelight. He stays at his workbench until his eyes are so heavy that he can no longer keep them open. But there is only so long he can fight the inevitable. His beloved puppets cannot protect him from the demons that pursue him through the darkest shadows of the night.

His dreams always come for him in the end.

2

A Rude Awakening

RAT-A-TAT-TAT.

Guillaume Blanc sits up in his bed, his heart smashing against his ribs, his breath quick, sharp, urgent. He stares at the door, waiting for the next angry tattoo.

The whispered words he heard through the door scream at him now: Three days.

Rat-a-tat-tat.

His shoulders slump. There is nobody knocking, not this time. The noise is coming from somewhere closer. Guillaume turns and squints through the window above the bed. The first blush of early morning sunlight smears the sky. From up here on the sixth floor, the rooftops of the city stretch out beneath him, a glinting cornucopia of slate and glass, a tapestry of cupolas and towers. There is the culprit: a woodpecker, richly plumed in blue and yellow, perched halfway up the window frame. It is staring beadily at the wood, as if trying to remember what it is supposed to do next.

Rat-a-tat-tat.

It is early, too early for anything good.

The shock of adrenaline subsides enough for Guillaume to register that his temples are pounding. He rolls over, spies a glass of cloudy water on the floor next to the bed, and drinks it thirstily. He rubs a dirty palm against his forehead. An ocean of pain to drown in. An empty wine bottle lies on its side in the middle of the small room. He stole it from the back of Madame Cuillasse's kitchen cupboard when he staggered in last night. It was covered in dust and long forgotten, not even good enough for her *coq au vin*, but by then Guillaume was too drunk to care.

Rat-a-tat-tat.

It feels as if the woodpecker is perched on the tip of Guillaume's nose and is jabbing its sharp little beak right between his eyes. It's typical of his luck, he reflects. The bird has no business in the dirty, narrow streets of Montmartre. It should be flying free with its brothers and sisters in the Bois de Boulogne, hammering joyfully away at tree trunks, rather than attacking the window frame of Guillaume's studio. And yet here it is.

Rat-a-tat-tat.

The woodpecker's head is a ferocious blur, then perfectly still again. What goes through its head, Guillaume wonders, during those moments of contemplative silence? Is the woodpecker asking itself: who am I, really, if I am not pecking wood? Am I, God forbid, just a *bird*?

Three days.

Guillaume lets out a small moan. There are lightning bolts erupting behind his eyes. He casts his mind back to the previous night. He was wandering through Montmartre, anxiously trying to outpace his problems, when he had seen Emile Brataille sitting alone in the bar at the end of his street. Brataille is an art dealer who spends most of his time at the *zinc* of the Closerie des Lilas, schmoozing with collectors and artists, striking deals, and skimming his fat commission off every painting he sells. He has no business in Montmartre anymore: all the painters whose work hangs on the walls of his palatial gallery on Boulevard Raspail have left Guillaume's *quartier* for the leafy boulevards of Montparnasse, where the wine is better, the oysters fatter, and the women more beautiful. Guillaume pushed open the door and slid onto the chair next to Brataille.

The alcohol lingers sluggishly in his veins. How much had they drunk, in the end?

After they were three or four carafes to the good, Emile Brataille made his mournful confession: he'd come to Montmartre to declare his love for Thérèse, but she wanted nothing to do with him. And so here he was, drowning his sorrows.

Thérèse is a prostitute who works at the corner of Rue des Abbesses and Rue Ravignan, next to Le Chat Blanc. Guillaume knows her, albeit not professionally: he has painted her many times. Lubricated by the wine, he embellished this acquaintance into a devoted friendship, and suggested to Brataille that he might be able to intercede on his behalf. At this, the art dealer began to weep drunken tears of gratitude. How can I ever repay you? he asked. Guillaume scratched his chin. I don't suppose you know any rich, art-loving Americans, he said.

Brataille began to laugh.

And so a deal was struck. Guillaume would talk to Thérèse, and in return Brataille would send some rich foreigners his way. And who knew what might come of that? Miracles happened: that sozzled goat Soutine had convinced an American doctor to buy every damn painting he'd ever made. Guillaume raised his glass toward the art dealer, a man he did not particularly like, and with every swallow of wine the way forward became more beautifully clear. His drunken imagination hurtled headlong toward a future of fame and untold riches.

He does not remember staggering home.

His euphoria has not survived the night.

That whispered voice through the door. *Three days*.

Today is the third day.

3

Rhapsody

JEAN-PAUL MAILLARD CLOSES his eyes and dreams of America.

The needle touches the spinning vinyl with the gentlest sigh of static.

He listens, spellbound.

That clarinet! The first low trill, fat with promise—then the solo ascent to the heavens, soaring smoothly through the registers. By the time that ecstatic high note, limpid and beautiful, pours into his ears, Jean-Paul has made his escape.

He sweeps through the open window onto Rue Barbette and hurtles down the cobbled streets of the Marais, streaking westward across the city. In a moment he is flying over the dark waters of the Atlantic.

The music beckons him on.

He soars high over the city's skyscrapered silhouette, his for the taking. He hears the rumble of the Harlem-bound A train in the orchestra's propulsive rhythms, low and sweet. He hears new worlds in the piano's blistering, arpeggiated attacks. Images streak past like the onrushing traffic hurtling down the arrow-straight avenues. Perfect lines of shimmying, high-kicking chorus girls, their cherry-red lips glistening in the spotlights. A liveried doorman striding onto the busy street, his hand outstretched for a yellow cab. Elegant matrons pushing through the door at Bergdorf's.

Sharp-dressed men with two-tone shoes, hats pulled down low, huddled close on a street corner.

When Jean-Paul Maillard dreams of America, he dreams of New York City.

But those dazzling syncopations do not last forever. The music ends, and the spell is broken. Reluctantly, Jean-Paul opens his eyes. America has retreated, as it always does, and his shabby French apartment remains. He looks around. The place used to be so bright and tidy, so clean. Now every surface is coated with a patina of ancient dust. The wallpaper is staging a slow escape from the walls. A dark brown stain has annexed a corner of the ceiling. The gramophone is still going around. The silence is gently punctuated by the soft, rhythmic bump of the needle against the spinning vinyl, as regular as a tiny heartbeat. He does not get up to switch it off. He likes the sound.

Jean-Paul looks at the dim morning light creeping across the apartment window. It's been years since he has slept through the night. In the early hours of every morning his ruined leg drags him from sleep. Then he sits in his armchair, listens to George Gershwin, and thinks about the lights of Manhattan.

The first Americans he met were soldiers. Assigned to report on foreign troops who had come to France to fight in the war, he had visited a military hospital where wounded men were recuperating. Their bodies were ruined, but they were bafflingly cheerful. These young men were from places Jean-Paul had never heard of—Maine, Missouri, Montana—on the first grand adventure of their lives. Fighting for freedom on foreign soil— what could be more exciting than that? They were so tall, so handsome, so unencumbered by doubt. Not even their injuries could eclipse these men's belief in their own marvelous destiny. Jean-Paul was trapped by his memories of the slaughter on the battlefields to the north, but the Americans turned effortlessly away from all that, distracted by what the future held.

When Jean-Paul Maillard thinks of America, he thinks of hope.

Hope: those young soldiers built whole worlds in their heads while they convalesced in their hospital beds. They dreamed of money, of cars, and of love—but mostly of money. *Le rêve américain* scrolled unstoppably across their febrile imaginations. They spun futures for themselves, elaborate edifices of unlikely fantasy, buttressed against dour reality by the force of their young wills. They did not care how improbable it all was. Optimism on such a cosmic scale was an art. And those wounded cadets were no fluke: the whole country seems to possess a magnificent, perplexing talent for it. There's none of the world-weary cynicism that flattens the people of tired, ancient France; America is too callow to know any better. So, of course, Jean-Paul is in love with the place. He knows all about slim chances. He's been playing diminishing odds ever since Easter Sunday 1918.

With a grimace, he hauls himself to his feet. His knee crackles in bright agony. By now he should have discovered some warped comfort in the brutal familiarity of the pain, but every morning it still draws a gasp of fresh dismay from his lips. He hobbles toward the bathroom.

It is time to begin another day.

4

Ritual and Remembrance

THE WOMAN AND HER DAUGHTER walk out of the Métro station and stop for a moment at the top of the steps. The woman stares into the cloudless blue sky. When they had left the hotel earlier, the streets of Saint-Germain were washed in pale predawn light. Now the sun is shining brightly. It is going to be a warm day.

There is a café on the other side of Boulevard de Ménilmontant, empty at this hour save for one or two early risers, hunched over steaming cups of coffee, and a waiter polishing glasses behind the counter. The buttery smell of freshly baked croissants floats by on the morning breeze. The girl grips a slim posy of camellias. In contrast to the beauty of the morning, her face is a thundercloud. The woman looks down at her daughter's pinched scowl, and—not for the first time—regrets insisting that she come along this morning. For a moment she contemplates abandoning the whole enterprise. She can always come back later, on her own.

The girl points across the road. "Can I have a croissant?" she asks.

It's a miracle, thinks the woman, how the young can distill so much sullen resentment into five simple words. She feels a fresh resolve, a stiffening of the spine. "No, Marie," she says sharply. "No croissant. Come along."

The sigh that follows is equal parts fury and triumph. Of *course* there was to be no croissant.

At this hour Avenue Gambetta is deserted but for a flock of pigeons that peck idly at the sidewalk. The pair walk up the hill in silence. The high walls of the cemetery cast the street into shadow. The place will not open for another few hours, but there is a small gate in the northwest corner, half hidden behind a crumbling wall, that is never manned and never locked.

"I still don't understand why you put flowers on the grave," says the girl, for perhaps the tenth time that morning.

"Because, *ma chérie*, that is how we honor the dead."

"It's not as if he will know they're there."

"Perhaps not. But everyone else who visits his grave will see them."

Another incredulous sigh. "Who visits his grave except you?"

"I think you'd be surprised."

Marie is silent. She is never surprised. She is ten years old. She knows everything.

The gate, at last. The woman looks up and down the street, and then steps inside, ushering her daughter in ahead of her.

At this time of day the cemetery is the most peaceful place in Paris. There are no slump-shouldered mourners traipsing between the tombstones on their meandering trails of sorrow. The birds have not yet begun their day of song. Even the leaves are motionless in the trees.

A sea of crypts and mausoleums crests the hill in front of them. The woman looks at the wave of polished marble that shimmers in the morning sun. The cemetery is its own city, with neighborhoods and thoroughfares, permanent residents and visitors. She sets off down the gravel path. Marie follows, her sighs reaching a quiet crescendo of outrage.

Just once, thinks the woman sadly. I wanted her to come just once. I wanted her to understand.

She strides ahead, not stopping to read the epitaphs of strangers or to admire the grand family memorials of Parisian aristocrats. She walks past the ranks of weeping stone angels without a second glance.

"*Maman!*" gasps Marie, struggling to keep up. "Wait for me!"

But she will not wait.

Finally she reaches her destination, an elegant rectangle of black marble, with simple gold lettering:

MARCEL PROUST

1871–1922

That is all. Amid these elaborate bids for immortality, not so much as a modest "*écrivain*."

Nineteen twenty-two, she thinks. Five years already, she's been coming here.

Her daughter arrives behind her, out of breath. She has been running. She does not want to be alone in the cemetery.

"Look, Marie. You see? Someone else *has* been here." A handful of irises has been scattered across the tomb, but the flowers have withered and died, their petals a sorry mosaic of faded lavender. The woman sweeps them away. She takes the camellias from her daughter and arranges them on the marble.

Then Camille Clermont kneels down in front of the tombstone of her dead employer, and begins to weep. She turns away from her daughter, but too late.

"*Maman,*" whispers Marie. "What's wrong?" At the sight of her mother's tears, the child's hostility has evaporated. Now she is worried, solicitous, scared, and this makes Camille cry harder still.

"I miss him, Marie," she says. "I miss him every day."

"Was he a nice man?"

"Oh yes. He was very nice. Very kind. I wish you could have known him better." She smiles down at her daughter. "But he thought children were best enjoyed at a distance."

"He didn't have children himself?"

"Goodness, no." Camille laughs and shakes her head. "He had the characters in his books, though. They were his children, I suppose."

"Did you love him?" asks Marie.

"Very much."

"More than *papa*?"

"Oh no. Never more than *papa*. And in a very different way."

"Different how?"

"It's more like you and Irène."

Marie's eyes grow big. "He was your best friend?"

"In some ways. We shared secrets, just like you and Irène. We told each other things nobody else knew." She pauses. "That's why I come and put flowers on his grave. I come to say hello, and to tell him that I miss him, and to say thank you for his friendship."

And, she thinks but does not say, to tell him that I'm sorry for my betrayal. And to forgive him for his.

Marie nods. "I would put flowers on Irène's grave, too."

Camille takes her daughter's hand. "Come on," she says. "Perhaps it's time for that croissant."

5

Passacaille I

EVERY MORNING THE PIANO rescues Souren Balakian from his dreams.

The same low notes gently tug him away from everything that he has left behind. The ghosts that haunt his sleep are chased away by the music floating up through the floor from the studio below. He opens his eyes.

The workbench on the other side of the room. The empty stares of the puppets on the wall. A small gasp of relief escapes his lips.

His head falls back onto the pillow as the music washes over him.

The first theme emerges from the depths of the piano, no more than a whisper. Souren hears a heavy melancholy in the stately procession of low, single notes. Every morning he wonders what the composer has lived through, to have drawn such sadness out of himself.

And then, through the dark clouds, a shaft of brilliant sunlight. A new melody emerges, high and clear and heartbreaking. This is what Souren waits for. The tune cleaves the gathering shadows and wraps itself brightly around his heart.

Those first brooding tones retreat, but they do not vanish. Now the music is two intertwined melodic lines, one low, one high, one sad, one full of hope. They meet and diverge, echoing each other, dual counterpoints of darkness and light. Sometimes they come together in sweet harmony; sometimes not.

Finally, the music resolves back to its first theme, that simple, forlorn elegy. The pianist's left hand stretches down the keyboard into ever-lower registers, until there are no more keys to be pressed, no more notes to be played.

Silence crowds in.

Souren lies still, staring up at the ceiling. From the room below comes the scrape of a piano stool. A moment later, the same low notes echo up once more through the floor. He listens to the piece a second time, then a third.

This is the only music the invisible pianist ever plays. There are no scales, no taxing etudes. Every morning he comes to his studio and performs the same tune over and over again.

When Souren sees his neighbor from downstairs in the hallway, the two men exchange polite nods, but they have never spoken a word to each other. The musician is a short, middle-aged man, always impeccably dressed. From his perfectly combed hair to the tips of his polished shoes, he projects an aura of unruffled elegance, but Souren knows better. His solitary repertoire betrays a quiet unraveling within.

Souren knows the comfort of the familiar all too well: like the pianist, he gives one identical performance after another. He tells the same stories, day after day. This is how he survives. That is why later on today he will pack up his puppets and cross the city to his usual spot in the Jardin du Luxembourg, beneath the chestnut trees. Then he will wait for the children to come.

The sound of the piano continues to float up through the floor. The melody breaches his defenses and buries itself inside him. He feels the mournful pulse of those low notes deep in his bones. The music quickens his blood, and he thinks of Thérèse—her soft body beneath his, her red mouth on his. He has not seen her in months. If the audience is generous today, perhaps he'll pay her a visit this evening.

There is the gentlest knock as the lid of the piano closes.

Souren moves to the window and looks down onto the street. In front of the apartment building there is a small fountain. An unsteady trickle of water emerges from the top of the stone column at its center. Beneath the fountain's surface is a carpet of coins, tossed in by superstitious passersby. From Souren's window they catch the reflection of the early morning sun, winking up at him.

After a moment the pianist appears. He walks past the fountain and crosses to the opposite sidewalk. He is wearing a perfectly cut gray overcoat and an elegant hat. There is a dark flash of color, a silk scarf, at his throat. He leans forward as he walks, as if he is heading into a strong wind.

This man's music has become part of Souren's mornings, as essential as the sun rising over the rooftops of the city. The familiar melody offers him a moment of quiet grace, and this gives him strength for the day ahead. The pianist knows nothing of this, of course. He plays only for himself. Souren wonders how the arc of the man's own days is changed by creating such beauty each morning. He watches as the pianist makes his lonely way down the street. The man looks tired, defeated. He does not play for joy, thinks Souren. He plays for survival.

The silence that follows is almost as sweet as the music it replaces. Souren sits down at his table, languishing in the space left behind by the piano's notes.

Then comes a lovely echo: a woman's voice, low and warm and rich. A second voice joins in, higher and sweeter than the first. The singers navigate the piano's melody in perfect unison. A song without words. Gone is the tune's melancholy. Now the music is reborn, full of life and bursting with hope.

Souren clears a space at one end of the table and lays out two plates. He unwraps a small parcel of heavy wax paper. Inside is a wedge of pale cheese, its rind a dusty gray. He bends down and sniffs. I've found a new one for you, Augustin told him last night when he stopped in at the *fromagerie* on Rue des Martyrs. A Saint-Nectaire, from the Auvergne. I think you'll like it. Souren places the Saint-Nectaire between the two plates, and waits.

A few minutes later, there is a knock on his door.

Standing in the corridor is a young girl. She is wearing a blue tunic and has long, dark hair. Big gray eyes gaze up at him.

"You'll never guess what!" says the girl at once.

"*Bonjour*, Arielle. What?" Even after all these years, Souren's French is awkward and cautious. It is a language, he has discovered, fat with grammatical and idiomatic peculiarities. Even the simplest sentence contains traps for the unwary. At least he knows that his young visitor will not judge him for his mistakes.

"*Maman* has agreed to take me to the Jardin du Luxembourg today. *Enfin!*"

Souren smiles at her. "That's very good news."

"I'm finally going to see your puppet show!"

"I like our little shows here," says Souren. "They remind me of a girl I used to know. Her name was Amandine."

"It's not the same, though," says Arielle. "I can see you, for one thing. And that's not right."

Souren inclines his head, conceding the point: seeing him is not right. He gestures for her to enter. "We have something new to try today."

Arielle sits down at the table and looks at the cheese in front of her. "*Qu'est-ce que c'est?*"

"It's called Saint-Nectaire," says Souren, as he cuts two slices and puts one on each plate. "Tell me what you think."

They eat the cheese in silence.

"It's not as smelly as some of the other ones," says Arielle. "May I have some more?"

Souren cuts them both another slice and then turns to the wall of puppets. "*Alors*, who do you choose today?"

Arielle considers for a moment. "Those two." She points to a young boy and a handsome knight. Souren takes the puppets off their hooks. He sits back down. Arielle eats her cheese and waits.

All of a sudden the puppets burst into life from beneath the tabletop. The knight is regal, serene. The boy, in contrast, flies back and forth along the edge of the table. He wants to become the knight's apprentice. He begs, he implores. Arielle watches, rapt. If you wish to be my page, says the knight, you must prove your loyalty and your bravery. Of course, of course, agrees the boy at once. And how do I do that?

Just then there is a knock on the door. Souren breathes a sigh of relief. Sometimes when he begins a story he knows how it will end, and sometimes he does not.

"Come in," he calls.

The door opens and a woman steps into the room. She smiles at them both. "How is the cheese today?" she asks.

"*Maman*, you're interrupting the story again!" complains Arielle.

Her mother looks unperturbed. "Oh, Saint-Nectaire! How delicious!" She picks up a crumb of cheese off her daughter's plate and pops it into her mouth. "We have some grocery shopping to do this morning, Arielle. Perhaps we'll buy some for ourselves."

"I heard you both singing this morning," says Souren.

"Oh, I hope we didn't disturb you!"

"Not at all. I love to hear you sing."

The woman smiles. "It's a beautiful melody, *n'est ce pas?*"

"I hope he will always play that tune," agrees Souren.

"I'm sure he will, until he writes something else."

Souren frowns, unsure he has understood correctly. "Until he writes—?"

"Didn't you know? He's not really a pianist. He'd be the first person to tell you that. He says his hands are too small."

Souren thinks of the elegantly dressed man and his well-manicured fingers. "He sounds like a pianist to me."

She shakes her head. "He's a *composer*. His name is Maurice Ravel."

Souren has never heard of him.

"*En tout cas*, they say that he has not written a note for months. He comes here instead, to his studio, and plays the same piece every day." The woman pauses. "Can you imagine how it must feel, to be put on earth to do one thing, and then not to be able to do it?"

Souren remembers the man's slumped shoulders as he walked down the street, away from his piano. "Perhaps that is why the music is so sad," he says.

The woman bends down and kisses the top of her daughter's head. "Did Arielle tell you that we're coming to the Jardin du Luxembourg this afternoon?"

"She may have mentioned it," says Souren, grinning. From the edge of the tabletop, the knight performs a deep bow. "Arielle knows the puppets so well, but she'll see a very different show this afternoon." He nods at the knight and the little boy, who both appear to be listening closely to every word he says. "Nobody else has ever heard the stories I tell you here," he says to Arielle. "They are just for you."

"What kind of stories do you tell at the show?" asks Arielle.

He shrugs. "Some you will know, others you will not."

"Stories from where you came from?" guesses her mother.

Souren thinks of the new tunic for Hector's puppet that he sewed together in the small hours of that morning, and nods.

"Well, we can't wait!" She smiles. "And if that wasn't enough excitement, tonight I'm going to hear one of the greatest jazz musicians in the world play." At this Souren pulls a face. "You don't like jazz?" She laughs.

"Don't the musicians just play whatever notes they want?"

"Well, they improvise, yes, so every time it's different. But that's what makes it so sweet."

Souren points to the floor, at the invisible piano in the room below. "I like things the same each time."

"Oh, Souren! Where's your sense of adventure?"

He does not respond. He has left his sense of adventure behind him, far away from here.

6

A Promise Abandoned,
A Promise Delivered

THEY WILL TELL YOU that Alphonse Lecroq is the most handsome man in Paris. Tales fly around the city of his extraordinary beauty. Every woman he meets falls in love with him; many men, too, so the stories go. People whisper about his face as if it is a work of art more astonishing than *La Joconde*—and like the *Mona Lisa*, he is better known by a nickname: Le Miroir, because rumor has it that even he cannot pass any kind of reflective surface without admiring himself in it.

Guillaume Blanc stands on Rue Nicolet, watching the front door of the apartment building on the opposite side of the road. There is a small fountain on the sidewalk. A limp trickle of water splashes into its shallow stone dish. He shivers, despite the warmth of the early morning sun. He has been thinking about Alphonse Lecroq for three days.

He never wants to see the man's face, no matter how lovely it may be.

Le Miroir runs a network of crime and larceny that stretches across the capital, from rat-infested squats in Belleville to the lavish opulence of town houses in the 8th arrondissement. Mostly he peddles whores, guns, and dirty heroin, but he is not averse to blackmail and extortion of the affluent and influential when the opportunity arises. An army of ruffians and hoods, poisonous and violent, does his thuggish bidding.

As so often in Paris, beauty cannot be separated from its own mephitic stink.

Guillaume had no idea whom he was dealing with when, after making a few inquiries, he sat in a café across from a man with a narrow, rat-like face who pushed a grimy envelope of cash across the table toward him. A small loan, just a few hundred francs, enough to tide him over until his luck changed. Once the money was in his hands he barely listened as the man set out the terms of the loan. He hadn't eaten in days. All he could think about was the cassoulet he would soon be ordering at his favorite restaurant, and the half-bottle of something crisp and cold that would accompany it. He did not care about the preposterous rates of interest, compounded daily. He was not concerned about the promises of retribution that would be visited upon him if he failed to repay the money in a timely fashion. It would never come to that, not for him. He would sell more paintings soon enough.

That was two months ago. Guillaume has not sold more paintings, and now the money has gone. The day stipulated for repayment by the rat-faced man came and went. Soon after that, angry notes began to appear beneath his door, demanding ever-growing amounts—his original debt was quickly dwarfed by the ballooning interest. After a while he began to burn the notes in the grate without opening them. Then the hammering on his door began, at all hours of the day and night. Guillaume lay in his bed, too afraid to move or make a sound. He stayed awake, every bulb and candle extinguished, waiting for the menacing *clomp* of boots on the staircase.

Three nights ago, after the customary thump on the door, a man's voice rasped through the darkness.

"I know you're in there, *mon gars*." Guillaume felt the terrified prickle of ice in his veins. "But you can't run forever. You know that, don't you? Le Miroir won't let you make him look like a fool."

It was only then that Guillaume understood how much trouble he was in.

"With interest, penalties, and late fees, you owe twelve hundred francs," whispered the voice. "You've got three days. We'll leave you alone until then. But have the money ready when we come for it. Down to the last centime. *Au sérieux*." A pause. "Three days."

After a moment the footsteps retreated down the corridor. The voice did not say what would happen if he didn't have the money. There was no need.

Today his time is up, and he has six francs in his pocket. Enough, Guillaume thinks morosely, for a condemned man's last meal.

His hangover has worsened. Poison malingers in his veins. He watches the door on the other side of the street. If this is, indeed, to be his last day, he has come to bid a final, silent *adieu*.

Guillaume knows all the residents who live in the building across the street. The elderly couple, stiff-backed and regally slow. The pretty woman who leaves for work at precisely the same time each day, her heels clicking as she hurries toward the Métro. The young man with the black beard who appears every morning with a large suitcase in each hand and a fierce look in his eye. The small, immaculately dressed man who comes and goes frequently, never staying for long. Guillaume watches them all, but he is waiting for somebody else.

The next time the door opens, a woman with long hair the color of burnished copper appears, a young girl at her side. Guillaume breathes in sharply. There is a wicker basket on the woman's arm: they are going to the market. The girl is talking excitedly to her mother. She is wearing a new coat that Guillaume has not seen before. They turn and walk down Rue Nicolet. Guillaume longs to run after them, but he just watches them go, as he always does, and his heart performs its familiar tango of longing and regret.

Five minutes later, Guillaume is walking back toward his studio. He gazes at the familiar landmarks of the *quartier*, wondering if he will never see them again. How he has loved this place! He peers into the windows of his favorite shops, admiring their wares one last time.

Guillaume Blanc is no fool. He knows that if he stays in Paris, Le Miroir's thugs will hunt him down and kill him. And so this morning he will go to Gare Montparnasse and spend the last of his money on a train ticket back to his childhood home. La Rochelle is an old port town on the Atlantic coast. His parents, he reflects grimly, won't be surprised to see him. They've been expecting his return since the day he left. His father has enjoyed an undistinguished legal career writing wills for the town's aging population, and his mother's ambitions have never been loftier than a nicely kept home and a well-seasoned pot-au-feu. When Guillaume announced his intention to become a painter, they looked at their only child as if he'd sprouted an extra head. Such a bohemian aspiration was a personal affront to their own provincial, clamped-down lives, and they did not trouble to hide their feelings from him. Guillaume sighs, imagining his parents' sour satisfaction at his return, penniless and without prospects. The thought makes him briefly contemplate taking a train to Nice instead. The weather will be more pleasant there, for sure—but then he remembers the six francs in his pocket. With all those triumphant *I-told-you-sos* comes food and his childhood bed. It is a price he has no choice but to pay.

He walks slowly through the streets, reluctant to return to his studio. As he pushes open the door to the building, Madame Cuillasse is standing in the middle of the hallway, her lumberjack arms folded across her chest.

"There you are," says the concierge crossly. "I've been looking for you."

Are Le Miroir's men here already? "What is it?" asks Guillaume. "What's wrong?"

"Nothing's *wrong*, apart from the fact that I've just walked up six flights of stairs to deliver this to you, and you weren't there." She brandishes an envelope at him. "Apparently it's urgent."

Guillaume looks at the letter in her hand. The stationery is heavy, ivory-hued, expensive. His name is scrawled across the envelope in purple ink. He does not recognize the hand. It is not, he concludes from the purple ink, another demand for payment.

"Thank you," he says, putting the envelope into his pocket.

Madame Cuillasse stares at him with her small, suspicious eyes. She wrinkles her nose, smelling the alcohol seeping through his skin. "You don't know anything about a bottle of wine that disappeared from my kitchen last night, by any chance?"

"Absolutely not," says Guillaume, doing his best to look offended. The concierge stares at him for a long moment, and then turns to make her way back to her lair with a pointed harrumph. Guillaume walks up the stairs to the top of the building. He closes the door of the studio behind him and opens the envelope.

Blanc, you hound—

Dear God, I feel like a steaming pile of horseshit this morning. If there's any justice in this world, your hangover will be at least as bad as mine.

Anyway, look, I have some news. I've found your wealthy, art-loving American, just like you asked. She's a strange bird, fancies herself quite the connoisseur. The walls of her apartment on Rue de Fleurus are covered with decent stuff. Some Matisses, a few Cézannes. Her name is Gertrude Stein. Perhaps you've heard of her. I called her last night when I got home and talked about you. She'll be at your place this morning, at about 10 or so. Show her your best work and keep your fingers crossed.

Consider your back well and truly scratched, old son. No need to thank me—just make sure you uphold your end of the bargain with the lovely Thérèse.

E.B.

Guillaume reads the letter twice, blinking in astonishment. In the sober light of morning, he assumed that Emile Brataille had forgotten about their deal of the previous night, but the art dealer has made good on his promise.

He reads the letter a third time, his delight and disbelief growing with every word. Gertrude Stein! They say she possesses a limitless appetite for new art, and the means to finance such a habit. Guillaume's heart begins to race again. There is none of last night's drunken elation, but there is a

flicker of cautious hope. Suddenly he can see a possible way out of his pre-
dicament. Guillaume starts to make plans for this rich, gullible American:
he'll charm her, delight her, and then fleece her for every franc she's got.
By lunchtime he'll have enough money to pay off his debt and more to
spare. The prospect of a humiliating return to La Rochelle retreats. Perhaps he'll be able to stay in Paris after all.

He'll be able to watch the woman and her daughter walk down the
road again.

Guillaume closes his eyes, and pictures Gertrude Stein taking down a
Cézanne to make room for one of *his* paintings. Her guests will inquire
about it. She will confide in them, making them promise not to tell others
about this brilliant artist she has discovered.

But genius will out. Soon the world will come running to his door.

Then Guillaume thinks: this morning!

He looks around him. The room is a mess. He scrabbles through his
supplies, and swears. There are no nails. He'll have to prop the canvases
up against the walls and hope for the best. Perhaps the American will be
bewitched by the poverty in which he lives. She'll admire his struggle to
bring his art into the world. None of the exotic fripperies of those lazy
wastrels in Montparnasse here! He starts to pull his canvases into the middle of the room. He arranges them first one way, then another. Some on
the bed, others on the floor. The best ones he puts near the window, where
they will get the morning light.

There is a knock on the door.

Rat-a-tat-tat.

Guillaume looks at his watch. It is ten o'clock.

7

Ritual

JEAN-PAUL MAILLARD LIMPS THROUGH the gate of the small city park, as invisible as the air.

Two old men sit on a bench, a chessboard perched between them. They are hunched over the pieces, two small Rodins, each with a cigarette hanging from one corner of their mouths. They do not look up at the uneven crunch of Jean-Paul's footsteps on the gravel. A flock of pigeons swarms across the pathway in front of him, the birds' heads a bobbing sea of hopeful pecks. They ignore him as he approaches, and he does not want to disturb their frantic hunt for food; he maneuvers around them. Mothers stand sentry on the periphery of the well-manicured lawn, too busy watching their children play on the grass to notice Jean-Paul's heavy progress past the blooming banks of bougainvillea.

This is how he likes to live his life; to see, rather than to be seen.

There is a bandstand in the middle of the park. Jean-Paul has never heard music performed there. It is where he likes to sit. He chooses one of the empty metal chairs and arranges it just so. He lights a cigarette and pulls the smoke gratefully into his lungs. From his elevated perspective he can see most of what he wants to see—the benches, the grassy area, and the ornamental lake beyond, its surface a dark mirror.

It is early. He can still taste the coffee he slung back at the *zinc* of the small café on Rue de Bretagne. He's been coming here so long that he no longer needs to order; his espresso is already brewing by the time he sits down at the counter. It is strong and bitter on his tongue.

Jean-Paul knows this *quartier* well. The military sanitarium is two streets away. The place had been an elementary school before the war began. For six days he stared at the same patch of wall, dodging the bullets and bombs that were still exploding inside his head. Iron beds were packed together where children's desks had once been, the air thick with the cries of the wounded. A teacher had written the words "TROIS CHEVRES" in chalk in the top left-hand corner of the blackboard at the front of the room, the legacy of a final, long-ago lesson. Those three goats saved Jean-Paul's life while he convalesced. For hours every day he pictured them gamboling peacefully together on a green hillside, somewhere far away from the blood-soaked fields of Verdun.

Today there are children everywhere, delighted with this new summer's morning. Jean-Paul sits back in his chair and surveys the scene before him. He and Anaïs used to come here every Sunday after Elodie was born. He liked to sit on the wooden benches and watch the world go by, dazzled by the baby sleeping in his arms. Now his eyes roam up and down the pathways, watching, searching, hoping.

There is a group of young girls playing jump rope. They laugh and chant and clap hands as they take turns to hop in and out of the rope's looping orbit. Jean-Paul looks at the face of every girl. Their games become faster, louder, more joyful. He finishes his cigarette, and then smokes another.

After a while he pulls his eyes away from the children and reaches into his coat pocket. He pulls out a black notebook, opens it at random, and begins to read. He knows every word by heart. The notebook contains the story of a life unlived, resurrected from the ashes of despair. Its telling was an act of love, of desperation, and of survival.

There were not enough memories to be had, and so Jean-Paul created more.

With a sigh, he closes the notebook and contemplates the day ahead. A month previously, France was gripped by Charles Lindbergh's solo flight across the Atlantic. Over a hundred thousand Parisians swarmed to Le Bourget to greet the *Spirit of St. Louis* when it landed. Roads around the aerodrome were gridlocked for hours. The following morning Jean-Paul stood among the excited crowd of cheering Frenchmen as Lindbergh appeared briefly on the balcony of the American embassy. They stayed for hours after the famous pilot had disappeared, chanting his name and waving their hats in the air. Jean-Paul realized that he was not the only one of his countrymen who was obsessed with the United States. The idea came to him then: a series of profiles of American expatriates now living in Paris. He made a list of potential subjects, and pitched the idea to his editor, who agreed to it at once. Today he has two interviews. He hopes his English will be up to the job.

He glances at his wristwatch. It is time to leave for his first appointment, but he does not want to quit his post just yet—there's no knowing when his hopeful vigilance might be rewarded. He sits back and watches the children play for a few moments more.

Jean-Paul does not even know the face he is looking for, but he is sure that when he sees it, he will recognize it at once.

8

Jealous of the Dead

THE HOTEL ON RUE DES CANETTES is a modest establishment for visitors to the city who are on a budget. The rooms are small and neat, with low ceilings and a great deal of dark wood. Guests share a communal bathroom at the end of each corridor. Camille Clermont scrubs and dusts from morning to night, but no amount of cleaning can eradicate the faint whiff of better times that lingers in every corner. Still, she could not be prouder of the place.

When Camille and Marie return from the cemetery, many of the guests have not yet appeared for breakfast. During the summer months the hotel's visitors are mostly tourists, and they tend to start their days in a leisurely manner.

Camille's husband is standing at the entrance to the small dining room. He watches the handful of guests who are already eating. Some talk quietly; others scrutinize guidebooks and make lists of the day's destinations.

"There you are," says Olivier Clermont.

"Here we are," agrees Camille. She kisses the top of her daughter's head. "You may go and play now, Marie," she says. "Later on we'll polish the silver together. You always enjoy that."

The little girl nods and runs up the staircase.

Olivier watches her go. "How did she like the cemetery?" he asks.

Camille shrugs. "She's ten years old."

"I did wonder."

"I wanted her to see the grave," says Camille. "That's not so terrible, is it?"

"It's been five years since he died," says Olivier. "That's half Marie's lifetime. She knows nothing of all that."

"Anyway, we're back now," replies Camille briskly. She is uninterested in having this argument yet again. She unties the scarf from around her head and shakes her hair free. "I'll get started on the rooms."

Olivier turns his attention back to the dining room. Berthe is taking orders and delivering pastries and coffee. She is young and pretty, and her black skirt is perhaps a little too tight. Camille notices that there is a small run in Berthe's stockings, just above the left knee. She turns away and climbs the staircase to the top floor, where she can hear Marie singing quietly to herself in her tiny bedroom under the eaves. Camille walks into the family bathroom and closes the door behind her. Next to the sink is a small chest of drawers. She crouches down, pulls open the bottom drawer, and removes an armful of impeccably laundered white sheets, which she carefully places on a wooden chair. She reaches back into the drawer. Her hand slips under the remaining bed linens and inches forward, the polished wood beneath her fingers. She is waiting for the touch of old leather.

There is nothing there.

When her fingers hit the back wall, she pulls out the remaining sheets and stares at the empty drawer.

"*Eh oui.*"

Her husband is standing in the doorway, watching her.

"Where is it?" she demands.

"Gone."

She straightens up to face him. "Where is it, Olivier?"

He puts his hands in his pockets. "I sold it yesterday."

A wave of nausea. With an effort she remains upright.

"You have no idea what you've done," she says.

"*Au contraire.*" He is exultant. "I know precisely what I have done, and I don't regret it, not one little bit. I got two hundred and fifty francs for it! What do you think of that?"

She stares at him. "Who did you sell it to?" she asks.

"*Tiens*, do you think I'm going to tell you that? Exactly how much of a fool do you take me for?"

"We need to get it back at once, Olivier. It's very important that nobody else ever——"

"It's gone, Camille. You'll never see it again, I promise you that."

"How could you be so cruel?"

"I wasn't being cruel. I just want you to pay some attention to me and Marie."

She looks at him in stupefaction. "What do you mean?"

"Do you even see us, Camille? Do you even know we're here?"

"Of course I do!"

"Really, though?" Olivier shakes his head. "It's bad enough that you visit his grave every week with fresh flowers, but that's not the worst of it. You creep up here all hours of the day and night." He sees her stricken face. "What? Did you think I didn't know where you've been disappearing to all these years?" He pauses. "It's time to stop mourning him, Camille. It's time to become a mother and a wife again."

Her husband is jealous. In any other circumstances this news would amuse her, but now terror is roiling in her gut. Finally she speaks, quietly and calmly. After all, there are the hotel guests to consider.

"Olivier, listen to me," she says. "You need to tell me what you did with it. We absolutely have to get it back."

He shakes his head. "I'm not telling you a thing."

"But you have no idea what you've done!"

"Tell me then, Camille. Tell me what I've done."

They're going to lose everything that is precious. Their lives will be destroyed, but she cannot tell him this, because it is she who has brought all this upon them.

She is the one who told their secret.

"Did you look at it?" she asks.

"Of course not. I didn't open the damn thing. I just wanted it out of our home."

He does not know. He does not know.

She walks out of the bathroom.

"Wait," he says, grabbing her arm. "Where are you going?"

"I'm going to find it."

A momentary panic ghosts across Olivier's face, but he quickly regains his composure. "Paris is a big city, Camille."

"If you think that's going to stop me, you don't know me very well."

"This is madness! He's been dead for five years!"

They stare at each other.

"I have to go," she says.

"But there are rooms to clean!"

"Have Berthe do it once breakfast is over." Camille hurries down the stairs. Is she already too late?

Olivier's office is in the basement of the hotel. Behind his desk sits an iron safe. Camille retrieves the key from its hiding place under the carpet, and unlocks it. There is a pile of banknotes nestling in a brown envelope. She counts out two hundred and fifty francs and replaces the rest.

Back in the lobby, she puts on her coat and reties her headscarf. Then she steps out into the street. As the door closes behind her, she realizes that she has no idea where to go next.

9

Eastern Anatolia, 1916: A Mother's Dress

THEY MARCHED ALONG THE BANKS of the river. Every step forward was a step closer to their deaths.

They had been walking for weeks, the bayonets of the Ottoman soldiers at their backs. The plains of Eastern Anatolia were brutally harsh. There was no shelter, and little food. At the end of each day the marchers collapsed in exhaustion, and every morning there were some who did not get back to their feet. The clothes of the dead were quickly stolen. Naked corpses were stacked up by the side of the road, left to the circling crows. The old and the infirm fell first, then the children. Souren Balakian remembered a young mother digging a grave for her infant baby with her bare hands. Deranged with grief, she pawed at the soil like a dog burying a bone. When the hole was half finished, she was dragged away into the nearby forest by a group of laughing soldiers. Souren did not see her again.

In this way his village was annihilated.

Throughout the region Armenians were being forced from their homes and driven eastwards, into the Syrian desert, to die.

The Euphrates ran red with their blood.

. . .

Souren did not leave his mother's side. Misery and exhaustion had erased the woman he used to know. She walked with her eyes fixed firmly on the ground, mumbling about the home that they had left behind. She did not talk about her greater loss, the one that opened up a hole in Souren's stomach every time he thought of it. Grief had cauterized something deep within her.

The villagers were forced to sleep under the stars, unshielded from the cold of the night. Each evening Souren's mother fell into a deep sleep, too tired for nightmares. He lay by her side and watched the breath spill from her lips in small white clouds. On the far side of the camp, tents were set up for Kamil Ömer and his thuggish cohorts. Lamps burned warmly from within, and the sound of the soldiers' merriment drifted across the cold air. Late at night, the men staggered drunkenly up and down the lines of sleeping villagers, looking for young girls to take back to the tents.

At least he did not have a sister, thought Souren.

Most evenings the soldiers roasted an animal over coals. Souren hungrily watched the meat turn on the iron spit, and dreamed of killing every man inside those tents.

He was seventeen years old.

Days turned into weeks. Still they marched. His mother was growing weaker and weaker by the day. He urged her to eat her rations, but she shook her head and turned away, leaving the food for him. In the end he wolfed down her share, frightened that someone else would steal it if he did not.

And then, one night, he was shaken awake. The camp was almost completely dark, save for the glowing embers of a few small fires that kept the guards warm during the night.

"Souren! Wake up!" His mother.

"What is it?"

"Here," said his mother. "Take this." She thrust something at him. It was the dress that she had been wearing since they left the village.

He looked at her and was horrified to realize that she was nearly naked. "What are you doing?"

"Put the dress on," she told him.

"What? Why?"

"Because you're going to escape."

He shook his head. "I want to stay with you."

She held his chin in her hand and looked at him. "I'm not going to lose you to these monsters as well."

"But—"

"I want you to put on the dress, Souren. Then I want you to leave. You have several hours until sunrise. That should give you time to put some distance between you and the camp."

"Where will I go?"

"Head back the way we came. Follow the course of the river. The next time you see a bridge, cross it, and start heading west. Travel only by night. Sleep during the day, somewhere out of sight." She paused. "You need to leave the country, do you understand? You must make your way to Europe."

"But there's a war going on in Europe. Won't that be dangerous?"

"Nothing could be as dangerous for you as staying here. Just keep moving until you feel safe. You'll know when."

"But I feel safe with you."

She smiled sadly at him. "Put on the dress, my love."

He struggled to his feet and did as he was told. His mother's dress was a tent over his teenage bones. She handed him a scarf and showed him how to wrap it around his head.

"Why do I have to wear this?" he asked.

"It's a disguise."

"Why do I need a disguise? Nobody knows who I am!"

"It's not *who* you are," said his mother. "It's *what* you are."

He frowned. "What am I?"

She patted his cheek. "You're almost a man, Souren. I've been watching the soldiers. They've started to look at you. They only want women and children on this march. You're getting too big, too strong. They're waiting for an excuse to put a bullet through your head."

He plucked miserably at the folds of the dress. "I don't want to leave you."

"Souren, you must do as I say. Use your wits and be careful. Don't take any risks, and everything will be fine."

"But I want to stay with you." He began to cry.

"Souren, my dearest, stop your tears and listen to me." She gripped his arm. "You have to do this, do you understand?"

He nodded, unable to speak.

"Good. Now take this." She stuffed some dirty banknotes into his hand.

"Where did you get these?" he asked, astonished.

"Never mind about that. Just spend them wisely. Buy food if you must, although it's safer to steal it. Don't let people see you unless it's absolutely necessary." She pointed into the night. "Go now," she said. "Remember, head west once you cross the river. And when the sun comes up, take cover and get some sleep. You have a long journey ahead of you." She kissed him on the cheek. "You're a good boy and a brave boy. And, Souren?" She took his hand and squeezed it tightly. "Never forget who you are. Never forget that you are an Armenian." She released her grip. "Now go."

Souren stumbled into the night.

He did exactly as his mother told him. A good boy and a brave boy. He walked by night and slept by day. He retraced the route of the death march. He scavenged for food in the moonlit shadows of silent farmhouses. He wrapped the scarf tightly around his head. For the first few days he could still smell his mother in the material. He inhaled her scent as he walked, and felt a little safer.

It took him three days to find a bridge across the river. There were few clouds that night and the moon hung low in the sky. Souren hid in the shadows of a nearby wood, his heart beating loudly in his chest, and watched the bridge. It was a simple, functional structure, constructed from roughly hewn timber, unadorned by a single decorative flourish. He waited for an hour, terrified: there would be nowhere to hide once he was out in the open. Just as he was summoning the courage to make a run for it, he heard the rhythm of approaching horseshoes, and froze. A moment later, a solitary rider appeared from the south—from the direction of the march. Souren felt his heart begin to pound. Perhaps his absence had finally been noticed. Perhaps this man was an assassin, on a mission to track him down and kill him.

But the horseman was not thundering ahead with murderous intent. He slouched lazily in the saddle, and was allowing his mount to amble along at its own pace. Whatever he was doing at this time of night, the man was not searching for an escaped prisoner.

Still, Souren did not want to be heading in the same direction as the man and his horse. He held his breath as they neared the bridge. To his relief, they did not turn to cross the river, but continued their plodding course northwards. Once rider and horse disappeared from view, Souren counted to a hundred, then two hundred, and then three hundred. Then he stepped out from his hiding place, hitched up his skirt, and began to run. He scanned the darkness in all directions as he went, although by then it was too late to hide.

He did not slow down as his feet hit the wooden planks of the bridge. The noise of his footsteps ricocheted through the still night air, gunshots beneath his shoes. He was sure he could be heard for miles. His eyes were fixed on the far bank of the river. There was a gravel road that began where the bridge ended. The road was hemmed in on both sides by thickly clustered pine trees—a forest, dark and inviting. His pace quickened.

The bridge was longer than it looked. The Euphrates ran beneath his feet, quiet and strong. When Souren reached the far bank, he did not stop running, but headed for the shadows of the forest. He crashed through the undergrowth, heading farther into darkness. Finally, he stopped moving and gulped air into his lungs, his chest heaving.

He was safe.

His journey became more difficult after that. The forest was thick with obstacles that slowed his progress—unyielding thickets of bramble that scratched his legs and ensnared his dress, invisible tree roots that caught his feet and tripped him up. When the moon was hidden by clouds, what little light remained did not penetrate the roof of trees above him, and he was scarcely able to see his hand when he held it in front of his face.

Without the river to guide him, Souren no longer knew where he was going. He just kept moving forward. Sometimes he did not see a dwelling for days. Without scraps of stolen food to sustain him, he was ravenous.

It was his hunger, in the end, that drove him into danger. He started to walk closer to the road, scavenging for food left by other travelers. Souren hurried out of the woods, took what he could, and retreated again to the safety of the trees. Pickings were paltry—he mostly found stale crusts of bread and apple cores—but there was just enough to survive.

One evening, he hungrily watched from the shadows of the forest as two men devoured a feast by the side of the road. An endless procession of food emerged from the leather sacks that hung from the flanks of the men's horses. Boiled eggs, thick slices of roast beef, tomatoes the size of a man's fist, an entire loaf of bread. The men uncorked a bottle of wine and passed it between them. As he watched, Souren had never felt so alone, or so hungry. After an hour, the men clambered back onto their horses, their bellies full. Souren forced himself to wait several minutes before emerging from the trees. He did not take his eyes off the spot where the men had been eating. A large chunk of crusty bread lay on the ground. Souren stuffed it into his mouth. He picked up the discarded bottle and raised it to his lips. A few drops of red wine fell onto his parched tongue.

"You!"

Souren froze. A man sat on a horse, not more than twenty yards away, the curved blade of a scimitar strapped to his back. He wore a fez so filthy that its original color was impossible to guess. A Turk. Slowly Souren turned to face him.

A mouthful of rotten brown teeth spread into an ugly grin.

"What's a pretty girl like you doing out here all alone?" said the horseman.

Souren had forgotten that he was wearing the dress. He quickly pulled the fabric of his mother's scarf over his face.

"Oh, there's no need to be shy," said the Turk as he dismounted. He was a short man. His belly fell over the front of his belt. "I'm not going to hurt you. At least not if you're a good girl and give me what I want."

Souren recognized the look in the man's eye. It was the same hungry look that the soldiers wore when they trawled the camp for girls to take back to their tents.

"What's the matter?" said the man as he approached. "Cat got your tongue?"

Souren took a step backward.

"Stay where you are!" The man whipped the sword out of its sheath. The tip of the blade was less than twelve inches from Souren's chest. "You and I are going to walk into the woods," he said. "Not too far. Just so we're out of sight of the road. Try and make a run for it and I'll kill you before you can scream for help, do you understand?"

Souren nodded.

"Good girl," said the man. "Now move."

Souren stumbled through the trees, the scimitar at his back. He knew what would happen when the Turk discovered that he was a boy. He contemplated running. He was younger and quicker than his captor, but the man would catch him easily on his horse.

"That's far enough." The Turk held his sword in one hand, and with the other he pulled at his belt. His trousers fell to his ankles. "Quickly, now," he grunted. "Off with the dress."

But Souren did not take the dress off. Instead he turned around and dropped to his knees. The Turk's penis emerged stiffly from beneath the folds of his tunic. It was long, thick, and purple. Souren reached out and closed the fingers of his left hand around the shaft.

"Well now," murmured the man.

Souren drove his right fist between the Turk's legs with every ounce of strength that he could muster. The punch smashed through the man's testicles and continued up into the softness of his abdomen. He collapsed, tripping over the trousers entangled around his feet. As he hit the ground he dropped his sword, and Souren lunged for it. The weapon was heavier than he expected, and he needed both hands to pick it up. The Turk didn't notice. He was rolling on the ground in agony. Souren plunged the sword into the man's neck. There was an immediate eruption of dark blood. Souren closed his eyes and pictured the scowling face of Kamil Ömer. He pushed the sword through the flesh and tendons of the Turk's neck and held the weapon in place until the man's body stopped thrashing, and was still.

The Turk's mouth was open in a silent scream. Souren put his foot on the man's chest and pulled the scimitar free. He dragged the corpse farther into the woods, and stripped it naked. He put on the trousers, tunic, and coat, even the dirty fez. The clothes were too big for him, but he did not care. He wiped the blade of the sword clean on his mother's dress, dropped the bloodied garment next to the dead man's body, and returned to the road.

The horse was still there.

Aleppo, Sis, Kayseri. These cities marked the start of Souren's true journey. His progress was faster and safer than before. The horse was a fine beast, young and strong. Souren could outrun anyone who found him suspicious—although traveling on horseback seemed to render him invisible. People did not give him a second glance as he rode by.

Now he traveled by day.

He gave the horse a name: Hector, of course. He bent down low over the animal's straining neck, talking into his ears as they galloped through the countryside toward Constantinople. Words poured out of him, an unceasing flow. He could not stop talking, as if the horse would pull up the moment he drew breath. He was simply grateful for the companionship of another living thing.

There were supplies for both him and the horse in the dead Turk's saddlebags, but they did not last long. He began to steal food again, but now he had to feed Hector as well as himself. Sometimes he spent a little of the money that his mother had given him—but only to buy food for the horse. The other purchase he made was a map. Souren studied this map for hours by the light of the small fire he set every night to keep himself warm.

He dreamed of riding through the countries beneath his fingers. Bulgaria. Serbia. Albania. Montenegro. Bosnia and Herzegovina. He whispered the names into the cold night air, a hopeful incantation. His finger moved north across the paper.

There was Italy.

There was France.

10

The Deal

GUILLAUME OPENS THE DOOR.

Standing in front of him is a middle-aged man in a brown corduroy suit. He is short and barrel-chested, with a handsome face that, Guillaume fancies, has seen a thing or two. The man's eyes shine with amused intelligence from beneath the rim of a pristine fedora.

"Monsieur Blanc?" says the man. "I hope you're expecting us. We have an appointment." He speaks excellent French, with just the faintest echo of an American accent. He gestures behind him, and there in the corridor stands Gertrude Stein. She is wearing a screamingly loud floral dress and a bright blue hat. She carries a large handbag in front of her, bearing it like a shield. In contrast to her companion, she is spectacularly unattractive. Her skin is sallow, her eyes dull, and her nose is shaped like a monstrous crow's beak.

"Of course," says Guillaume. "Won't you come in?" He takes a step back and ushers the couple inside. The man removes his hat as he walks into the room, and runs a hand through his short-cropped steel-gray hair. His eyes fall on a painting propped up against Guillaume's still-unmade bed, a grittily beautiful scene from the streets of the Marais. He turns and says something to Gertrude Stein in English. She shrugs her shoulders but says nothing. The couple stares at the painting in silence for several moments. Then the man shakes his head.

"I don't like this at all," he says.

Who is this bossy, ignorant fellow? The demonic pounding of Guillaume's hangover returns. "Miss Stein?" he asks, turning toward her. "What do *you* think?"

Those big ugly eyes goggle at Guillaume in mute horror. He feels an anxious twist in his gut, a vague sense that everything is unraveling, but he doesn't know why.

"Excuse me," says the man. "But *I* am Gertrude Stein."

Guillaume blinks. "Pardon?"

"I am Gertrude Stein," repeats the man. He points to the woman. "This is my companion, Alice Toklas. You're welcome to ask her opinion, monsieur, but I can assure you it will be the same as mine." He produces a small, embossed card from an inside pocket of the corduroy suit, and hands it to Guillaume. It reads:

GERTRUDE STEIN

27, RUE DE FLEURUS, PARIS

écrivaine

Guillaume feels the blood rushing to his cheeks and hopes that he doesn't look as confounded as he feels. He looks at Gertrude Stein again, more closely this time, recalibrating everything he sees.

Confoundment, still.

"Emile Brataille said that you had some superior portraits," says Gertrude Stein. "Perhaps you could show us those?"

The portraits are propped up against the wall by the window. Guillaume leads the pair over to inspect them. His subjects are a motley crew; whenever he can afford it, he pulls people off the streets with a promise of a franc or two for their time. A street cleaner, a grave digger, the trumpet player from the house band at Le Chat Blanc. There are two or three of Thérèse in various states of undress. The two Americans scrutinize each painting, then whisper to each other before moving on to the next one. Gertrude Stein is doing most of the talking. Guillaume has learned enough English while dashing off charcoal portraits in Place du Tertre to follow most of the conversation, but he pretends not to understand a word.

Finally Gertrude Stein turns toward him. "What else do you have to show us?" she asks.

Guillaume feels his world tilting precariously. "There's nothing here of interest to you?" he croaks.

She shakes her head. "I'm afraid it's all quite derivative and second-rate." Before Guillaume can respond, the American clomps across the studio and stands in front of the painting hanging on the wall opposite his bed.

"Ah, now," she murmurs. "This, on the other hand. Alice, come and see!"

Alice scuttles across the room. They look at it together.

"This one is all right," says Gertrude Stein. She turns to him. "How much do you want for it?"

Of all the paintings in the room, this is the one that she wants.

Guillaume closes his eyes. He thinks of Le Miroir and his thugs.

"Twelve hundred francs," he says. The words are ashes in his mouth.

Gertrude Stein considers this number, her head cocked at a thoughtful angle. "I'll give you nine hundred for it," she says.

Nine hundred francs will not help him. Nine hundred francs will still get him killed. Guillaume curses silently. Of course the American wanted to haggle. He should have asked for two thousand and then allowed himself to be beaten down. He shakes his head. "The price is twelve hundred," he says, hoping she won't hear the fear in his voice.

Gertrude Stein looks at him with interest. After a moment she says, "Well, in that case you might as well show us what else you have."

Guillaume doesn't know whether to feel despair or relief.

For the next half hour the two women pick over what remains of Guillaume's inglorious career. They are unmoved by his landscapes. They do not like his still lifes. His brief dalliance with collage leaves them cold.

They move toward the final canvas. They stand in front of it, their heads almost touching. There is a final shake of the head from Gertrude Stein, and the game is up.

Guillaume makes a decision.

"One moment, please."

Gertrude Stein turns to him. "Yes?"

"I accept your offer," he says miserably.

"My offer?"

He points to the painting on the wall. "It's yours for nine hundred."

"No, thank you," she says.

Guillaume stares at her. "Pardon?"

"I've changed my mind," she says. "I don't want it anymore."

"But you said you liked it!"

"Did I?" Gertrude Stein puts the fedora back on her head. "Come along, Alice."

Alice moves past Guillaume and into the corridor, not looking him in the eye. He watches them go, numb. Just before the door closes behind them, Gertrude Stein steps back into the room. There is a new, hard glint in her eye. She points to the painting on the wall.

"I'll give you six hundred for it," she says.

Guillaume stares at her. "But you just offered me nine hundred!"

"An offer you rejected. This is my new offer."

"But that's daylight robbery!"

She doesn't blink. "Do you accept or not?"

Six hundred francs. Exactly half of what he needs. He is bleeding, on the floor.

Gertrude Stein stands in his studio and calmly waits for him to agree to her terms.

She watches him.

She does not look away.

11

An American in Paris

THE AMERICAN OPENS THE DOOR HERSELF.

She is wearing nothing but a nightgown. Her body— that dark, lithe thing, the talk of the city—is sheathed in pale pink silk. Jean-Paul does his best not to stare at those famous breasts that make men dream of forbidden delights as they lie next to their unsuspecting wives. She stands in the doorway, well aware of the spectacle she is creating.

"Yes?" she says.

Jean-Paul coughs. "Mademoiselle Baker?"

She inclines her head, although it is not really a question that requires a response. Everyone in Paris knows who Josephine Baker is. "And you are?"

"Jean-Paul Maillard. From the newspaper." He hands over his card.

She doesn't look at it. "Do you speak English?" she asks. "I want someone who speaks English. My *français* is not so *bien*."

"I do."

"All right, then. Come on inside, why don't you?" With that she turns on her heel and sashays down the corridor, her hips swinging in silent, sultry rhythm. Jean-Paul limps along the hallway in pursuit. She leads him into a sitting room bigger than his entire apartment. She sits down on a green velvet couch and unleashes a dazzling smile. It is early in the morning, but her hair is already fixed in its famous shiny helmet of tight black waves, and her fingernails are flawlessly painted silver. She is twenty-one years old. "I am *trying* to learn French," she says. "I've been reading books of fairy tales." She rolls her eyes. "Those French stories are *beaucoup* more strange than the ones my mother told me when I was growing up."

Jean-Paul sits down and looks around him. Abandoned clothes are draped over every piece of furniture, and there are piles of unopened letters everywhere. A large bust of Louis XIV sits on the marble mantelpiece. Next to it there is a cage containing two elaborately plumed parakeets. They shuffle up and down their perch, squawking crossly at each other.

"What are we supposed to be talking about today?" asks Josephine Baker.

Jean-Paul takes out his notebook. "I want to know about your life in France," he says. "How you came here, why you decided to stay."

"*J'adore la France.*" She smiles. "And France adores me, too."

"Why do you think that is?"

A shrug. "Because I'm different. *Exotique.*"

Jean-Paul nods. "Paris's very own African princess."

She looks at him. "You know I've never been to Africa, right?"

"But the city loves you all the same. *Un Vent de Folie* is sold out every night of the week. The Folies-Bergère has never been more popular. And it's all because of you."

"The show is fine, don't you think? I like the costumes."

"The costumes are spectacular," agrees Jean-Paul politely, although he does not in fact believe this. You've seen one skirt made out of bananas, he thinks, and you've seen them all. "Where did you first learn to dance?"

"In St. Louis, Missouri. There were large riverboats that took passengers up and down the Mississippi—you know, day trips, just for fun—and every boat had a band. A lot of musicians came up the river from New Orleans, looking for work on those boats. I heard Johnny Dodds play, and Pops Foster." She smiles. "There was so much dancing going on back then! New steps were being invented all the time, and I learned them all." In another room, a telephone jangles. She jumps up and leaves the room in the softest rustle of silk. Jean-Paul looks at the parakeets and wonders what stories they could tell. Then he wonders if they speak English or French.

"Hello? Hello?" Her voice carries through from the other room. "What? I can't—what? I don't understand. I don't—*parlez-vous anglais*? Hello?" There is a small pause, then the rattle of the telephone receiver being slammed back into its cradle. Then the owner of the most recognizable face in Paris returns, all smiles.

"Silly man didn't speak a word of English," she says. "I hate the telephone, don't you? It's a pain to hear a person's voice and not see him! Although you probably use the telephone all the time, don't you? Isn't that what you journalists do?" Before Jean-Paul can answer, she continues, "I know a journalist. An American. He writes for a newspaper in Canada. He writes stories, too. His name is Ernest Hemingway. Perhaps you know him."

"Of course. That is, I know *of* him. *The Sun Also Rises* is a very good book."

"Ernest thinks so, too. I haven't read it, though." She winks. "It drives him crazy."

"I've written a book," says Jean-Paul, to his own surprise. He has never told anyone this before.

"How *magnifique*! What's it about?"

He pauses. "It's the story of a girl named Elodie."

"That's a pretty name," says Josephine Baker.

"Yes," agrees Jean-Paul sadly.

"What's the title? I'll go out and buy it this afternoon."

"Oh, it's not for sale." He looks at his shoes. "I just wrote it for myself."

"Well, if you ever want to get it published, perhaps Ernest can help. I'm sure he knows everyone in the book world. He's terribly important these days, or so he tells me." She grins. "A word or two in the right ear might make all the difference, don't you think?"

"Didn't he just get married again?" says Jean-Paul, who is eager to change the subject.

"Ah, yes, to the lovely Pauline." Josephine Baker leans forward. "She doesn't approve of me," she whispers.

"Oh? Why not?"

"Ernest still likes to dance with me when he can. But he holds me a little too tight for Pauline's taste."

"I see."

"It's not so bad." Her eyes twinkle. "He's a very handsome man." She sits back and considers him languidly. "How did you learn to speak such good English?"

"I met some American soldiers at the end of the war. I gave them cigarettes in exchange for English lessons. And I love American music."

"You do?"

"Of course. I especially like George Gershwin. And Bessie Smith and Louis Armstrong. I learned a lot of English, listening to those two." He sings in a full-throated Satchmo rasp:

Mama I'm so sad and lonely
Just for you only
I'm blue

Josephine Baker howls in delight. "Well, *that* sure beats reading fairy tales! And learning the blues will help you more than handsome princes and evil stepmothers will ever help *me*."

"But you never know when a handsome prince might come along. And it would be a shame not to know what to say, if he did."

She smiles at him. "You sure know how to make a girl feel better."

"Perhaps I should throw away my Louis Armstrong records and pick up the Brothers Grimm instead. Are there many evil stepmothers in America?"

"Oh baby, you have no idea!" She slaps her knees in pleasure. "You've never been to the States?"

"Never. But I'd love to go."

"The women will go wild for your accent."

He changes the subject again. "Do you miss America?"

She shakes her head. "They call my country the land of the free, but

I was born poor and black, and there wasn't much that was free about *that*."

"Tell me," says Jean-Paul.

"When I was six, we woke up before dawn every day and walked two miles to the Soulard Market. That was where farmers would go to sell their crops each morning. The stalls were overflowing with fruit and vegetables, but we couldn't afford any of it. Instead I crawled beneath the tables and picked up food that had been dropped in the dirt. The stallholders saw me do it, but they paid me no mind. Sometimes they felt sorry for me and gave me a fresh apple or apricot. Other days, my brother and I went to the railway freight yards near where we lived. We picked up lumps of coal and sold them for a penny." She breaks into that famous smile. "In France, though! I got sparkling rings as big as eggs, one-hundred-fifty-year-old earrings that once belonged to a duchess, six chairs from China, and a pair of shoes made out of gold." She laughs. "Somebody gave me a car with seats that were upholstered in snakeskin. I don't know how to drive, though, so now I've got a chauffeur with big gold buttons on his uniform."

"France has been good to you," says Jean-Paul.

"Far better than where I came from, that's for sure." She sits forward. "I came here on a ship called the *Berengaria*. I was part of the original company that put on *La Revue nègre*, you know. We had actors, musicians, dancers, all sorts. We were kind of a big deal, but the ship was American, and that meant we had to travel in steerage. They didn't want black folks mingling with the first-class passengers. It was only when we got to Paris that we were treated just the same as everyone else." She watches as Jean-Paul scribbles in his notebook. "Have you ever heard of Lloyd Waters?"

"No."

"Lloyd is a friend of mine. When the war began, even before America got involved, he wanted to fight, so he joined the French Foreign Legion. He got wounded, and then he trained to become a fighter pilot. He was very brave. The French called him the Black Swallow of Death. But when America joined the war, he was transferred to a US military unit, and never flew again."

"Why not?"

"Because America doesn't trust its Negroes to be pilots. After the war was over the French awarded him fifteen medals. Fifteen! It's no wonder he never went back to America."

"He's still here?"

"Of course! Why would he ever go back? In France he is treated with love and respect. These days he runs a club in Montmartre. Le Chat Blanc. Do you know it?"

"I've heard of it."

"I like to go there after the show at Les Folies. It's a fine place to relax. They have good music."

"Jazz?" guesses Jean-Paul.

She nods. "Sidney Bechet is playing there this week."

"Bechet? Really?"

"Sure. He just got back into town. He's been playing all over Europe. We're good friends, me and Sidney. He writes to me from every city he visits." She stands up and walks across the room to a small bureau. "Look." She hands Jean-Paul a bundle of postcards. He flicks through them. Greece, Turkey, Sweden. "We performed together when I first arrived in France."

Jean-Paul nods. "I saw that show. He played a peanut vendor. He pushed a cart on stage and then played the blues while a couple danced."

She smiles, radiant at the memory. "You should come to Le Chat Blanc tonight. As my guest. I'll introduce you to Lloyd Waters, and Sidney, too. I'll invite Ernest as well. He likes to go to the *boîtes* to drink and watch the dancers. There'll be lots of Americans for you to interview."

"That would be wonderful."

"You'll all get along famously, I know. You could ask Ernest about your book, if you want. And you'll hear Sidney play, of course." She pauses. "He's another one who would rather live in France. It's funny, isn't it? Look at us—me, Sidney, Lloyd, Ernest. All of us escaped America. But here *you* are, wanting to go the other way."

"Everyone is running toward somewhere," says Jean-Paul lightly.

"Except you're not, are you? You're still here."

Jean-Paul inclines his head. "That's true."

"What's stopping you? Why don't you get on the next boat and leave for the States?"

"I have to stay here."

"Why? What's keeping you in Paris?"

"It's a long story."

Josephine Baker crosses her arms. "So tell me a story."

And, to his own astonishment, he does.

12

Auxillac, 1913: Country Girl

CAMILLE GINESTE GREW UP in a tiny village in the Lozère. Her family's large, low-ceilinged mill in the center of Auxillac was her whole world. Not many people came to the village, and not many people left, so when a visitor arrived, people paid attention.

A man came to stay at her cousins' house. His name was Olivier Clermont. He lived in Paris, and was ten years older than her. She liked his open, honest face. He had a thick mustache which she thought gave him an air of raffish sophistication.

She asked about him.

Here is what she learned: he had grown up in La Canorgue, a village five miles away down a winding country road. When his mother died, he and his brothers moved to Paris to live with their elder sister. He owned a car, an elegant beast called a Unic, and he worked as a chauffeur in Paris, and Normandy, and Monaco, depending on the season. He was staying in the Lozère for the summer, while his clients were away from the capital on vacation.

There were some large family dinners, a festive picnic or two. Olivier Clermont had a fine tenor voice, and could sometimes be persuaded to sing. Camille liked the way he carried himself when he performed, the amused twinkle in his eye. She liked that he did not take himself too seriously. She wore her prettiest dress and hoped that he would introduce himself. Sometimes she felt his eyes resting on her, but he kept his distance. Then one afternoon he appeared at the door of the mill, his cap rolled up in his hand.

They went for long walks through the nearby meadows, and told each other stories about themselves. She liked to listen to his tales about life in Paris, and wished she had something more interesting to tell him in return. Auxillac was all that she knew.

Sometimes he arrived in his car, and they would drive to nowhere in particular. The air rushed past her so quickly as they sped down the narrow roads that she could hardly catch her breath.

At the end of the summer Olivier returned to Paris. They wrote to each other. She enjoyed reading his news from the city, but didn't give him much thought in the weeks between his letters. She held out no particular hope. She knew that in Paris the women were beautiful, and she was a simple country girl. She would never catch the eye of a man like him.

The next summer, Olivier Clermont returned to Auxillac. Most days he would appear at her parents' front door.

At the end of July, one of Camille's cousins married a cattle farmer from Mende. That evening a grand feast took place in the center of the village. Long tables were pushed together under the stars and were piled high with plates of food and jugs of wine. After dinner a band began to play, and the whole village danced late into the night.

Olivier found her sitting alone, watching the crowd. She smiled at him as he approached.

"I've been watching you," he said. "You haven't danced once!"

"It's more fun to watch other people." She pointed into the middle of the melee, where her father was spinning her mother under his arm. She was laughing, her head thrown back in delight.

"How do you know if you never try it yourself?" he asked.

She looked up at him, amused. "Monsieur Clermont," she said, "are you asking me to dance?"

He shook his head. "No, Camille," he said. His voice was thick. "I'm asking you to marry me."

She was so surprised that she could not speak.

"Camille?" said Olivier. "Did you hear me?"

She nodded.

"And? What do you say?"

She had never traveled farther than twenty miles from the spot where she'd been born. Her life was here, with her parents. She had never imagined that a different future might be hers for the taking.

"Yes," she whispered.

He took her hand and led her into the middle of the throng of dancing wedding guests.

Camille was twenty years old. As they twirled across the village square in time to the band, Olivier's strong hands at her back, she wondered what on earth she had done.

In the spring of 1913, they were married in the small church in the center of the village. Her mother and father tried to hide their dismay, but Camille saw their red eyes and heard their whispers. They were sure that she would never return to Auxillac. No amount of her ardent promises could convince them otherwise.

The day after the ceremony the newlyweds boarded a train to Paris. Camille sat next to her husband and watched the countryside outside the carriage window. So many miles between her past and her future.

The train pulled into Gare de Lyon early the following morning. Camille had not slept well, her restless night not helped by Olivier's beatific snoring in the bunk above her own. Her mother had made her a new hat for the trip. Camille held it firmly on her head as she stepped off the train. The fumes on the platform were so strong that she could taste them, sharp and bitter, at the back of her throat. A white cloud of steam hissed from the engine on the neighboring track. There was a shrill whistle blown by an invisible guard, then a lusty shout. She turned in panic to look for Olivier. He was standing right behind her, a suitcase in each hand.

"Welcome to Paris, Madame Clermont," he said with a smile.

She glanced up at the roof of the railway station, a giant lattice of iron and glass that soared over their heads. She reached for her husband. He put down the suitcases and wrapped an arm tightly around her shoulder. She felt a little braver under his touch. Passengers swarmed around them.

"Everyone is in such a hurry," she said.

Olivier laughed. "Ah, yes. Wherever you're going, there's no time to lose."

"Where *are* we going? How far away is Levallois from here?"

"It's out to the northwest. You'll get a little tour of the city on the way. Come on." They walked out into the cold Parisian morning. Dark clouds hung low in the sky. Camille shivered, already missing the southern sun.

They found a taxi. Olivier pointed out famous landmarks as they trundled down the city's wide boulevards. When they arrived at the apartment, Olivier bounded up the stairs, carrying the suitcases with him, leaving his new bride to follow in his steps. In the parlor Camille took off her new hat. Then she put her head in her hands and burst into tears.

The first weeks were not easy.

Camille did not know how to do anything. She had been spoiled by her mother, spared from even the simplest household chores. She could not cook, she did not know how to light a fire. She did not know how to be a wife. Her sister-in-law showed her how things were done. She learned how to select the ripest melons at the market, how to tell when the *poulet rôti* was ready to bring to the table. Her husband was patient and kind. He watched as she tried to marshal their apartment into some semblance of order, never reprimanding or rebuking her. He wrapped her in his bear-like arms whenever she became discouraged, and whispered in her ear that she was doing beautifully, that she would get used to everything soon enough. For weeks he stayed with her in the apartment because she was nervous about being left alone, but finally he told her that he needed to return to work. The rent, he said gently, was not going to pay itself.

"Let's go out for a little while," he said.

"Where to?"

"Boulevard Haussmann. One of my clients lives there. I want to pay him a visit to let him know that he can call on me at any time, now that I'm back at work." He paused. "He's a writer. He'll be pleased to meet you."

"Will I be pleased to meet him, do you think?"

"Oh yes."

"And why is that?"

He patted her cheek. "Because he's one of my best clients."

At 102 Boulevard Haussmann, the young couple climbed the service stairs to the second floor. The door was opened by a smartly dressed man.

"Clermont!" he barked in pleasure. "You're back!" He shook Olivier's hand warmly and then turned to Camille. "And this is the beautiful bride that you've brought back from the Lozère?" he said, looking her up and down with approval. "How delightful."

She blushed and performed a curtsy, just as she had practiced. Both men burst out laughing. "What excellent manners they have down south!" exclaimed the man.

"Camille, this is Nicolas Cottin," said Olivier. "He's the valet."

She looked between the two men in confusion, her cheeks hot with embarrassment. "The valet?" she stammered.

Cottin looked at her kindly. "Yes, I'm just the hired help, I'm afraid," he said with a grin. "My wife, too. She's the chambermaid." He clapped Olivier on the shoulder. "It's good to see you! I'll go and let him know that you're here. Come, follow me." He led them down a corridor to the kitchen. "Give me a moment, if you will," he said, and disappeared.

Camille looked around the kitchen. The fireplace had been swept spotless and was filled with a fresh stack of kindling. Every work surface was pristine and uncluttered. Shining nests of copper saucepans were arranged neatly on shelves in order of size, each handle set at the same precise angle. The stovetop gleamed as if it had been installed that day. She turned toward her husband. "Does anybody actually *cook* in here?" she asked.

Before Olivier could reply, the door swung open.

The man who walked into the kitchen was wearing a beautiful smoking jacket with velvet lapels, and a white shirt so freshly laundered that the creases from the smoothing iron were still visible. He was not wearing a collar or a tie. A single curl of hair fell across his forehead, and in the middle of his moon-like face was a dark and luxuriant mustache. His eyes were calm and limpid. He carried himself with hesitant reserve. Every gesture was cautiously restrained, as if he were reluctant to engage too completely with the world in which he found himself. He was a man of half steps.

He greeted Olivier, and then he held out his hand toward Camille. "Madame," he said. "May I introduce Marcel Proust, in disarray, uncombed, and beardless!"

Now that it was the correct time for her to curtsy, Camille could manage no more than a self-conscious half-bow. Marcel Proust looked her up and down with a disarming lucidity. His smile was a curious contortion of lips and teeth, but it did not reach up as far as his eyes. "You know your husband is invaluable to me, don't you, Madame Clermont?" he said. "He is the only driver I trust. Nobody else will do, nobody." He turned to Olivier. "I hope you've come to tell me that you're ready to start work again."

"Whenever you need me, monsieur." Olivier produced a piece of paper from his pocket. "This is the number of my sister's restaurant," he said. "You can call me there whenever you need me."

"Excellent," said Proust, taking the paper and folding it neatly in half. "I shall be calling you soon, have no doubt."

Olivier inclined his head. "However I can be of service, monsieur."

"Thank you, Olivier. I have been quite lost without you." The writer turned back to Camille. "On that subject, Madame Clermont, I have something of the utmost importance to tell you."

She nodded, suddenly apprehensive.

"It is critical," said Marcel Proust, "that your husband is not too happy at home."

There was a long pause.

"Not too happy?" repeated Camille.

Proust nodded. "He needs to be available for me whenever I need him, you see. I don't want him lounging about at home with his pretty young wife! If you look after him too well, he'll never want to drive me any-where, do you see? I want him standing by the telephone, ready and wait-ing for my call!"

A joke. She smiled weakly.

"In fact, perhaps I should give *you* a job here," he mused. "That would make Olivier more willing than ever to come to Boulevard Haussmann!"

"What an excellent idea!" exclaimed Olivier. "You'll never find a better employer than Monsieur Proust, Camille."

She shook her head. "You don't want me working in your home, mon-sieur. I can't even boil an egg."

Marcel Proust was looking at her closely through his hooded, reptilian eyes.

"I don't like eggs," he said.

13

Sons and Brothers

AFTER ARIELLE AND HER MOTHER have left, thanking him for the cheese and promising to see him in the Jardin du Luxembourg that afternoon, Souren Balakian stares out of the window. He lives for Arielle's visits each morning. She is a tiny sun, filling him with warmth and light.

He smiles at Arielle's excitement about the puppet show. Souren stretches his arms high above his head and thinks about the pianist from downstairs. Not just a pianist, he reminds himself. A *composer*—although one who no longer writes anything new. The man has been caught in a melancholy trap, stilled by the beauty of his own music. Perhaps he is scared that he'll never write anything as perfect again. Tomorrow, thinks Souren, he will knock on the door of the ground floor studio. He will tell Maurice Ravel that he has a devoted audience who waits for him to play each morning. Perhaps that will be enough to set the music within him free.

Humming, Souren begins to fill his suitcase.

Every evening he hangs each puppet on its designated hook on the wall, and every morning he reverses the process. He always takes his time with this daily packing and unpacking, relishing this private act of communion with his puppets before the public spectacle that is to come. His audiences watch from a distance, but his own relationship with the puppets is visceral, immersive, wholly tactile. This is what he knows, what he loves: the smoothness of the tiny garments; the weight of those burnished wooden heads; the faint smell of lacquer and old paint. His hands inhabit these creatures. His fingers twitch and snap beneath their skins and bring them to life. Not once has he left them in the suitcase overnight. He could not fall asleep staring at a wall of empty hooks. His puppets keep him company when the dreams crowd in.

After he has arranged his strange workfellows in tight, well-regimented rows, Souren lowers the lid of the suitcase and pushes the brass clasps shut. The other suitcase, the one containing his theater, waits by the front door. He picks up both and makes his way out onto the street.

It is a beautiful morning. Souren walks through the streets of Montmartre, enjoying the warmth of the sun. On Rue des Martyrs, the shops are busy. Housewives wait in line outside their preferred fishmonger, butcher, and grocer. As always, Souren steps inside the *fromagerie* to admire the fragrant abundance of cheese on display. From behind the counter Augustin greets him with a cheerful wave.

"How did mademoiselle like the Saint-Nectaire?" he asks.

"She approved," replies Souren. "We both did."

"Excellent!" Augustin grins. "I have something special for you this evening. A lovely Chaumes." He pinches the tip of his nose between his fat fingers. "It's good and pungent. We'll see what your little friend makes of *that* one."

Souren grins. "I'll look forward to it."

"*Alors, à ce soir,*" says the cheesemonger.

With a wave, Souren steps back out onto the street. At the bakery next door, children press their noses up against the window, hungrily staring at the cakes, the *tartes aux pommes*, and the perfect pyramids of chocolate-glazed éclairs. A boy bends down to feed the crumbs of his croissant to a stray dog.

Souren heads south down the hill. He stops in front of Younis's grocery and pushes open the door. Inside, he puts down his suitcases and inhales deeply. Most of the stalls on Rue des Martyrs smell of fresh fruit and vegetables, but here a heavy aroma of spice lingers in the air, delicious and foreign. Rather than the usual bountiful displays of food for customers to admire, the day's produce sits in battered cardboard boxes on the floor. A dark-skinned old lady with a bright scarf wrapped around her head bends down stiffly to examine a heap of gnarled yams. There are no lines of well-turned-out French ladies here, politely waiting their turn to be served; the shop is a chaotic, tumbling circus of marauding children. They run back and forth, laughing and shouting. There are at least twenty adults in the shop, too, although nobody seems interested in buying anything; they are all too busy talking. Souren can hear several different conversations, all being conducted at considerable volume. He can understand none of them.

Next to the cash register at the far end of the room stands a tall man with his hands on his hips, deep in conversation with two other men. He has a handsome brown face. He looks up when the door opens, and, seeing Souren, excuses himself. As he crosses the shop, his smile is one of unqualified joy, as if he has been waiting all morning for Souren to walk through the door. The two men clasp hands firmly. Apart from little Arielle, Younis is the only friend Souren has made in ten years of living in Paris. (His relationships with Augustin and Thérèse, while warm enough, are strictly transactional.)

"Younis," says Souren. "*Tout va bien?*"

"Of course, of course," replies the man. His French is as awkward and as thickly accented as Souren's own. Their friendship has been built, at least in part, on the perilous leap they take every time they open their mouths to speak the language of their adopted country: each knows that the other will never judge him for how he talks. And that is not nothing, when everyone else is ready to brand you as different.

Younis gestures around him, still smiling. "It's business as usual here, which means that everyone is too busy gossiping to buy anything. But it makes my father happy, so who am I to argue?" He gestures to the far corner of the shop, where an old man sits on a wooden chair, one hand placed on each knee, silently surveying the busy scene before him. Younis's father, Bechir, is wearing a tunic buttoned up to his weathered neck. His small, dark eyes are set deep into his face, but Souren doesn't suppose they miss too much. A plume of thick white hair sprouts from the old man's chin, which always reminds Souren of the goats that he used to herd on the grassy slopes of Anatolia. Souren raises a friendly hand toward the old man. Bechir smiles in response, showing off three or four teeth that poke up at improbable angles around the periphery of his gums.

Just then, a small boy clatters into one of Souren's suitcases, knocking it over and sending himself sprawling across the floor. Younis bends down and pulls the child to his feet, speaking to him softly in Arabic. The boy is dismissed with a gentle pat on the behind.

"Sorry," says Younis.

"Don't be," says Souren.

"He's a good boy. Just a bit careless, that's all."

"You're very kind to him."

Younis shrugs. "He's my little brother," he says, as if this explains everything.

When Souren first visited the shop he assumed that all of the children who played (and sometimes, grudgingly, worked) there were Younis's sons and daughters, but in fact they are his siblings. Bechir may be as old as the hills, but according to Younis he is still a randy old goat, and improbably fecund with it. He is presently married to his fourth wife, a supremely fertile specimen herself, who is pregnant with what will be his seventeenth child. Younis—the eldest of the tribe—complains that he is too busy running the shop and looking after his brothers and sisters to find himself one wife, let alone four. Meanwhile, his ancient father spends his days watching the fruits of his prodigious loins run amok across the shop floor, and his nights copulating with his poor, exhausted wife. Souren thinks that this is why Bechir always remains so still as he watches his swarming progeny: he is preserving his energy for later.

Younis has told Souren his family's story many times. His father was a successful cloth merchant in Tunis before the turn of the century. He ran a lucrative business out of the largest souk in the city, until one day he saw a photograph of the Eiffel Tower that had recently been built for the 1889

World's Fair. Bechir stared for hours at the tower's gorgeously curving parabolas, stretching high above the city's skyline. Hardheaded business-man though he was, he discovered a hitherto undetected romantic streak within him. He understood instinctively that he needed to live in a country that could build such a beautiful, useless, and flagrantly priapic monument on such an enormous scale. He stared at the massive wrought-iron erec-tion thrusting unambiguously into the sky and thought: that's the place for me. A few months later he had sold all his business interests and was making his way to Paris with his four eldest children and bemused wife in search of a different life.

Of course, in the end things were not so different in France. Bechir had commerce in his blood, and could no more stop trading than he could stop breathing. He purchased the grocery on Rue des Martyrs, and has been there ever since, working and procreating with equal degrees of success—although Younis runs the business now, leaving his father free to focus his efforts exclusively on the latter. The photograph of the Eiffel Tower is still tacked onto the wall behind the register. Souren once asked Younis whether his father has ever actually visited the famous monument. His friend shook his head. He doesn't need to, he explained. What's im-portant is that he knows it's there.

Younis picks up the suitcases and moves them closer to the door, out of danger. He smiles at Souren. "Two apples?" he says.

Souren inclines his head. Every day he buys the same thing. An apple for lunch, another one to eat later.

"Take your pick," invites Younis, gesturing toward to the cardboard boxes along the floor of the shop. Souren peers into each box. The goods on offer vary from day to day, depending on what Younis finds at market, and sometimes there is a fruit or vegetable that Souren has never seen before. He enjoys these exotic new discoveries, warmed by the strange otherness of it all. Like him, Bechir and Younis are refugees from else-where, and so he feels kinship with these men. The only difference, thinks Souren as he bends down to inspect today's offerings, is that they are sur-rounded by family, and he is not.

Younis follows Souren as he walks along the line of boxes, talking in his halting French about his younger brother, a tall, handsome fellow who sometimes works in the shop. Souren has seen him occasionally, sullenly slumped against the register.

"He's always getting into fights," complains Younis. "He cannot walk away from an argument, that's his problem. He doesn't need to go looking for trouble. Trouble will find him easily enough, you know?"

Souren knows.

"He's twenty-four years old and hasn't learned that everywhere he goes, people see him. Or rather, they don't see *him*. They see the color of his skin." Younis pauses. "I keep telling him he needs to learn to be invisible."

Souren nods. He may perform in public every day, but he is always hidden behind the striped awning of his puppet theater. Out of sight is the only place he feels comfortable.

"He won't listen, of course," continues Younis gloomily. "Unlike me, he was born in France, and he believes that he has as much right to be here as anyone."

"You don't agree?"

"There's one big difference between you and me, Souren. You can walk down the street and nobody will look twice at you. But me or my brother?" Younis gestures to the street outside. "Most of Paris just sees our dark skin." He sighs. "Of course, my brother is right. He *does* have as much right to be here as anyone. But being right and being safe are different things. And I know which is more important." Younis pauses. "He's my brother. All I want to do is protect him."

Souren bends down and chooses two apples. "He's a grown man, Younis. There's only so much you can do."

Younis looks at him. "Do you have any brothers?"

"No," says Souren. The word barely escapes his lips.

"Well, I have eleven of them," says Younis. "And I can tell you: brothers, especially *younger* brothers, all know much more than you do. You try to give them the best advice you can, of course. And they listen politely, or sometimes not so politely, and then they go and do exactly as they please anyway. But I'd die for my brothers in a heartbeat."

Souren stares down at his shoes.

Younis claps him on the shoulder. "You and I will never get too comfortable here, my friend. We'll always be from somewhere else, won't we?"

"That's true," agrees Souren.

"I'll never forget landing in Marseilles for the first time. I'd never been on a boat before, and I'd felt ill for the whole journey from Tunis. The moment my feet hit dry land in France I vomited all over my shoes—that was how I celebrated my arrival here. The docks were madness. What a circus! We lined up to have our papers inspected and all around us there were officials, traders, thieves, and whores. My poor mother took one look at them all and begged my father to get back on the ship. He refused, of course." Younis shakes his head in rueful remembrance. "They spent their first three days in France not speaking to each other." He looks at Souren. "And you? Do you remember your arrival?"

"Oh yes," says Souren.

14

Paris, 1915:
The Circus Medrano

Guillaume Blanc arrived in Paris with no more than a notebook, some paintbrushes, and bucketfuls of hope. He made his way directly to the cobbled streets of Montmartre, where he rented a tiny room in the cheapest lodgings he could find. He had come to the city with only one purpose: he was going to paint.

He spent those first days wandering up and down the boulevards of the city, absorbing every sight and sound. After each excursion he returned to his room and drew everything he had seen. Young children playing by a fountain. A woman, her back bent with age, carrying home groceries. The tall, dark windows of Saint-Sulpice. A hungry dog scrounging for scraps in the Passage Jouffroy. He filled page after page with his visions of the streets. As he committed Paris first to his memory and then to paper, he could feel the place flowing into his veins. La Rochelle grew more distant with every passing day.

In the evenings, Guillaume prowled the *quartier*. The streets of Montmartre were swarming with artists, the atmosphere febrile with genius. André Derain held court in a café on Avenue Junot, dressed like a peacock in a fancy vest and colorful cravat. Sometimes Guillaume would see Juan

Gris or Francis Picabia walking toward him on the sidewalk and it was all he could do to keep his starstruck feet moving forward. He learned to linger unobtrusively at bars over a single cup of coffee while he listened to artists at neighboring tables bicker and gossip with their friends and colleagues. It was during one such overheard conversation that he learned that Pablo Picasso was fond of spending his evenings at the bar of the Cirque Medrano.

Pablo Picasso!

Guillaume returned to his room and counted out his money. He could barely afford to feed himself, let alone buy a ticket to the circus. But he had come to Paris to paint, and the circus had always been a welcome home to artists. Toulouse-Lautrec and Degas had made masterpieces there. Seurat, too. And if he found Picasso at the bar, well, so much the better.

The following night Guillaume walked down Rue Dancourt wearing his best hat. As he turned onto Boulevard Rochechouart, he saw the crowd milling about in front of the circus's grandly proportioned arches, and his heart ballooned. A cart was selling bags of sweetly roasting chestnuts, and Guillaume's stomach rumbled. He had not eaten that evening, a token of frugality to compensate for the extravagance of this adventure. His hunger was eclipsed by excitement.

Once he'd purchased his ticket, he went in search of the famous Spaniard. The floor of the circus bar was polished marble and the walls were painted gold. Mirrors stretched up to the ceiling. People jostled good-naturedly against each other, yelling to make themselves heard. Guillaume tacked back and forth through the sea of drinkers, looking for Pablo Picasso, but he was not at the Cirque Medrano that night.

Trying not to feel disappointed, Guillaume took his seat in the circus arena a few minutes before the show was due to begin. Vaulted ceilings soared over the heads of the spectators. In the center of the huge room was a circular stage. All around him audience members were chattering and laughing.

Once the show began, Guillaume forgot about Pablo Picasso.

A daredevil Mexican with black hair flowing down his back stood blindfolded on the back of a snorting stallion as it cantered around the circus ring. Jugglers threw blazing batons in ceaseless arcs of tumbling light. A riotous posse of clowns made the crowd howl with laughter. A strongman in a red tunic paraded around the arena, balancing a woman on each of his upturned hands. A magician sawed one of the women in half, and turned the other one into a rooster. The rooster ran in circles before itself being transformed into a rabbit. There were knife throwers, fire eaters, and a troupe of acrobats who tossed each other through the air, landing on each other's shoulders and then somersaulting off again. The climax of their act was to create a human Eiffel Tower. Guillaume cheered along with everyone else.

But it was the trapeze artists who changed everything.

Two women, one white and one black, walked to the center of the circus ring. Unlike the other performers, they did not smile and wave at the audience. The white woman wore a black costume, a snorting dragon's head of silver sequins glittering on her back. Her kohl-rimmed eyes and darkly painted mouth made a perfect triangle on her face, and a long mane of black hair fell down her back. Her partner was her perfect monochromatic opposite—she wore a white costume, decorated with a black dragon. Both were beautiful.

The women scaled twin rope ladders until they reached small wooden platforms that had been built on opposite sides of the arena, high up near the roof. Guillaume craned his neck upward and watched as one of the acrobats took the end of a rope in her hands and launched herself over the heads of the audience, swinging into the void in long, graceful arcs. The second woman stood perfectly still on the opposite platform, until in a quicksilver flash of movement she threw herself headlong into nothingness. Guillaume held his breath as her outstretched hands reached through the empty air for her partner's ankles, and then they were swinging in tandem over his head, a human rope of interlocking limbs.

There was no safety net.

The women flew high above the circus ring. Their tricks became more elaborate and more dangerous. They swung in perfect synchronicity, every twist and half turn measured to perfection, every grip and release timed to the millisecond. The smallest of errors would have been fatal.

When the acrobats climbed back down to the circus ring to take their bows, the audience rose to its feet and roared. Soon afterward Guillaume hurried back to his studio and put a fresh canvas onto his easel before he had even taken off his hat and coat. He needed to paint the trapeze artists while his heart was still racing. He wanted to capture their bravery, their strength, their fluid grace. He worked long into the night.

When he woke the following morning, Guillaume was dismayed to discover that nothing he had painted the previous evening came close to the dazzling spectacle he had witnessed. The acrobats' lithe bodies and taut muscles were executed well enough, but the thrilling poetry of those death-defying stunts had escaped his brush.

That evening he returned to Boulevard Rochechouart. He could not afford another ticket, but he knew he had to watch the acrobats again. After the performance had begun, he crept down the alleyway behind the circus building, hoping to find an unguarded back entrance. As he made his way through the shadows he could hear the cheers and applause of the audience inside.

The first door he tried did not yield, but the second one did. He stepped inside. The backstage area was dimly lit and unfurnished. The aromas of freshly cut straw and sour horse piss hit the back of his nostrils. Exotically dressed performers waited for their turn to go onstage. None of them noticed him—they were all too busy watching the show from the wings. Guillaume skirted the periphery of the room, staying in the shadows, until he could see into the arena. The watching crowd of performers blocked his view of the circus ring itself, but he didn't mind. He didn't care what was happening on the ground. He was waiting for the acrobats. When they began, he would just have to look up.

That night, as the women swung high over the audience, he was mesmerized afresh by their need for constant perfection. Once again, he returned to his room and painted until he could no longer keep his eyes open.

Guillaume began to spend three or four nights a week at the Cirque Medrano, creeping through the back door after the show began. He returned to his studio each night and tried to capture the acrobats' strength and beauty on the canvas, but every morning brought the same disappointment.

He was no longer interested in the other glories that Paris had to offer. All he wanted to do was to paint the acrobats. He sketched them compulsively, their elegant forms appearing on every piece of paper he touched. Soon their bodies became as familiar to him as his own hands. He went back to the circus night after night and wondered about the women as they flew over the audience. Were they lovers? He pictured the two of them together. His paintings took on a vivid, erotic charge.

And then one night, the white woman lost her footing as she climbed down the rope ladder at the end of the act. She was thirty feet from the ground when she fell. Guillaume heard her cry when she landed on the ground. The audience murmured anxiously, but he could not see what was going on. When she was carried out of the circus ring on a makeshift stretcher, Guillaume put on his hat and left.

He returned the following night, but the trapeze artists did not perform.

He never went back to the circus again.

Nobody wanted to buy Guillaume's paintings of the trapeze artists in miraculous flight. Reluctantly, he turned his attention to other subjects. Without the acrobats of the Cirque Medrano to inspire him, he painted the chaotic aggregations of empty bottles that littered his studio and street scenes that unfolded daily around Pigalle. He sold dashed-off cartoon caricatures of tourists strolling through the streets of Montmartre for a franc or two, just so he could eat.

A year passed. One morning Guillaume was sitting in a café on Rue Lepic, sketching while he waited for his coffee to cool. He had spent the previous afternoon wandering through the Montmartre cemetery, and now he was idly filling a page of his notebook with an army of weeping stone angels.

"That one is beautiful." An elegant fingertip on the paper.

Guillaume looked up. A woman was standing next to him. Her hair cascaded around her shoulders in russet waves. She was looking at the page with beautiful gray eyes.

"Thank you," he said. Then he added: "It's just a sketch."

"But a good one." The woman bent down to look more closely. Guillaume caught the faintest hint of citrus. "You've captured them perfectly."

"Would you like it?" he asked.

The woman laughed in surprise. "I would *love* it!"

Guillaume tore the sheet of paper out of the notebook and handed it to her.

"Are you quite sure?" she said.

"Of course."

"You must let me give you something for it."

He shook his head. "I'm happy for you to have it."

"Well, thank you." The woman smiled at him. "I shall cherish this." With that she began to walk toward the door of the café.

Guillaume did not want her to leave, but he was too shy to ask her to stay. "You're most welcome, madame," he called.

She stopped and looked back at him. "Actually," she said, "it's mademoiselle." Then she pushed open the door without another backward glance. Guillaume stared through the window as she made her way toward Rue Véron. She walked with a slight limp. So, he thought, not entirely perfect.

Once she had disappeared from view, Guillaume sat back and drank his coffee. He remembered her limp, and that was when he realized that he had seen her before.

He began to look for her.

For weeks he prowled the streets of Montmartre, peering hopefully into every bar and café. How could he not have seen at once that she was the trapeze artist from the circus? He had drawn her face and body so many times! Even with her hair a different color, he should have recognized her. Drawing a person is first and foremost an act of looking. He had stared at her for countless hours, both in the flesh and on canvas—but when it mattered most, he had failed to see her.

And then, one morning, there she was, sitting alone on a bench in front of Sacré-Coeur. Guillaume came to a halt several paces away. Her hands were clasped together on her lap. She had tilted her head back so that her face met the full embrace of the sun; her eyes were closed against its glare. Guillaume watched her for several minutes. Finally, he walked up to her.

"Excuse me," he said.

The woman opened her eyes and looked at him.

"Do you remember me?" he asked.

She gave him a radiant smile. "Of course I remember you," she said. "I look at your angels every day, monsieur. They're beautiful."

He blushed. "Guillaume Blanc." He held out his hand.

"Suzanne Mauriac," she said. Her hand was warm and strong. "Won't you join me?"

Guillaume sat down next to her on the bench. Paris stretched out in front of them, vast and beautiful, the city's rooftops twinkling in the sunlight. "I've been hoping I would see you again," he said.

She smiled. All around them mothers kept a close watch on their playing children, vigilant shepherds of their flocks. Men strode by in twos and threes, gesticulating in earnest conversation. "I like to sit here and watch the world go by," she said. "If you wait long enough, most of life will pass under your nose. It's quite the show."

"Any street or square in Paris would give the Folies-Bergère a run for its money," agreed Guillaume.

"In Montmartre especially," she said. "Always a spectacle!"

"You live here?"

She nodded. "I wouldn't live anywhere else."

"I realized after you left the café the other day that I've seen you before," said Guillaume.

"Oh yes?"

"It was at the Cirque Medrano. You were an acrobat."

Suzanne Mauriac pressed her hand against her throat as she let out a gleeful laugh. "*Enfin!*" she exclaimed. "My terrible secret is out!"

"I saw you fall and hurt your foot."

She looked at him. "You were there that night?"

"I was there most nights. There was a back door to the place that was always open. I used to creep in and watch your act from the wings. Then I went home and painted you."

"Goodness," said Suzanne.

They were silent for a moment.

"What happened to the other girl?" asked Guillaume.

"Hélène? She left. I broke my ankle in that fall, and I was no good to her after that. I couldn't walk for months, let alone swing on a trapeze. She found work somewhere else, and left soon afterward. I haven't seen her since."

"That's too bad."

Suzanne shrugged. "Do you still have any of the paintings you made of us?" she asked. "I'd love to see them."

Guillaume shook his head. "Not a single one."

"You sold them all?"

"I painted over them."

"Ah, *non*. Why?"

"Because they were terrible."

"I doubt that. I've seen your work, remember."

"I could never capture the thrill of it all, the excitement."

She turned to look at him. "Would you like another chance?" she asked.

"Another chance to what?"

Her gray eyes dancing. "To paint me."

He had one unused canvas in his studio. He pulled a chair into the center of the room, and motioned to Suzanne to sit.

"I have a question," she said.

"Of course."

A small smile played around the edges of her mouth. "Should I take my clothes off before I sit down?"

Guillaume swallowed. He had spent countless hours thinking about the acrobats, obsessively drawing them in infinite permutations and configurations. Night after night he had dreamed of their lithe, supple bodies. He had often imagined what lay beneath those outfits.

"That would be fine," he croaked.

He studiously arranged his easel and began to mix paints while Suzanne stepped out of her dress. She sat down on the chair and looked directly at him. Guillaume's fingers hovered above his paintbrushes, paralyzed by the sight of her. Her limbs were still sleekly muscled, her body lean and strong.

"Here I am," she said. "Paint what you see."

He worked for hours. Suzanne sat in the chair and watched him, not saying a word. By the time he had finished, it was late afternoon. He went to the window and looked out over the city's rooftops. Suzanne stood up. She crossed the room and put a hand on his shoulder. He did not turn around.

"Are you happy with your work?" she asked.

He nodded. "Would you like to see it?"

"If you want to show me."

He led her to the easel. Suzanne looked at the painting.

"Do you like it?" asked Guillaume.

Finally she turned toward him. "I love it," she said. "Do you?"

"It's the best thing I've ever done."

Suzanne's face was serious. "I told you to paint what you saw."

"Yes."

"And this is what you saw?"

"Yes."

She put her hand on his chest.

"Do you like it?" he asked again.

She undressed him then, and took him to bed.

• • •

When it was over, they lay in each other's arms and listened to the sounds of the city's streets floating in through the open window.

"I should go," she said.

He wanted her to stay forever. "Must you?"

"Oh yes." She rolled away from him and climbed out of the bed.

Guillaume watched her collect her clothes. "Can I see you again?" he asked.

Suzanne buttoned up her dress and smiled at him. "I don't think so."

He propped himself up on one elbow. "Did I do something wrong?"

She shook her head. "Not at all. I've had a wonderful time. I'll treasure the memory of it. But some things are better left just as they are."

Guillaume frowned. "I don't understand."

"This has been perfect, don't you think?"

"Yes, but—"

"And that's how I want to leave it." She sat down on the edge of the bed and stroked his cheek with a fingertip. "I want to remember us exactly like this. No fights, no disappointments. No broken hearts. Just a perfect memory."

She had given the speech many times before.

"A perfect memory." He sighed.

Suzanne kissed him lightly on the lips and stood up. She walked over to the painting, which was not yet quite dry, and ran a finger along the top of the canvas. "And you'll always have this to remember us by."

With that, she was gone.

Guillaume hammered a nail into the wall and hung up the painting so that he could stare at it from his bed.

For the next week, he languished in his room, crucified and bewitched. The rest of the world retreated, cast into shadow.

He stared at the painting for hours on end.

When he finally left the studio, he turned every corner beset by anxious elation. He wanted to see Suzanne more than anything in the world. He longed to stare into those eyes again.

It was about a week later when he finally spotted her on Boulevard de Clichy. Guillaume stopped and stared across the busy thoroughfare.

She was not alone.

A man walked by her side, gesticulating comically. Suzanne's head was thrown back in laughter. Guillaume could have been standing right in front of them and she would not have noticed him. He remembered that laugh all too well, so full of unabashed delight.

The couple turned down Rue Houdon and disappeared.

Guillaume stood on the sidewalk.

After that there was no escaping her. Suzanne was everywhere he turned. Sometimes she was alone, but she was usually in the company of a man—although never the same one twice. Guillaume wondered if she had given each of them the same little speech.

There was a quiet change in register to Guillaume's longing. He understood that his memory of their hours together would have to be enough.

The painting helped. He could look at it whenever he liked, for as long as he liked. He knew every brushstroke by heart. That, at least, nobody could ever take away from him.

Ah, but what tricks fate plays on the beleaguered heart!

As the months passed, Guillaume noticed an unmistakable swell to Suzanne's belly. The following spring, a baby carriage.

A little girl.

He looked at the calendar. He counted the months. And, because men are fools, with the little girl there came fresh hope.

Guillaume waited for a knock on the door. He imagined Suzanne standing there, the baby in her arms, begging for help. He would welcome her in, and together they would raise the child and become a family.

But there was no knock. Suzanne did not come looking for him. She did not want his help.

There were no more men scurrying devotedly along by her side. Now it was just Suzanne and her child.

One afternoon he saw them on Rue Custine. Unable to help himself, he followed them until they disappeared into an apartment building on Rue Nicolet. Guillaume stared up at the building's windows. He wondered which ones belonged to them.

In the ten years since then, he has spent countless hours on Rue Nicolet, waiting for them to appear. He gleans what information he can from these brief sightings—new shoes for the little girl, a different hairstyle for Suzanne. These glimpses remind him how little he knows about their lives.

Guillaume has watched his daughter grow from an infant to a beautiful, long-haired sprite. The sight of her never fails to pull his heart to a standstill, but not once has he approached them. He is a penniless artist, after all. He watches as his daughter skips happily down the street. He longs to follow her, but his feet are stilled by shame.

Still, he cannot stay away.

After each sighting Guillaume retreats to his studio and stares at the painting on his wall.

This is what Guillaume Blanc painted that long-ago afternoon as he gazed at Suzanne Mauriac from across his studio:

A small house, in the middle of a wood.

On either side of the house erupts an army of trees, streaking upward into swirling knots of darkness, black stars of mordant energy. Ranks of lichen-wrapped trunks surge toward each other, a sinister labyrinth of shadows. There is no sky: the dark forest marauds across the canvas, annexing every square inch.

There is a strip of lawn in front of the house. On the grass stands a solitary wooden chair. An owl is perched on the back of the chair. Its feathers are silver and purple. It is gazing off into the distance.

A path leads to the house, but there is no door there, just a wall.

The walls of the house are painted white. All the light gathers here, a radiant defiance against the encroaching shadows. But we cannot see what lies within Guillaume's little cottage in the forest, because it has no windows.

No windows, no door . . . but no, there *is* a door. It is a rich, deep blue, and it sits in the very center of the building's façade, suspended halfway between the ground and the roof.

The door is the only way into the house.

Every night Guillaume lies in his bed and looks across the room at the painting. The last thing he sees before he goes to sleep is the blue door, beautiful and unreachable.

This is the painting that has saved his life, over and over again.

This is the painting that Guillaume Blanc swore he would never sell.

This is the painting that Gertrude Stein has just purchased for six hundred francs.

This is the painting that must save Guillaume's life, one last time.

15

The Language of Flowers

JEAN-PAUL MAILLARD STANDS in the hallway of the apartment, pulling on his coat and saying his embarrassed good-byes. It is the interviewee who should confess secrets, not the journalist.

There is a crystal vase standing on a table near the front door, full of perfect red roses. Josephine Baker grabs the flowers and thrusts them into his hands.

"Here," she says. "Take these."

He shakes his head. "Really, there's no——"

"I don't need them. Some man sent them to me. I don't even know who. Wait." She disappears down the corridor and returns a moment later with an old newspaper. She wraps the dripping stems in it and hands them back to him. "There." She pats his hand and opens the door.

No further words or instructions are needed. Jean-Paul knows what he is to do with them. "Thank you," he says.

Josephine Baker smiles at him. "We'll see each other at Le Chat Blanc tonight?"

He nods. "I'll look forward to it."

"*Alors, à ce soir.*"

Jean-Paul limps down the staircase. A moment later he steps out onto the street. The grim-faced concierge of the building opposite is sweeping the sidewalk with a stiff broom. A cloud of dust dances around her thick ankles. Jean-Paul raises the bouquet of red roses to his nose and inhales deeply. They smell of sunlight and hope. His leg is aflame, mortification salting the old wound. At the entrance to Parc Monceau, he turns in through the ornate iron gates. He is agitated by his encounter with Josephine Baker, and is not yet ready for the claustrophobic embrace of the Métro. He needs fresh air and some time to think. As he makes his way down the winding gravel paths and past the overflowing flower beds, his pace slows. Finally he stops in front of a marble bust of Guy de Maupassant, who looks sternly off into the middle distance.

Josephine Baker was so young, so pretty, so kind. When she looked at him with those big, dark eyes and asked what kept him in Paris, the words had poured out of him. She sat quite still as he told his story. Behind her famous face, Jean-Paul saw the little girl who scrabbled around beneath tables for bruised fruit at the market. She knew the fragility of happiness, and for this reason he trusted her.

Now, though, he feels nothing but dreadful embarrassment. How unprofessional he has been! He looks up at the statue of Maupassant—now there, he thinks ruefully, is a *proper* writer—and shakes his head. He is so appalled by his indiscretion that he contemplates ignoring her invitation to Le Chat Blanc this evening, but decides against it. He cannot slink away from his mistakes. Tonight is an opportunity to make things right, to show her that he is a professional, after all.

There is a sweet kiss of honeysuckle on the morning breeze. The damp stems of the roses have soaked through the newspaper, and a few drops of water have fallen onto his shoes. Jean-Paul glances at his watch. With a nod to Maupassant, he turns and makes his way back toward the park's entrance and disappears down the steps of the Métro station.

As he waits for his train, Jean-Paul holds the roses out in front of him, so as not to drip any more water on himself. When the train pulls in, he becomes aware that some people are casting furtive glances in his direction. He looks straight ahead. At Place de Clichy a small group of women board the train. They nudge each other and point at him. One or two stare at him with indulgent looks on their faces. They are remembering a time when men traveled across the city to bring *them* flowers.

The women would not be looking at him like this if he were carrying lilies, reflects Jean-Paul. Flowers have their own silent vocabulary. There are blooms for love, for friendship, for sorrow, and for joy. He inspects the roses he is carrying. Long-stemmed and elegant, they have been grown, selected, arranged, and purchased for a single, unambiguous purpose: to seduce. Jean-Paul considers unwrapping the newspaper and handing a single flower to each woman who is jumping to such wrong conclusions about him. He thinks about Josephine Baker's devoted admirer who has pinned so much hope on these twelve roses. They are so identical, so perfect, they must have cost a fortune. She does not even remember his name.

Pigalle, Stalingrad, Belleville. Jean-Paul looks at his reflection in the carriage window as the darkness rumbles by. Finally, his destination. He steps off the train and makes his way toward the exit, his uneven footsteps echoing along the tile-wrapped tunnels. He emerges blinking into the sun and sets off down the street.

Clutching the flowers, Jean-Paul walks through the gates of the cemetery and into the labyrinth of tombs. His pace slows as he nears his destination. He does not want to read the terrible, granite-inscribed truth that awaits him there.

As he walks along the familiar paths, he notices that someone has left a spray of fresh camellias on the tomb of Marcel Proust.

16

The Search Begins

OLIVIER IS RIGHT. Paris is a big city. A beautiful, glittering haystack.

Where to start looking for such a precious needle?

On Boulevard Saint-Germain, Camille passes in front of Les Deux Magots and Café de Flore. Waiters move with regal grace between the tables, full trays of drinks balanced on their upturned hands. She has heard that famous writers like to spend whole days in these establishments, drinking coffee, arguing with strangers and acquaintances, and perhaps sometimes jotting down a sentence or two. She sniffs. Monsieur Proust would never have contemplated such an unserious existence. His work was too important to be conducted in public.

Camille walks on, clutching her handbag tightly. The money she took from the hotel safe is as heavy as rocks. Men are such imbeciles, she thinks. Her husband is jealous of a man already five years in the grave! She cannot forget the look of defiant triumph on Olivier's face as he stood in the bathroom doorway, watching her. It is a look that throws into doubt everything that has gone before. With every step comes a recalibration of the last fourteen years. The cumulative effect of these microscopic adjustments is devastating: she looks back and no longer recognizes her own marriage.

She crosses the river at the Palais Bourbon. She is going by blind instinct. Where would you go to sell something that is priceless? To where the most money is, of course. She heads toward Rue du Faubourg Saint-Honoré.

It is a *quartier* she knows well. Boulevard Haussmann is not far away, and before the war she and Olivier liked to explore the area after their work for Monsieur Proust was over for the day. They held hands as they strolled up and down the streets, dazzled and bewitched by the fairy tales on display in every shop window. Other worlds existed beyond the glass. There were ankle-length fur coats, of sable and fox and mink. There were impossibly beautiful dresses, shimmering with light and promise. There were strings of perfect pearls, made for the neck of a princess. Olivier used to nudge and tease her, urging her to step inside the shops, but Camille remained frozen on the sidewalk. She was a country girl from the Lozère! She could no more cross those thresholds than fly to the moon.

Now she walks past those same shop fronts, but no longer stops in wonderment in front of every boutique. Today she is shopping to save her own life.

Camille walks the neighborhood for an hour. She gets lost and regains her bearings. She retraces her steps. Finally she finds what she is looking for. She pushes open the narrow door and steps inside.

There is only one person in the shop, an elderly man who is standing behind a counter at the far end of the room. The walls are lined with shelves from ceiling to floor, every one of them bursting with books. Volumes are crammed into every available inch of space, some horizontal, some vertical, some poking out at peculiar angles. The building could disappear, thinks Camille, and there would still be an edifice standing, its walls made entirely of paper. She breathes in the comforting smell of old books, and wonders how many lifetimes of stories are held here.

"Can I help you, madame?" asks the man behind the counter. "Are you looking for something in particular?"

Camille walks to the back of the shop. The shopkeeper has a certain shabby gentility. His white hair is a little longer than it should be. His tie is marginally askew. He is wearing a dapper pinstriped vest, but Camille can see the ghost of his breakfast smeared just above the breast pocket. She wonders how many of these books he has read.

"Do you buy books, as well as sell them?" she asks.

"If they're of good quality, then *bien sûr*. I reject a great deal of what people bring in because it's in poor condition." The man shakes his head sadly. "You wouldn't believe the way people treat their books these days."

Camille nods anxiously. "Have you bought anything recently?"

"Of course, every day. Are you looking to sell something yourself, madame?"

"Oh no. Quite the opposite, in fact. I'm looking to *buy* a book."

"What is it you're looking for?"

Camille looks around. "Do you know every volume on your shelves?" she asks.

"Of course." The bookseller taps the side of his head. "It's all up here."

"I'm looking for a book by Marcel Proust."

The man's eyes light up. "Ah! What a treat you have in store for you, madame! Or perhaps you're already familiar with his work?"

Camille falters. "Well, I—"

"Oh, I'm quite jealous! Such a journey you have ahead of you! Seven volumes of wonderment! Seven volumes of consummate mastery of the literary art! Forget Voltaire, or Dumas, or Flaubert, or even Victor Hugo. Never has the French language been so blessed by the craft of such a genius!" The shopkeeper beams at her. "Of course, you'll want to start with *Du côté de chez Swann*." He steps out from behind the counter and walks down the shop, scanning the spines of the books. "I believe I have several copies here for you to choose from." He runs his hand along the shelves as he goes.

"As a matter of fact," says Camille, "that isn't the book I'm looking for."

"So you've already begun! *Alors*, which volume do you need?"

"Actually, I'm looking for a different kind of book altogether."

"A different *kind* of book, madame? What do you mean?"

"I'm looking for a notebook."

The shopkeeper frowns. "Marcel Proust's notebooks were never published."

"Yes, I know. This isn't a published book."

"Then I'm afraid I don't understand."

"I'm looking for an actual notebook," explains Camille. "One that he wrote in."

The man gives her a small, condescending smile. "You can visit every bookstore in Paris, madame, but you'll never find what you're looking for. Marcel Proust's notebooks are preserved at the *Bibliothèque nationale*. All the ones that survived, that is." The bookseller taps the shelf next to him thoughtfully. "I heard a rumor that there were many more, but that he had them destroyed some years before he died. Such a tragedy! I can only imagine what treasures one would find within those pages!" He smiles. "But, of course I am being greedy. Monsieur Proust has given us gifts enough."

"Thank you very much, monsieur," says Camille, turning to go. "You've been most helpful."

The man looks disappointed. "You're quite sure there's nothing else I can help you with?"

"No, thank you."

Back out on the street, Camille remembers her husband's words. *Paris is a big city, Camille.* She had thought nothing of Olivier's absence the previous afternoon, but now she remembers that he was away for several hours. In that time he could have gone anywhere. There must be hundreds of bookshops he might have visited.

The thought heralds a fresh storm of despair. She considers returning to the hotel now and making a full confession to her husband. When Olivier understands what is at stake, he will tell her where he sold the notebook. But she does not want to admit the danger she has put her family in, not yet.

She decides to give herself the day. If she does not find it by this evening then she will tell him everything, and explain what lies in those pages that he has so carelessly sold to a stranger.

Still, the thought of the notebook out in the world makes her veins run cold with dread. Camille stares up at the sky, remembering the first time her disbelieving eyes fell on the terrible words, the warmly familiar handwriting sharpening their treachery.

Betrayal, she learned that day, can go both ways.

17

Vaucluse, 1917:
The Kindness of Strangers

THE VILLAGE LOOKED LIKE a hundred other places he had passed through over the last several months. As Hector trotted gently down the road into the valley, Souren gazed down on the church spire that emerged from the uneven chessboard of terra-cotta and slate rooftops below him. The buildings were clustered close together, hemmed in on all sides by dark forest.

Souren had dreamed of France every night during his trek north. The first time that he studied the map of Europe, he knew that he needed a destination, somewhere to aim for. He remembered his mother once telling him that there were more than three hundred types of cheese made in France. Souren had solemnly replied that one day he would go there and try every one of them.

There were worse reasons to choose a place to begin a new life.

The thought of those cheeses had kept him company on every step of his long journey from Anatolia. Every day the outrageous number dazzled him afresh. He tried to imagine living in a country blessed with such abundance. How happy the French must be! It was this idea of jovial, contented Frenchmen, their bellies full of delicious dairy product, that made him climb back into Hector's saddle each morning. Once Constantinople was behind him he could have stopped anywhere, but those three hundred cheeses beckoned him on, through months of lonely travel, across borders and mountain ranges.

And for what?

It was over a week since Souren had crossed the border into France. He and Hector had ridden deep into the new country, the imperious Alps now at their backs. The countryside was windswept and craggedly beautiful. The roads were punctuated by a string of isolated villages. He waved to the natives and received nothing but suspicious glares in return. The French did not seem so happy, after all. Worse still, he was yet to taste a single bite of cheese. But he could not turn back now.

By the time he reached the edge of the village, the sun was starting to set behind the hills to the west. The first houses he passed were closed up, doors locked and wooden shutters latched tight. There was not a soul to be seen. The streets were silent but for the tattoo of Hector's hooves on the cobbles. Not even a dog barked.

"Did we stumble on a ghost town?" Souren whispered in the horse's ear. They stopped in the village square, in front of the church he'd seen on his descent into the valley. In the middle of the square there was a small fountain, and Souren allowed Hector to drink from its basin. He was hungry, and had been looking forward to a good meal, but the place was deserted. Souren sighed. It wouldn't be the first time that he had gone to sleep with an empty stomach. He decided to ride on a mile or two into the woods on the other side of the village and set up camp for the night. He patted Hector's neck. "Come on," he said. "There's nothing for us here."

Just then he heard a sound he knew all too well. The staccato one-two click, the gritted bite of steel on steel: the chambers of a shotgun being loaded. At once he was back in Anatolia, trudging onward into nothingness, the barrel of a soldier's rifle trained on the back of his head.

He turned in the direction of the noise. Thirty feet away from him, a man stood, his gun aimed at Souren's chest.

Souren dropped the reins and slowly put his hands above his head. He did not take his eyes off the end of the weapon, which was weaving unsteadily in a small figure of eight. The gunman shouted something unintelligible at him. When Souren did not respond, the man took a step forward. He stumbled on the uneven cobbles, and as he tried to regain his balance, there was a flash from the barrel of the gun. The bullet streaked harmlessly into the darkening sky, but the noise of the shot obliterated reason. Hector rose up on his hind legs, snorting in terror. Without the reins to hold on to, Souren was thrown off the horse's back. His body twisted in panic as he fell through the air.

When Souren awoke, he was lying in a bed, enveloped in fresh white sheets. He could not remember the last time he had enjoyed such a luxury—ever since his escape from the death march, his nights had been spent sheltering under bridges or shivering on the floor of cold, deserted barns. He lay quite still, enjoying the kiss of the cotton against his skin and the softness of the mattress beneath him. He shifted beneath the sheets, and a lacerating fissure exploded down one side of his body. He cried out at the pain.

A middle-aged woman was sitting next to the bed, a book in her hand. She looked up from its pages and said something that he could not understand. Souren tried to sit up, and this prompted an even fiercer jolt of agony. At this the woman reached out a hand and touched his shoulder. She spoke again, more urgently this time.

"Where is Hector?" Souren asked her. "Where is my horse?"

At this the woman leaned back in her chair and called out. A moment later a man appeared by the side of the bed. He peered down at Souren and began to speak. Again, Souren did not understand a word he said.

"Where is Hector?" he asked.

"*Hector*," repeated the man, his eyes flashing in recognition. He pointed at Souren. "Hector?"

"No, no," said Souren. "Hector is my *horse*. Have you seen him? Is he all right?"

The man murmured something to the woman, and then started to speak, slowly and clearly. Souren shook his head to show that he did not understand, but even this small movement made him wince. The man pointed to himself. "Philippe," he said. He pointed to the woman. "Françoise."

"Françoise," whispered Souren.

Later that day Françoise ushered a tall, unsmiling man into the bedroom. He carried a leather bag, which he placed between his feet as he sat down in the chair next to the bed. Souren watched the man anxiously. Was he a policeman, come to take him into custody? The man said a few gruff words. When he reached down to open his bag, he did not produce handcuffs, or a gun. He removed a stethoscope.

The doctor performed a careful examination, speaking quietly to Souren as he worked. Souren found the meaningless words strangely calming. When the doctor finished, he talked at some length to Françoise, and handed her a piece of paper. Then he was gone.

The medicine that the doctor prescribed was appalling, a toxic syrup that made Souren's lips pucker whenever Françoise brought it close to his mouth, but it served to dull the pain.

Each day Françoise sat by the bed and pointed at things, saying the word in what he supposed was French. Bed. Table. Window. Book. She wrote each word down on a sheet of paper and, once he was well enough to prop himself up, made Souren copy out each word ten times.

Souren drew a picture of Hector and showed it to Françoise. "Have you seen my horse?" he asked her, in Armenian.

She smiled and shook her head.

Three times a day Françoise brought Souren food on old plates, their elegant patterns faded by years of use. She served up hearty stews, thickly sliced hams, slabs of roasted chicken, the crisp golden skin salty and delicious. She brought mountains of sweet, fresh vegetables, bowls of piping hot soup, and crusty baguettes as thick as Souren's forearms. Each night she gave him a sliver of cake, a crumbling pastry, or a delicate slice of tart. And, yes, she brought cheese: creamy white triangles; stout, blue-veined

wedges; and unctuous concoctions that oozed across the plate, their vol-
canic fumes catching at the back of his nose.

Souren ate as if he had never eaten before.

Françoise sat next to the bed and watched him.

After a week Souren was well enough to climb out of bed. His shoulder
still hurt, but he was able to make his way down the stairs. The house was
modest, but elegant in its simplicity. The kitchen was the largest room in
the house. He sat at a long wooden table and watched Françoise prepare
their meals. She moved with calm assurance as she cooked. Souren thought
of his mother, who had always fretted unhappily in the kitchen, a never-
ending stream of gloomy predictions about the meal to come passing her
lips. Everything was served with the same air of resigned defeat. Her despair was often justified, but Souren's father never failed to shower each
dish with extravagant praise and always asked for a second helping, which
he ate with as much ostentatious relish as he did the first. Souren had done
his best to carry on the tradition after his father disappeared, but sometimes he would fall silent when he saw his mother and brother looking at
him in silent misery.

Each morning and afternoon, Souren walked through the village and
into the countryside beyond. It was early spring. Clusters of flowers
bloomed on the verges of the lanes, tiny explosions of yellow and purple.
A chorus of exquisite birdsong filled the air. Souren saw and heard little of
this, however. He was looking for his horse. He peered into every pasture
and searched every unlocked barn, but Hector was nowhere to be seen.
When Souren became too tired to go any farther, he turned and traipsed
back to the village.

The main square had a butcher's shop, a baker, a hardware store, and
two vegetable stalls. Most of the day's business was concluded by the middle of the morning. In the afternoon old men gathered on the wooden
benches beneath the ash trees to smoke and grumble at each other. Sometimes they hauled themselves upright long enough for a round of *pétanque*.
Souren liked to watch these games. The men's lethargy vanished when it

was their turn to play. They crouched forward, suddenly lithe and alert, considering their shot. The metal balls caught the sunlight as they flew through the air. In the group was the man who had appeared out of the shadows with his shotgun on Souren's first night in the village. Souren felt his suspicious eyes linger on him, and would quickly walk away.

At his new home, the French lessons continued. There were so many things to put a name to. They identified words by pointing and pantomime. Françoise helped him write down each word and corrected his attempts at pronunciation.

Merci, he said. *S'il-vous plaît.*

It was months since Souren had spoken to anyone other than his horse, and he was determined to learn this new language. He was a diligent student, and before long he could communicate in a rudimentary fashion with his hosts. One night he showed them his map, tattered and torn from the constant folding and unfolding during his long trek north, and pointed to where he came from.

"Armenia," said Françoise softly.

"You know there is a war going on, don't you?" asked Philippe.

Souren nodded.

"The other villagers think you're an escaped soldier." He mimed firing a rifle. "They think you are German."

"German?" said Souren.

Philippe pointed to the map. "I have told them that they're wrong, but the less men know about a thing, the harder it is to make them change their minds about it."

"But I do not speak German!"

"All they know is that you do not speak *French*," replied Philippe.

Françoise patted the back of his hand. "You're welcome in our home, Souren, but you should always remember that you're a stranger in this town."

Souren thought of the old man who appeared out of the shadows with his shotgun on the night he and Hector arrived. He could still see the look on the villager's face as he raised the weapon to his shoulder. Souren's only crime was to be from somewhere else.

18

Thérèse

GUILLAUME SITS DOWN on the bed and stares at the empty wall. There is a pale rectangle where Suzanne's painting has sat for the last ten years. His hangover has returned with a vengeance, sharpened by loss and regret.

What a fool he has been.

He thinks of the artists who used to live in Montmartre after the war. They had painted together, laughed together, drank together, and fought together. Each pursued his art with rare singularity of purpose. It was a time of gallant, impoverished idealism and fraternity, ripe with the promise of possibility. But they had all left, one by one, beguiled by the more refined comforts of Montparnasse and the Left Bank. Over there, patrons bought their work before the paint was dry, and to hell with the price. There were enough art collectors in Paris to make rich men of all of them. All it took was a chance encounter with the right benefactor, and a career was made. Guillaume has watched his friends' success until now he is the only one left in the old *quartier*. Of course, there's nothing he wants more than to join his old friends for oysters and a glass of something expensive and delicious at the *zinc* of La Rotonde, but he manages to find a certain painful satisfaction from the fact that he cannot. He wears his poverty like a badge of honor, even as his stomach rumbles. Guillaume does his best to submerge his jealousy beneath a veneer of self-righteous disdain, but it does not always work. Integrity does not pay the bills—or street thugs. He puts his head in his hands. Gertrude Stein's six hundred francs will not save him from Le Miroir's henchmen. Where is he going to get the rest of the money? Then he thinks: Brataille.

Guillaume should have asked the art dealer for a loan the previous evening, but he'd had too much pride. There is no time for such indulgences now. He thinks about Brataille's lovesick tears as he drank himself under the table last night. If Guillaume can persuade Thérèse to give him another chance, he can probably name his price. Unfortunately he knows that his chances of success are practically nonexistent. She is not a woman who changes her mind.

Thérèse is beautiful in a sultry, exotic way. Her body is made for pleasure, all delicious curves and ripe flesh. She is the most popular whore working at Le Chat Blanc. Customers have been falling in love with her for years. Guillaume has heard many stories of her clients' lust-addled buffoonery. They promise her the world: money, diamonds, even, once, a small apartment on Rue du Cherche-Midi. One or two have begged for her hand in marriage. Thérèse has no patience for such nonsense. When customers start to act like besotted fools, they become more trouble than they are worth, and she refuses to see them again. Brataille appears to have fallen into this trap. Guillaume is sure that nothing he can say will make Thérèse change her mind, but he needs to try. Without another six hundred francs, he'll be on the train back to La Rochelle before the end of the day.

He cannot look at the empty wall where Suzanne's painting hung for another moment. He needs to escape, to turn away from what he has lost. He stands up, stuffs Gertrude Stein's money beneath the mattress, and hurries down the stairs.

The cafés and restaurants of Montmartre are filled with people. Guillaume traipses along the streets, thinking about the empty patch of wall where Suzanne's painting used to be, stunned that he will never see it again. He remembers Suzanne, buttoning up her dress, getting ready to make her escape. *You'll always have this to remember us by.*

He lets out a small bleat of anguish. He starts to walk toward Rue des Abbesses.

Thérèse is already at work. Her leather skirt clings to her rump as closely as a second skin. Her top is lacy and black. Dark hair falls down her back, alluringly unkempt. There is a dark red slash across her mouth. She is at her usual spot, leaning against a brick wall next to Le Chat Blanc, watching the street, a smoldering cigarette between her long fingers. Some of the women stroll back and forth along the sidewalk, whispering come-ons to the men who shuffle by, but Thérèse stays at her post. She doesn't have to go looking.

She watches him approach. "Well, if it isn't my favorite starving artist," she says, taking a languorous drag on her cigarette. "What brings you around these parts, *chéri?*"

"Actually," says Guillaume, "I wanted to talk to you."

"How exciting," says Thérèse. "But don't take long. They don't like it when we talk too much."

"They?" Guillaume glances up and down the street. "Is someone watching?"

Thérèse gives him a sad smile. "Someone is *always* watching."

"I'll be quick, then," says Guillaume. "It's about Emile Brataille."

"Never heard of him," says Thérèse.

"He's a client of yours."

She shrugs. "They don't tell me their names."

"He's an art dealer. He has a gallery on Boulevard Raspail. I'm sure he told you about *that.*"

"Oh, *mon dieu.* Yes, I know who you mean." She exhales a luxuriant plume of white smoke. "His cock is the size of a *cacahuète,*" she tells him.

"Is that so." Guillaume cannot stop a smile spreading from one ear to the other.

"The silly man won't leave me alone," says Thérèse.

"That's why I'm here. He says he's in love with you."

"Of course he's not in love with me," she scoffs. "He needs a bucket of cold water thrown over him, that's all."

"I saw him last night," says Guillaume, who is not willing to give up just yet. "He was weeping over you. Real tears. I saw them."

Thérèse looks at him, unimpressed. "And?"

"Well, when I told him I knew you, he begged me to come and talk to you, to see if you might change your mind. And so here I am."

"What's it to you?"

"Oh, nothing." Guillaume tries a shrug. "He's an old friend of mine, that's all."

"An old friend of yours?" Thérèse looks suspicious.

"The art world in Paris is small, you know," he hedges.

"And you've come to plead his case?"

"All I know," Guillaume says, "is that he's crazy about you."

"Let me explain something to you, *chéri*. These men come here and pay cash for twenty minutes in a room with me." She points toward Le Chat Blanc. "When the door closes they don't get down on one knee and recite poetry, no matter how much they say they adore me. They want one thing, and only one thing, and that is what they get." She sighs. "Why do you think they come here at all?"

Guillaume says nothing. He watches as Thérèse lights another cigarette.

"Because they're terrible people," she continues. "Every last one of them. That's why they have to pay strangers for sex. They're needy and angry and bitter as hell." She looks at him. "Now can you understand why I never want to spend more time with any of them?"

Guillaume can feel hope slipping away. "Please, Thérèse? As a favor to me?"

"I'm sorry, *chéri*." She reaches out and puts a hand on his arm. "You'll have to tell your friend that I'm flattered and everything, but the answer is still no. I don't want to see him or his tiny peanut dick again."

"Hey, you," says a voice in his ear.

Guillaume turns. A huge man has materialized, seemingly out of no-where, and is standing right next to him. He appears to have been built for the specific purpose of inflicting the maximum amount of pain on other people in the most efficient manner possible. His hands are mon-strously huge. His ill-fitting jacket bulges with granite slabs of muscle. He looks capable of tearing Guillaume limb from limb without breaking into a sweat—and would probably do so with a contented smile on his hard, flat face. "She's not here to talk," grunts the man. "Either pay up or move on."

Thérèse shoots the man a look of disgust. "Relax, would you, Léon? He's a friend of mine."

"I don't care if he's the reincarnation of Emperor Napoleon, *ma poule*. Rules are rules." The man gives her an ugly leer and turns back to Guil-laume. "You've had your free look, my friend. Make your decision, or I'll make it for you." He takes a step forward, so close that Guillaume can feel the man's stale breath on his neck.

"I'll go," he mutters.

"It's always good to see you, Guillaume," says Thérèse softly.

"I don't suppose you've got six hundred francs you could lend me?" he says.

Guillaume can still hear her laughter as he walks away.

19

Paris, 1918:
The Treble Clef

JEAN-PAUL MAILLARD STANDS in front of the small grave, lost in his memories.

Anaïs Maillard had an exquisite voice—the kind of voice, her husband used to say, that could charm the birds down from the trees.

Jean-Paul loved his wife most when she was singing. It was the ravishing vigor with which she performed that laid siege to his heart. Music coursed through her, a joyous river. It illuminated her from within, filling her with the light of a thousand suns. When there was a tune on her lips, his wife was always the most beautiful person in the room.

Had they lived in Lyon or Toulouse, Anaïs might have pursued a professional singing career, but in Paris there was no hope of that: the finest singers in the world traveled across the globe to perform on the city's stages. But she did not complain. Paris was bursting with music, and she joyfully plundered the riches on offer, joining all the choirs and choruses that she could.

Jean-Paul was sent home from the Western Front in late 1916. Soon after he returned to their apartment on Rue Barbette, Anaïs became pregnant.

She sang to her unborn baby from morning to night. The apartment was always filled with song. Arias, requiems, masses, lieder—the little life growing inside her heard everything. Anaïs continued to rehearse and perform as her stomach swelled, to Jean-Paul's quiet consternation—but he knew that his wife could no more stop singing than she could stop breathing. Her waters broke during a performance of Beethoven's Ninth Symphony. At the hospital she spent the next three hours belting out "Ode to Joy" while she waited for the baby to arrive. Toward the end, the familiar melody was punctuated by a disquieting variety of shrieks and grunts. When their daughter was finally born, her soft infant cries were beautiful, already in harmony with her mother.

Elodie's first months were an anxious procession of fevers and afflictions. She cried frequently and with impressive gusto. She's inherited your lungs, Jean-Paul told Anaïs as they were once again shaken awake by the window-rattling yells from the crib at the end of their bed. The only thing that could quieten the baby's screams was her mother's voice. Within moments of hearing Anaïs sing, Elodie would be cooing along in contented accompaniment. And while Jean-Paul could carry a tune, whenever *he* tried to sing his daughter back to sleep, her beautiful features contorted into a mask of wordless, red-faced fury.

A few months after the birth, Anaïs joined the choir at a nearby church, the Église Saint-Gervais. She took Elodie with her to rehearsals. The baby slept peacefully through it all, becalmed by her mother's song. Anaïs became adept at holding her sheet music in one hand and her sleeping daughter in the other.

Good Friday of 1918 fell on March 29. It was Anaïs's twenty-sixth birthday. That morning Jean-Paul gave her a silver brooch in the shape of a treble clef. She kissed him softly and pinned the brooch onto her blouse.

"Thank you, *chéri*," she said.

"Do you like it?"

"Look where I've pinned it." She pointed. "Over my heart."

"Will you wear it this afternoon?" The choir at the Église Saint-Gervais was to sing at the Good Friday Mass. Anaïs had been looking forward to it for weeks, humming the music to herself as she moved about the apartment.

"Of course." She smiled at him. "I'm going to wear it every time I sing."

Elodie was lying on their bed, cooing gently. Anaïs picked her up. The baby's hand reached immediately for the glittering brooch.

"Ah, someone else likes it, too," said Jean-Paul.

"Of course she does. Elodie has excellent taste, don't you, *ma chère?*" Anaïs began to hum the refrain from a Palestrina motet, rocking the baby gently in her arms.

"I'm sorry I can't come to the service today," said Jean-Paul.

"That's all right."

"You know how much I want to hear you sing, but these deadlines—"

"I know."

"Next time, I promise."

"You get to work. We'll go and enjoy ourselves." She tickled the baby under her chin. Elodie let out a small gurgle of pleasure.

Jean-Paul watched his wife and daughter, his heart full.

After Anaïs and Elodie left for the church, Jean-Paul settled down to work. On his return to Paris, he had resumed his job at the city desk of the newspaper, reporting on stories from across Paris, going wherever his editor sent him. It was tedious work, but it paid the rent. Still, every time he sat down in front of his typewriter he experienced a brief but intense moment of regret. He longed to write a novel, but had been unable to find a tale that he needed to tell. Instead he told other people's stories, rather than his own.

Jean-Paul soon lost himself in the details of a report about the thriving black market for truffles that had sprung up in Paris. War or no war, people loved to eat well, and were ready to pay for the privilege. He was wholly focused on the words on the page in front of him when a low, rolling boom thundered through the apartment. He put on his coat and hobbled out onto the street. People were pouring out of their houses and running in all directions. He made his way to Rue Vieille du Temple, his leg throbbing in foreboding. People were streaming northwards, away from the river.

He called out to a couple who were hurrying past. "What happened? What was that noise?"

"Some kind of explosion," panted the man.

There was a chorus of wailing klaxons in the distance.

"An explosion?" said Jean-Paul. "Where?"

The woman pointed behind her. "Somewhere near Rue de Rivoli."

Jean-Paul began to limp down the street as fast as he could. The shouts and the sirens got louder as he approached the river. He crossed Rue de Rivoli and turned onto Rue François Miron. How many times had he strolled this way, without a care in the world, on his way to Sunday Mass? The street was barely recognizable now. Eddying typhoons of debris floated in the air. People were emerging from the clouds of dust like ghostly figures materializing out of a dawn mist. They staggered down the street in small groups, leaning up against each other for support. Some were limping, others were bleeding.

On Place Saint-Gervais, the doors of the church were open. Jean-Paul climbed the steps, but was stopped by a policeman before he could enter.

"You can't go in," said the gendarme. "It's not safe."

"What happened?"

"A bomb. Direct hit on the north side of the roof."

"I need to find my wife and daughter," said Jean-Paul.

"It's too dangerous, monsieur. The place may collapse at any moment."

"My daughter is six months old," said Jean-Paul, as if this might change the policeman's mind.

"I'm sure your wife and daughter are quite safe, monsieur," said the gendarme. "Find them, and take them home."

Jean-Paul turned to survey the crowds in front of the church. People stood as still as statues, immobilized by the horror. Men yelled warnings. Mothers screamed for their children. He limped back down the steps and began to weave through the chaos, looking for Anaïs and Elodie.

They were not there.

He tried to remain calm, to think. If they had escaped unscathed, there was no reason for them to remain nearby. Anaïs would have taken Elodie back to Rue Barbette. They were probably in the apartment right now. Anaïs would be wondering where he was. He turned and began to retrace his steps. As he hurried home, Jean-Paul did his best to bury his fear. By the time he arrived he had almost convinced himself that he would be greeted with his wife's tales of a close escape and his daughter's gurgles of delight.

The apartment was empty.

For two hours he did not know whether to feel terrified or hopeful. He wanted to be there when the front door finally opened, when he could hold them tightly in his arms and breathe once more. But the waiting was torture. He couldn't sit there and do nothing. Finally he scribbled Anaïs a note, promising to return soon, and put his coat back on.

Back at Place Saint-Gervais, the crowds had disappeared. The doors of the church were open. Men hurried in and out. Jean-Paul climbed the steps and went inside. The floor was hidden beneath an uneven landscape of fallen masonry. He picked his way unsteadily toward the center of the church, the carpet of rubble shifting beneath his feet. Ahead of him he could hear men shouting to each other. As he reached the high-ceilinged nave, he could see dim silhouettes clambering over a mountain of fallen detritus.

Men, looking for bodies.

"Anaïs!" he yelled.

Above him there was a jagged streak of sky: the hole in the roof where the German shell had hit. As he moved forward, a shower of rocks fell on his shoulders. He picked his way toward the altar. There were men everywhere, straining and heaving to shift slabs of fallen stone.

Where were Anaïs and Elodie?

Jean-Paul chose his spot. He began to clear away the rubble.

Hours later, he was still in the church, working in the light of kerosene lamps that had been erected so that rescue efforts could continue into the night. His knuckles were scraped bloody and raw. His limbs were screaming in exhaustion.

There were people buried beneath the fallen stones. Their bodies had been pulverized, their faces bloodied and bruised. Working with another man, Jean-Paul uncovered corpse after corpse. Men, women, young, old; none were spared. A young girl, no more than six or seven years old, was missing her left arm. Without speaking—there were no words—they lifted the bodies out of the rubble and took them down to the front of the church, and delivered them into the care of a priest. Jean-Paul watched the other men carry their own gruesome cargo down the aisle. He looked at every body.

No Anaïs. No Elodie.

There was one last large slab of stone on the ground in front of the altar. Jean-Paul and three other men eased it onto its side and heaved it upright. A body lay beneath it. The force of impact of the falling masonry had twisted the victim's head, the neck gruesomely snapped. There was a black crater smashed into the side of the skull.

But Jean-Paul saw none of this. All he saw was the silver brooch that was pinned to the bloodied shirt.

Jean-Paul stood knee-deep in rubble while two strangers carried Anaïs's body down the nave to the waiting priest. He did not turn to watch. His eyes scanned the floor of the church, his gaze darting among the fallen stone.

He was looking for his daughter.

Nobody had asked Jean-Paul who he was or what he was doing in the church. Now, when he told the men that there was one more body to recover, he saw the ghosts of skepticism creasing into the corners of their tired eyes. Jean-Paul didn't care. He waded back into the debris and began to turn over every last stone, no matter how small. He moved with a manic desperation, the hours of back-breaking work forgotten. His ferocious energy dragged the other men into its irresistible vortex. Within minutes they had all wearily joined the search.

Elodie was not there.

Jean-Paul moved through the ruined church, speaking with every person he saw, asking the same question, over and over. Nobody had seen an infant.

It didn't make any sense. Bodies didn't simply vanish, not even tiny ones. Some trace of her would have remained. He finally stumbled out of the church. Anaïs was behind him, lying beneath a white sheet on the cold stone floor, but he had no time to mourn her, no time to say good-bye—not while Elodie might still be alive.

He limped to the nearest hospital. He went from one ward to the next, then one hospital to the next, interrogating nurses and registrars, asking if a baby girl had been admitted.

The answer was always no.

As the sun rose over the city's rooftops, Jean-Paul traipsed numbly down the deserted streets back to Rue Barbette. Inside the apartment, he picked up the note he had written to Anaïs and tore it into little pieces. His clothes were filthy with sweat and blood and grime, but he was too tired to undress. He lay on the bed and stared into the darkness.

Elodie's disappearance created a fathomless hole into which everything tumbled. His grief needed a body, a home. Without it, he was left suspended by the thinnest threads of improbable hope—threads that refused to break and set him free. A father's love was a bullish beast, immune to logic and reason. Without a body, there was the faintest possibility that Elodie was still alive, and while such a possibility existed, Jean-Paul had no choice but to cling to it with everything he had. Perhaps Elodie had been fussing before the service began, and Anaïs had asked a friend in the congregation to hold her while she sang. Perhaps the baby had been in a different part of the church when the roof collapsed, and she had been carried away to safety. Perhaps there would be a knock on his door tomorrow, and he would see his daughter again, delivered safely back to him.

He lay on the bed, and waited.

There was no knock on the door the next day, or the next. And then he realized: whoever was looking after Elodie would not know who she was or where she lived. Of course there would be no knock. Nobody would bring her to him. He would have to go and find her.

He returned to the hospitals. He visited every orphanage in the city. He papered the walls of the *quartier* with handmade posters, begging for information. He stopped people on the street. He stared helplessly into every baby carriage. He persuaded his editor to run a story about Elodie in the newspaper, listing his name and address. For two days he sat in the empty apartment and waited.

Nobody came.

His sister came to Paris to help with the funeral arrangements. It was she who picked out a coffin for Anaïs, she who chose the flowers, she who purchased the plot at Père Lachaise. The service came and went in a blur. All Jean-Paul could remember was his dismay when he saw the tombstone his sister had ordered.

The black letters carved into the white granite.

There were two names, not one.

It would take more than those thirteen letters etched into stone for Jean-Paul to relinquish the hope that lingered within him.

He filed a missing persons report with the police. He waited in line for hours to speak with city officials. Inquiries would be made, he was told, but there were proper channels to go through, protocols to be followed. Bored municipal employees handed him forms to sign and wished him a good day. But once he had wandered into the city's web, there was no escaping the clutches of bureaucracy. A succession of interviews followed, the same questions asked again and again. Jean-Paul numbly recounted the events of that Good Friday to a stream of unsmiling strangers. He wanted to find his daughter, but the city's officials just wanted the paperwork off their desks. Reports were filed, investigations conducted, conclusions reached.

At the end of it all, over her father's helpless protests, Elodie Maillard was declared dead, along with her mother. But still Jean-Paul believed that his daughter lived, and so he had no choice but to resurrect her.

Finally, he had his story.

He purchased a new notebook and began to write.

Grief robbed him of the sanctuary of sleep. He spent his nights at his desk, telling his daughter's tale—not her brief few months on Rue Barbette, but everything that was still to come. He conjured up the rest of her childhood, a marriage, even children of her own. The words poured out of him, an unstoppable flow. His pen flew across the page as his imagination hurtled toward an unreachable future. While he wrote, his daughter remained exquisitely alive, his words reincarnating her. Sentence after sentence, paragraph after paragraph, he wrote long into those lonely nights.

When he finished, he sat at his desk and wept as he had never wept before. Elodie lived within the pages of the notebook, but now her story was over. This was a second good-bye, almost as painful as the first.

The Good Friday bombing of the Église Saint-Gervais was the most lethal attack on Paris of the war. Eighty-eight dead, read the reports.

Jean-Paul Maillard still believes that it was eight-seven.

He still lives in the same apartment on Rue Barbette. He listens to Gershwin late at night, and reads his story of Elodie's life, and wonders what his daughter looks like now.

She will be ten years old.

This is who Jean-Paul is looking for every morning as he sits on the bandstand in the park by Rue de Bretagne, watching the children play.

As he walks the streets of the city, Jean-Paul is always searching. His eyes scan every crowd, hoping for an echo of Anaïs on a stranger's face.

This is the story Jean-Paul told Josephine Baker.

This is why he can never leave. He may dream of America, but he is lashed to this city, these streets, by ropes of impossible hope.

He will always be searching for his daughter.

20

Paris, 1913:
An Upside–Down Life

CAMILLE BEGAN AS A GLORIFIED postman. The first volume of Monsieur Proust's novel, *Du côté de chez Swann*, had just been published, and he wanted to send signed copies of the book to his friends. Nicolas Cottin, the valet, wrapped the books meticulously—blue paper for gentlemen, pink paper for ladies. Every morning she made her way to Boulevard Haussmann, where Nicolas would hand her the day's deliveries, always with precise instructions. She never saw her new employer during these visits. She tucked the parcels beneath her arm, climbed into a horse-drawn cab, and set off into the city.

In this way Camille discovered Paris. She learned to recognize different squares and thoroughfares. She especially loved to make deliveries across the river, on the Left Bank. Halfway across the Pont Royal, she would sometimes ask the cab driver to stop, just for a moment, so she could look out at the waters of the Seine.

When all the books had been sent out, Nicolas announced that Monsieur Proust still wanted her to come to the apartment every morning. There was usually a letter or two that needed to be delivered. Camille was pleased with this arrangement, and so was Olivier: he could see how much happier his wife was when she had something to occupy her days other than the lonely tedium of housework in the couple's apartment in Levallois. And it was true: she looked forward to taking the bus from Porte d'Asnières to Gare Saint-Lazare every morning. Sometimes there was something for her to deliver; sometimes there was not. Either way, she enjoyed the never-ending theater to be found on the streets of Paris.

One evening that December Olivier returned home late. "You'll never guess what's happened!" he said as he walked through the door.

He was like a big puppy when he became excited. Camille smiled at him. "What, *mon amour?*"

"Céline Cottin has fallen ill."

"Oh no. Is it serious?"

"It appears to be. She's in the hospital. Poor Nicolas is beside himself with worry."

"How awful!"

"Here's the thing, Camille. With Céline sick, Monsieur Proust has no chambermaid." His tone was stricken, as if the writer had lost both his arms. "He—Monsieur Proust—suggested that perhaps you might be able to come to the apartment during the afternoons to help him. That way Nicolas can be with Céline during her recuperation."

Camille wrinkled her nose. "To *help* him? With what? Can't the man exist on his own in the apartment for a few hours?"

Olivier laughed.

The next afternoon Camille appeared at Marcel Proust's apartment and was welcomed in by a harried-looking Nicolas. They stood in the middle of the kitchen.

"This is a nice place," she said, looking around. "I didn't realize that being a writer paid so well."

"Oh, he doesn't own it," whispered Nicolas. "The building belongs to his great-aunt. She lets him live here for almost nothing."

"Why are you whispering?" asked Camille.

"Because Monsieur Proust is asleep."

Camille snorted. "But it's four o'clock in the afternoon!"

Nicolas inclined his head ever so slightly, acknowledging the point. "Yes, well, he keeps peculiar hours," he said. "Now, pay attention. The most important thing you need to learn is how to make coffee."

"I know how to make coffee, Nicolas!"

The valet grunted. "Don't count on it. Everything has to be done in a very particular way." He looked at her. "*Very* particular." He opened a cupboard and took out a jar. "Here's the coffee. There's a shop on Rue de Lévis where you have to buy it. Nothing else will do. He likes the way they roast it there."

"Rue de Lévis," repeated Camille.

"You need to use a double boiler on the stove. The water has to pass through the coffee granules *slowly*. That's the only way you can be sure that the coffee is the strength he likes." He set a silver coffeepot down on the countertop. "Make enough to fill this, and absolutely no more. And don't even *dream* about serving him coffee in anything else." He turned back to the cupboard. A single coffee cup appeared, then a matching saucer. "This is the only cup he'll drink out of. The saucer is for his croissant."

"And this is the only saucer he'll use?" guessed Camille.

The valet nodded. "Purchase two croissants each day from the *bou-langerie* on Rue de la Pépinière. On no account should you buy them from anywhere else."

"How will he know?"

"Oh, he'll know, believe me. He rings the bell when he's ready for his breakfast. One ring means he only wants one croissant. If he wants two, he'll ring twice."

"Does he ever eat anything else?" asked Camille, looking around the spotless kitchen. The copper pans still hung from their hooks in perfect alignment. She was sure they had not been touched since she had first seen them.

"Rarely," said Nicolas. "Although you'll use the oven every day."

"What for?"

"His clothes. They need to be warmed to just the right temperature before he puts them on." Nicolas saw the look on her face. "Monsieur

Proust suffers terribly from the chills," he explained. "But he doesn't like the apartment to overheat, so you must be sure not to put more than four logs on the fire at any time."

Camille opened her mouth to speak, saw the expression on the valet's face, and remained silent.

"Sheets are to be changed every day, without fail, once he has left the apartment. That's when you'll clean, as well, because Monsieur Proust can't abide the smell of furniture polish." Nicolas turned to face her. "Most important of all, it's critical that there is no noise of any kind while he is sleeping or writing. Do you understand?"

"No noise of any kind," whispered Camille, rolling her eyes just a little.

"I'm being perfectly serious," said Nicolas. "He mustn't be disturbed. Deliverymen must never knock or ring the doorbell. And while we're on the subject of visitors," he continued, "anyone wearing perfume or cologne must not be admitted, under any circumstances."

"Why not?"

"Monsieur Proust is allergic to odors of any kind. That means no flowers, ever."

"When does he ring for his breakfast?"

"As soon as he wakes up."

"And when is that?"

"Around five in the afternoon."

Camille looked at him. "Pardon?"

Nicolas smiled. "That's the least of it," he said.

The following afternoon Camille arrived at the apartment on Boulevard Haussmann clutching a paper bag containing two warm croissants from the *boulangerie* on Rue de la Pépinière, as instructed. Nicolas showed her, again, how to make the coffee just as Monsieur Proust liked it, and then he put on his coat to leave for the hospital.

"You might do a little dusting while you wait for him to wake up," he said. "Just be careful not to make any noise." He closed the door silently behind him, and was gone.

Camille sat down at the kitchen table and took off her shoes. She had only ever met Marcel Proust once, and now here she was, alone with him in his apartment. The place was completely, eerily silent. There was not even a ticking clock to be heard. She had never gone beyond the kitchen before, and decided to explore the other rooms while her employer was still asleep. She opened the kitchen door and stepped into the hallway.

She guessed that the closed door at the far end of the corridor was Monsieur Proust's bedroom. She peered into the other rooms. Each was a jungle of wardrobes, divans, and chests of drawers. The furniture was packed so closely together that Camille could not see how anyone could comfortably spend any time in there.

Just then she heard the faint chime of a bell from the kitchen. A single ring.

One croissant.

Camille tiptoed back to the kitchen. While the coffee brewed, she anxiously arranged the cup and saucer on a tray. A few minutes later, she walked down the corridor and knocked on the bedroom door.

"Come in," said a faint voice.

She pushed open the door. The room was completely dark. She stood uncertainly on the threshold, the tray in front her, peering in.

"I'm over here, Madame Clermont," called the voice.

Camille took a cautious step into the room, then another. The only light came from the corridor behind her. As her eyes became used to the darkness, she saw long velvet curtains, drawn tight against the afternoon sun. There was a bed in the far corner of the room. At the end of the bed, emerging from the white sheets, was the disembodied head of Marcel Proust. His eyes glinted in the shadows, watching her from beneath a messy fringe of black hair. She crossed the room and put the tray down carefully on the table next to the bed. Those large, dark eyes watched her, not blinking once.

"Thank you," he whispered.

Camille performed an anxious curtsy and fled.

An hour later, Camille was pacing up and down the kitchen. She wondered if the coffee had been to his liking. Was the croissant acceptable? There had been no further rings of the bell—indeed, there had been no noise of any kind from the bedroom. She wondered if Monsieur Proust had fallen back asleep.

Finally she stepped into the corridor and was horrified to see dark wisps of smoke emerging from beneath the bedroom door. With a cry of alarm, she ran down the hallway and flung the door open. A wall of black cloud billowed into her face. Across the room she could just make out the silhouette of Marcel Proust, who was standing near the bed, bent over double.

"Monsieur!" she cried. "Can you hear me? I'm over here! There's a fire—"

"Close the door," wheezed Proust, not looking up.

Against her better judgment, Camille did as she was told. The curtains were still drawn. A small lamp next to the bed spilled a weak light into the room, but the smoke made it difficult to see what was going on. Her eyes began to sting.

"Are you all right, monsieur?"

"I'm absolutely fine, Madame Clermont. This is my daily treatment for my asthma. I burn Legras powder and inhale the fumes. The smoke clears the congestion in my chest. It's a marvel, I assure you." He began to cough. Camille watched in bewilderment as his rasping hacks filled the bedroom. When the fit passed, he said, "There's no need to worry."

The smoke was clearing a little. Like the other rooms in the apartment, the bedroom was crammed full of furniture. A grand piano stood immediately in front of a mahogany chest, so close that the drawers of the chest could not be opened. There were books piled high on every surface. All the other rooms in the apartment were decorated with ornate wallpaper, but the walls of the bedroom looked quite different. Camille looked more closely. They appeared to be covered with a lining of cork.

"For sound insulation." Marcel Proust had seen her staring. "I like to keep all the noise and light outside."

Camille flushed. "And here am I barging in and bringing both with me!"

"Ah, but you will always be welcome, Madame Clermont." He paused.

"But only you. If you could keep the rest of the world at bay, I'd be most grateful."

"I'll certainly do my best." She began to move toward the door.

"Oh, and Madame Clermont?"

She turned back to face him.

He smiled at her. "You make excellent coffee."

After a few months, there was no more Madame Clermont. Now there was simply: Camille.

She quickly became accustomed to Marcel Proust's domestic rituals. Such idiosyncrasies did not strike her as strange. She understood his desire that things should be exactly as he wanted them, and she did her best to abide by his every wish, never once passing judgment on his peculiar ways. Together, Camille and Nicolas looked after Monsieur Proust's domestic arrangements, and Olivier chauffeured him to his appointments and assignations across the city. The Clermonts spent less and less time in their apartment in Levallois. Their lives began to orbit increasingly around the needs and desires of their employer.

Then came the war.

Olivier was called up to serve as a driver, transporting food to the front. A week later, Nicolas also received his mobilization papers. The apartment on Boulevard Haussmann was suddenly empty.

"Come and live with me, Camille!" Proust begged her. "There's a spare bedroom here. Why spend so much time traveling back and forth to Levallois? It's not as if Olivier is waiting at home for you anymore. He's off at the front, poor man!"

And so Camille packed a suitcase and moved into the apartment on Boulevard Haussmann. She missed Olivier terribly, but escaped her worry about the war by devoting herself completely to Marcel Proust's every need. Such dedication was required due to the strange hours he kept. If he left the apartment, it would usually be after midnight, and he would not return until the early hours of the morning. It was during these late-night forays into the city that Camille put fresh sheets on his bed and aired out the bedroom. During the day the curtains were always drawn and the shutters kept tightly closed; while she cleaned the room, she opened the windows and let the cool night air in. The room had not seen a flicker of daylight in years.

Since Monsieur Proust refused to carry a key, Camille was required to stay awake to let him back into the apartment on his return from his nocturnal outings. His nights in the city were spent visiting acquaintances and attending glittering soirées thrown by the elite of Parisian society. He trawled these glamorous parties on the hunt for material for his book. He listened to gossip and noticed what people were wearing. After he hung up his hat and coat, he would regale an exhausted Camille with stories of what he had seen, whom he had met. Then he would retreat to his bed and begin the day in earnest—which was to say, he would write it all down.

Proust rarely moved from his bed while he worked. He wore white pajamas and lay with heavy wool sweaters wrapped around his shoulders for warmth and support. He used his knees for a desk. It looked absurdly uncomfortable to Camille, but he was able to write for hours on end without moving. Despite the lateness of the hour, Camille was not permitted to sleep while he was writing. If he needed something, she was expected to respond immediately, no matter what time it was. Every whim had to be catered to at once; nothing could interrupt or delay his work. She spent nights slumped over the kitchen table in a lonely vigil, just in case the bell might ring. One night she brought him a plate of fried potatoes just as the first hint of dawn mottled the dark sky. Proust was hunched over his work, scribbling furiously, surrounded by notebooks and a sea of scrap paper. He did not look up as she placed the food on the table by his side.

"Monsieur?" said Camille. "Is everything all right?"

With a sigh, he put down his pen. "I'm afraid it has begun," he said somberly.

"What has begun?"

"My slow shuffle off this mortal coil, Camille. There can be no more doubt."

She shook her head. "I don't understand."

"I'm *dying*, Camille. I'm terribly, terribly sick. Can't you see?"

"You seem perfectly healthy to me, monsieur."

"Well, I can assure you that I am *not*," retorted Proust, a little huffily. "My whole life I've been battling one illness and affliction after another. But this time, alas, I fear I am done for. I'm a condemned man."

"Whatever is the matter?"

"My lungs. Or my heart. Or perhaps my liver. It doesn't matter. All I know is that life is ebbing away. I feel it in my bones."

"Come, surely it's not as bad as that!"

He didn't seem to have heard her. "Do you know what I fear most in the world?" he asked.

"What, monsieur?"

He gestured to the papers on the bed in front of him. "I'm terrified of dying before I finish this book. That's all that matters now. My legacy."

"I'm sure there's nothing wrong with—"

"But there's so much still to do! I have so much more to write." He looked up at her. "That's why I'm so grateful for you, Camille! Without you, all this would be hopeless. I'm in a race against time, but at least I have you on my side. You look after me so beautifully. I don't know what I would do without you."

She smiled. "*Ce n'est rien.*"

"It might be nothing to you, Camille, but it's everything to me. Nothing else matters but that I finish this book before it finishes me."

And so her devotion to her employer grew. Marcel Proust locked himself away in his cork-lined prison cell, and with Olivier away at the front, Camille was a willing inmate with him. She committed herself to looking after his every need while he spent all his energies on completing his book.

The war did not result in the rapid French victory that many had predicted. It soon became clear that the troops would be locked in murderous stalemate for months, perhaps years. Camille missed her husband terribly, and worried constantly about his safety, but at least her work was a refuge from the slaughter on the battlefields to the north. In that strange, cluttered apartment on Boulevard Haussmann, she was discovering new worlds.

21

Vaucluse, 1917:
The Suitcase Under the Bed

ON THE SHELF ABOVE the fireplace in Philippe and Françoise's kitchen there was a framed photograph of a boy. He had fair hair, neatly trimmed and brushed. He wore a white shirt, buttoned up to the neck. He was staring directly into the camera, a solemn look in his eye. He looked about fifteen years old. One day Souren pointed at the photograph. "Who is that?" he asked.

"That is Antoine," replied Françoise. "Our son."

"Where is he?"

"He volunteered to go and fight in the war. We begged him not to, but he was determined to serve his country. He was killed in Belgium. At Ypres." Françoise put a hand on Souren's shoulder. "He would be about your age now," she said.

Souren was sleeping in the dead boy's bed. He was wearing the dead boy's clothes.

He began to explore Antoine's room. Philippe and Françoise had not thrown anything away; it was as if they were still expecting their son to return one day. His books were neatly arranged on a small bookcase. Beneath the bed were two wooden crates, brimming with forgotten trophies of childhood: a bow and arrow, parts of a wooden train set, an old bear with cracked buttons for eyes. Souren fingered these treasures in silent wonderment, as if he could conjure up the boy who played with them like a genie from a lamp.

Next to the crates there was an old suitcase. One afternoon Souren pulled it into the middle of the floor. The brass clasps popped open with a satisfying click. He lifted up the lid.

Inside was a troupe of hand puppets. He reached in and pulled one out. It was a round-faced man, a perfect circle of red paint on each of his fat wooden cheeks. Souren put his hand inside the puppet. The puppet looked at him quizzically, and then performed a deep bow. Souren reached back into the suitcase and took out a young girl with long, blond braids. He held the puppets up in front of him, and watched as they began to talk to each other. They were having an argument. The girl was singing, and the man wanted her to stop.

"Don't you like my voice?" asked the girl.

"No," snapped the man. "It's giving me a headache."

The girl put her head into her little wooden hands and burst into tears.

"There, there," said the man, patting her on the back. "Don't cry. Your voice is perfectly fine."

Souren could not take his eyes off them.

Over the days that followed, he worked his way through the suitcase, bringing the other puppets to life, one by one. A policeman declared his love for a buxom, rosy-cheeked cook, who pretended not to hear him, because she was busy making soup—although she was secretly delighted, and that day's soup was the most delicious she had ever produced. Two brothers staged a mock sword fight with twigs and were magically transformed into mighty warriors. An old woman said good-bye to her son as he left to seek his fortune in faraway lands, believing she would never see him again. Years later she discovered that she could fly, and immediately set off, swooping over seas and mountain ranges, to the new country where her son now lived. Souren watched their reunion with tears in his eyes.

The stories poured out of him.

He was building a time machine. With the puppets on his hands he could rewind the clock, back to a time of hope and happy endings.

In the house next door lived a couple with a little girl. Souren guessed she was six or seven years old. He often saw her playing with dolls in front of her house, chattering quietly to herself. Souren waved to her, and she waved shyly back, but they had never spoken.

One afternoon he closed up the suitcase and carried it across the grass to where the little girl was sitting. He put the suitcase down in front of him.

"Hello," said Souren in his best French.

"You live next door."

"That's right."

"My name is Amandine Nouvel," the girl told him.

"I am Souren."

She looked at him in frank appraisal. "My parents say you're a German soldier."

He grinned. "Would you like to see some puppets?" The French word, *fantoches*, sounded heavy on his tongue.

Amandine brightened at this. "*J'adore les fantoches!*" she declared.

Souren bent down and clicked open the suitcase. He pulled out a girl with red pigtails, and an old witch. Using the open lid of the suitcase as a rudimentary stage, Souren performed a story: the witch had turned her back on a life of evildoing and was trying to be nice to everyone. She offered the girl some candy, but the little redhead was very rude and ungrateful. It was all the witch could do to restrain herself from turning the horrible child into a toad, just to teach her a lesson. Instead she just smiled her crooked smile, scratched her huge, warty chin, and walked away.

Amandine watched in silence. When Souren lowered the puppets behind the lid of the suitcase, she raised her hand as if she were at school.

"Yes?" said Souren.

"What language were the puppets speaking?" asked Amandine.

"They were speaking in *my* language."

"Not German?" she guessed.

He shook his head.

Amandine smiled. "I liked it."

After that, Souren and Amandine met every afternoon on the front steps of her house, and he told her a different story with the puppets. The little girl watched each performance in complete silence, never taking her eyes off Souren's hands as they flitted back and forth along the top of the suitcase lid. Not once did she glance up at him: he was invisible to her. She listened closely as the puppets chattered to each other in Armenian, and Souren was sure that she understood every word.

One evening a few weeks later, Souren was about to push open the kitchen door when he heard Philippe and Françoise speaking inside. There was something about their tone, urgent and different, that made him pause. He stopped and listened from the other side of the door.

"Are you quite sure?" said Françoise.

"You know Nouvel," muttered Philippe. "As blunt as always. He left very little room for doubt."

"But Souren would never hurt a fly!"

"The man thinks we're harboring the enemy, Françoise. He's convinced that Souren is going to murder us all in our beds, Amandine included."

"Oh, this is too absurd! That little girl is his only friend."

"She's also Nouvel's only daughter," said Philippe.

"Yes, and Souren is performing puppet shows for her!"

"In a foreign language. Nouvel and his wife are beside themselves." Philippe paused. "Françoise, listen to me. They want Souren out of the village. Others feel the same way. The whole town wants him gone."

"I don't care what the town wants!" cried Françoise. "This is *our* house! This is *our* family!"

Souren held his breath.

"Françoise," said Philippe quietly. "Souren is not Antoine."

The silence that followed was amplified by the leathery tick of the grandfather clock in the hallway. Souren imagined the pendulum swinging precisely in its narrow, unchanging parabola, hidden within the clock's tall body like a beating heart, driving time on. The seconds knotted themselves into minutes, and still there was no sound from the other side of the door. Souren leaned against the wall. The silence breathed, exhaled, and expanded, obliterating everything except this:

Souren is not Antoine.

Later that evening, once he was sure that Philippe and Françoise were asleep, Souren tiptoed down the stairs. A note lay on his bed, one hastily scrawled word: *merci*. He had packed Antoine's suitcase with some of the dead boy's clothes and his puppets. At the bottom of the stairs he stopped, listening to the old house as it performed its nightly chorus of creaks and groans.

What a fool he had been.

He knew what he heard in Françoise's voice from the other side of the kitchen door earlier that evening: the despairing cadences of loss. The mourning couple and the hungry boy: they were bound together by nothing but mutual need. And such need had its limits.

Souren is not Antoine.

His instinct for survival had been dulled by comfort. The only way for him to be safe was to be invisible, and nobody could be invisible in so small a village. Clean sheets against his skin, delicious food, the delight on Amandine's face as the puppets weaved back and forth—these things had held him in place for too long.

The blue-white glow of the full moon fell through the kitchen window, bright enough to cast long shadows into the room. He crossed the flagstones to the back door, and reached for the iron key in the lock. He held his breath as he twisted it, waiting for the heavy click of release. When it came, the sound thundered through the room. He waited for a moment, blood pulsing in his ears. Then he turned the handle, pushed open the door, and stepped out into the night.

22

Best Served Cold

GUILLAUME WALKS AWAY FROM Rue des Abbesses, still feeling the insolent gaze of Thérèse's pimp between his shoulder blades. He puts his hands in his pockets and turns toward Boulevard de Clichy. The sun is high in the cloudless sky. Its brilliance provides a measure of clarity that cuts through the fog of his lingering hangover.

He is disappointed but not surprised by Thérèse's refusal to see Emile Brataille again. He does not blame her. She is a survivor. She does what she needs to do.

Guillaume wonders idly how many times he has painted Thérèse over the years. He probably knows that voluptuous body as well as her most devoted customers, but he has never touched her. He does not want her the way these other men want her. They may possess her for a fleeting moment—or be possessed, perhaps—but Guillaume is looking for something different. For him, Thérèse's body is where the story starts, not where it ends. They have spent hours together in his studio, the tableau never changing over the years. He is on one side of the easel; she is on the other. He is fully clothed; she is quite naked. He works; she watches. She stares out from every canvas with the same frank gaze, and the knowledge in that look eclipses the sensuous actuality of her nakedness. Guillaume has spent his life watching other people, but only when he is with Thérèse does he feel seen.

His pace slows until his feet stop moving. He is standing in front of a shop window, and considers his reflection in the glass. He is gaunt, unshaven, and looks exhausted. He thinks about the empty wall in his studio where Suzanne's painting used to be, the whispered threats through the door in the dead of night, the six hundred francs beneath his mattress, and the six hundred francs he still needs.

The train to La Rochelle is waiting at the platform, ready to take him to safety, and away from all that he loves.

As he walks south into the heart of the city, he contemplates the delicate encounter ahead. Brataille will be desperate for news about Thérèse, but Guillaume has to keep him in good humor long enough to ask him for a loan. Finally he reaches Montparnasse. There is none of the affable squalor of Montmartre down here. The streets are wider, emptier, and swept clean, both of trash and character. Lines of well-manicured trees punctuate the sterile sidewalks at precisely measured intervals. Well-preserved women parade up and down with small dogs. Guillaume arrives in front of Emile Brataille's gallery. There is just one painting in the window. On the left-hand side of the canvas is a crudely rendered terracotta vase, or rather, half of one. Opposite the vase is half a blue rabbit's head. An ornate Doric column is emerging out of the top of the head, next to the rabbit's ear. Guillaume peers at the painting. There is an embossed card next to the easel. It says:

FERNAND LÉGER
Blue Guitar and Vase

Guillaume looks back at the painting again. So, a guitar, not a rabbit. He shakes his head and pushes open the door to the gallery.

Inside the walls are adorned with more childlike paintings. The colors are bright and stupid. Guillaume has no idea what he is supposed to be looking at. There is a large wooden desk at the back of the room. Brataille sits behind it, smoking a cigarette. His tie is askew, his hair uncombed. He is a picture of elegant dishevelment.

"Good lord, it's a miracle," drawls the art dealer. "I didn't think it was possible, but you look worse than I feel." Brataille stubs out his cigarette in the heavy glass ashtray on the desk and looks at Guillaume with keen interest. "I wasn't expecting to see you again so soon, *mon ami*. Perhaps you have news of a certain deliciously proportioned whore from Rue des Abbesses?"

"Actually," says Guillaume, "I've just come from there."

"And?"

"She and I talked about you for some time."

"Oh yes? What did she say?"

"She told me your cock is the size of a peanut."

Brataille stares at him, and then bursts out laughing. After a moment, Guillaume starts laughing, too. The art dealer gestures at him to sit down, and he sinks into the soft leather chair in front of the desk. Both men are still giggling.

"Seriously," says Brataille after a moment. "What did she say?"

"Well," says Guillaume. "She knows who you are, of course." Brataille nods. Of course. Guillaume looks around at the overpriced paintings. "I reminded her, several times, that you own one of the most successful art galleries in Paris."

"Aha. She liked that?"

"Oh yes. I laid it on pretty thick, *mon vieux*."

"That's magnificent news. So, will she see me again?"

"Aren't you going to ask me how it went with Gertrude Stein this morning?" asks Guillaume.

"What? Oh yes, of course." Brataille doesn't bother to conceal his impatience. "How did it go? She's a funny old fish, isn't she?"

"She is quite," agrees Guillaume.

"Alice came too, I suppose?"

"Alice came too."

"And did she buy something?"

"As a matter of fact," says Guillaume, "she did."

Brataille beams at him. "*Alors, félicitations.* You know what this means, don't you?"

"I'm not sure that I do," says Guillaume.

"It means you've arrived. Everything will change for you now. Gertrude Stein bought your work!"

"Actually, she didn't so much buy it as steal it."

"What do you mean?"

"She beat me down on price. Gave me half what I asked for. She was merciless."

Brataille leans his elbows on the desk and temples the tips of his fingers. "Ah, yes," he says thoughtfully. "You have to watch the Americans. They do love a bargain." His tone suggests that of course *he* would never have agreed to such a deal.

"Here's the thing, Emile," says Guillaume. "If Gertrude Stein had paid what I'd asked for, I wouldn't mention it. But as it is, I'm in a difficult situation right now."

"Oh?" Brataille's eyes narrow. "Difficult how?"

"I need some money."

"Some money."

"Just a short-term loan," says Guillaume affably.

"How much?"

"Six hundred. If I don't repay it today, I'm done for."

"Done for? What do you mean?"

"They're going to kill me."

"Nobody's going to kill you for six hundred francs," scoffs the art dealer with a chuckle.

"I'd prefer not to risk it," says Guillaume tightly.

"What did you do, for heaven's sake? Borrow money from Le Miroir?"

"That's exactly what I did."

Brataille sits up. "*Au sérieux?*"

"Do I look like I'm joking?"

The art dealer runs a hand through his tousled hair. "*Putain,*" he mutters. "You got caught up with the wrong people."

"I realize that now. The thing is, I'm late on my repayments. If they don't get their money today——"

Brataille cuts him off. "I can't possibly help you."

Guillaume stares at him. "What?"

"There's no way I'm getting involved."

"But you probably have that kind of money just sitting in a drawer somewhere, don't you?"

"That isn't the point."

"No? What *is* the point?" asks Guillaume.

"The point is that I don't want anything to do with those bastards. They're criminals. Le Miroir extorts cash from people like me. Why would I ever want to get on his radar?"

"He would never know that the money came from you!"

"You'd never tell him?"

"Of course not."

"Even with a knife pointed at your throat?"

Guillaume is silent.

"Anyway, I'm an art dealer, not a bank. Lending money isn't my business. I sell paintings."

"So don't lend me the money. Just give it to me."

Brataille shakes his head. "And what if they still manage to trace it back to me?" He gestures at the walls of the gallery. "Look around you, Guillaume. I have too much to lose to get involved with people like that."

Guillaume feels the last breath of hope escape from him.

"I'm sure you understand. No hard feelings, eh?"

"No hard feelings," mutters Guillaume.

The two men are silent for a moment.

"Anyway," says Brataille. "You were telling me about Thérèse." He leans back in his chair and puts his hands behind his head, the small matter of the loan, and Guillaume's survival, already forgotten. "Has she changed her mind?" he asks. "Did you convince her to see me again?"

Guillaume thinks of Le Miroir's thugs, who will soon be hunting him down. Then he remembers Léon, the giant who stepped out of the shadows while he was talking to Thérèse this morning.

Léon, with his enormous fists.

"Yes," says Guillaume. "She will see you again."

Brataille thumps the desk in triumph. "I knew it!" he cries.

"Here's the thing," says Guillaume. "She wants you to go to Le Chat Blanc tonight."

"Tonight?" The art dealer actually licks his lips.

"She'll be waiting for you in her room. She said you should just go right up."

"Splendid," says Brataille.

"And if anyone tries to stop you, or asks what you're doing, she said you should ignore them. She's going to take care of it."

Guillaume has never been inside Le Chat Blanc, but he is confident that there will be an army of goons the approximate shape and size of Léon whose job is to stop people getting to the prostitutes without paying what is due. He is equally confident that none of those men will take kindly to being ignored by an arrogant prick like Emile Brataille.

Léon's proclivity for violence had wafted off him like cheap cologne. Guillaume imagines those giant fists smashing into the art dealer's face. He hears the crunch of cartilage; he sees the spray of blood.

23

The Bookshop

THE CAFÉ NEAR THE CEMETERY gates is almost empty. Jean-Paul takes a sip of the steaming coffee that the waiter has just delivered to his table, and flicks through the notes he took that morning in Josephine Baker's apartment. Except, he remembers, it isn't Josephine. It's *Joséphine* now. She was most particular about her newly acquired *accent aigu*, and had peered over his shoulder more than once to make sure that he was writing her name correctly in his notebook. So much more *chic*, don't you think? she asked him. So much more *French*. Jean-Paul scratches his neck in bemusement. All the Americans he has met in Paris seem so eager to become something other than what they are. Each of them has arrived in France hoping to forge fresh existences for themselves. The Americans' faith in the regenerative power of new geography astonishes him. It's a myth, this idea that you can change who you are simply by climbing on a boat or boarding a train. Some things you cannot leave behind. Your history will pursue you doggedly across frontiers and over oceans. It will slip past the unsmiling border guards, fold itself invisibly into the pages of your passport, a silent, treacherous stowaway.

He closes his notebook and sighs. His visit to the cemetery has summoned too many unwanted ghosts. He cannot concentrate. Anaïs and Elodie are his Sirens, luring him on to the perilous rocks of memory and regret, and he is helpless to resist their call.

His loss is a blanket that he can never shuck off. Sometimes it suffocates him, sometimes it keeps him alive. The space beneath the blanket is dark with shadows, but it is where he lives now.

His next interview is on the Left Bank. Another American, this one a bookshop owner. He checks his watch and decides to walk across the city to his appointment. Perhaps the stroll will clear his head. Today, he tells himself, he will become a *flâneur*, a modern-day Baudelaire, walking the streets of the city for no purpose other than his own pleasure. The waiter gives him a friendly nod as he pushes open the door.

As he walks down the street he can see the Eiffel Tower above the city's rooftops. The tower has dominated the city's skyline for almost forty years now. Many Parisians despise it. They complain that it serves no purpose whatsoever, but that is precisely why Jean-Paul likes it. The combination of first-rate mechanical engineering and such manifest uselessness strikes him as being particularly, deliciously, French.

At Place de la Bastille cars hurtle by him, belching clouds of black smoke in their wake, streaking the air with their angry horns. Men hurry past, clutching their hats to their heads. Women stroll by, languid and graceful. Jean-Paul walks at his own slow pace. He crosses the Seine at the eastern tip of Île Saint-Louis, and turns onto Boulevard Saint-Germain. At Carrefour de l'Odéon, he turns off the busy thoroughfare and walks up a quiet, narrow street. He stops in front of a shop whose windows are filled with books. They have been arranged on shelves with their covers facing out toward the street. No two volumes are the same. A metal sign hangs above the front door. It reads: SHAKESPEARE AND COMPANY.

The inside of the bookshop is dark. As the door closes behind him, Jean-Paul looks around the room. There are tables of various shapes and sizes, each of them bearing piles of books, some stacked precariously high. At the far end of the shop there is a fireplace, and on the wall above the mantel is a collection of framed photographs of serious-looking men.

There is a large desk next to the fireplace. Two men and a woman are bent over it, looking at a painting. Another woman is standing silently to one side, clutching a handbag in front of her. None of them turns around to see who has come in.

"What do you make of it?" asks a man in a brown corduroy suit. He is speaking in English.

The second man strokes his mustache. "It's a fine enough painting, I suppose," he says. "But I don't understand what it's about."

Jean-Paul stares. He recognizes the man's face. At once he picks up the nearest book and opens it at random, hiding behind its cover.

"I like the blue door," says the woman. "It's quite beautiful."

"Ah, but it's the blue door that makes me crazy," says Ernest Hemingway. "The stupid thing is halfway up the wall!"

"That's exactly what I love about it."

"But it doesn't make any sense! What possible purpose does it serve?"

"Must you always be so pedestrian?" asks the man in corduroy. "Since when does everything need to have a purpose?"

"I'm not saying *everything* needs to have a purpose, Gertrude," replies Hemingway crossly. Jean-Paul looks at the man in corduroy more closely, sees his mistake, and realizes whom he is looking at. "But it's a goddamn *door*. What's the point of a door if you can't go through it?"

"Well, I think it's charming," says the woman. Jean-Paul peers at her over the top of his book. She has a kind face. Her wavy brown hair is pulled in a severe part. Sylvia Beach, he guesses.

"In that case, dear girl, you should have it," says Gertrude Stein.

"What? Oh no, I couldn't possibly!"

"You could possibly," replies Gertrude Stein. "And you should."

"But you're too kind!"

"Not really. I don't actually like it that much."

"Why did you buy it, then?" demands Hemingway.

A shrug. "I can't resist a bargain."

"Well, I think it's lovely," says Sylvia Beach. "I accept your kind gift. Thank you."

"I'm glad," says Gertrude Stein gruffly. "Well, we need to get home. Come on, Alice."

Gertrude Stein and her companion march out of the shop without another word. Ernest Hemingway glares at their retreating backs.

"Here." Sylvia Beach hands him a book. "Your new treasure."

"Ah, yes!" The American's face brightens. He flicks through the book's pages, brings it up to his nose and inhales deeply. "My God!" he exclaims. "You can practically smell the genius wafting off it." He looks up with an unguarded grin on his handsome face. "Thank you, dearest Sylvia. You've made my week." He tucks the book into his pocket and looks toward the door. "Do you think it's safe to leave?"

"Honestly, I don't see why the two of you can't be more civil." Sylvia Beach sighs. "Your constant bickering is exhausting for the rest of us."

"Gertrude started it," says Hemingway, petulant.

"That's not what *she* says."

"No, well, it wouldn't be, would it?" The American raises his arm in a farewell salute, then turns to leave. As the door closes behind him, Jean-Paul finally lowers the book from his face. Sylvia Beach is still standing over the painting, examining it closely. He approaches and clears his throat. "Mademoiselle Beach?"

The woman looks up. "Can I help you?"

"Jean-Paul Maillard. I'm here for our interview."

"Of course," she says. "You're the journalist on the hunt for Americans."

"Perhaps I should just spend my days here," says Jean-Paul, pointing toward the front door. "I daresay they all come in eventually."

"It certainly feels that way," agrees Sylvia Beach with a smile. Just then a piano starts to play somewhere nearby. The notes clash together sharply. "A case in point," she says, pointing to the ceiling. "That's George. He's from New Jersey."

They listen for a moment. The music continues, angrily dissonant.

"Goodness," says Jean-Paul.

"I think that's supposed to sound like an industrial air turbine," explains Sylvia Beach cheerfully. The jarring piano chords crash through the ceiling.

"Although I wouldn't mind the occasional Chopin nocturne every now and again," she whispers, rolling her eyes.

"It's very——" Jean-Paul stops, unable to find the right word.

"Yes, isn't it? He never would have written such a thing in Trenton, you can be sure of that."

"Paris has inspired him to greater things?"

She pulls a rueful face. "There's a wonderful line in a poem by one of our American poets, Walt Whitman. It goes: *A thousand singers—a thousand songs.*"

Jean-Paul nods. "*Clearer, louder, and more sorrowful than yours.*"

She looks at him in surprise. "Yes! Well, it rather feels like that around here these days. Everyone is so busy singing their sorrowful songs that it can be difficult to hear yourself think." She picks up the painting. "I rather like this, though."

Jean-Paul looks at the painting of a little white house in a forest. It is quite beautiful. "This song seems a little quieter," he says.

"Perhaps that's why I like it," says Sylvia Beach. She carries the painting to the other side of the shop and puts it in the window. "There," she says. "That ought to brighten someone's day."

They walk back to the large desk at the back of the shop. Jean-Paul sits down and pulls out his notebook.

"Tell me about Paris," he says.

24

Paris, 1915: Confidences

OUTSIDE THE APARTMENT, the war raged. Olivier remained stationed at the front. Finding themselves increasingly alone, the two occupants of the apartment at 102 Boulevard Haussmann began to talk more and more.

"Tell me about Auxillac," Marcel Proust said one afternoon, watching Camille carry the tray of coffee and croissants across the bedroom.

"Oh, monsieur, you're not interested in where I came from," she demurred. "I'm a simple country girl from the Lozère."

He looked amused. "And?"

"You spend your evenings talking to duchesses in tiaras! What possible interest could my childhood be to you?"

"My dear Camille, why on earth do you imagine that those people are more interesting than you? Because they're duchesses? Or because they wear tiaras?"

"Now you're mocking me, monsieur."

"Not in the slightest. It was an entirely serious question." Proust reached for a croissant. "Most of those women are stupendously boring. They're obsessed with trivialities, they have no opinions of their own, and they are uniformly dim. An aristocratic pedigree is no guarantee of anything these days, least of all a discernible character." He took a bite. "You, though," he said, after chewing for a moment. "I see still waters running deep within you."

Camille blushed, quite undone.

"Never let anyone tell you you're boring, Camille. If they tell you that you don't matter, that you're of no consequence, don't believe it for one moment."

"*Oui*, monsieur."

"I like you so very much, Camille! Will you promise me something?"

She nodded, not trusting herself to speak.

"Be a strong woman. Most of all, be yourself! Don't ever let anyone tell you what to do. Especially not a man." He paused, a small smile on his lips. "Except me, of course. You should always follow my instructions to the letter."

"*Oui*, monsieur."

"So, tell me about Auxillac." He took another bite of croissant.

And so, hesitantly at first, she began to tell stories of her childhood. She was sure that Monsieur Proust would quickly become bored by the tedium of her family's simple, bucolic life, but he appeared quite enchanted, and asked for more. Once she was sure he was not teasing her, she obliged. She resurrected old family legends that she had heard told around the dinner table countless times as a child. She reminisced about the carefree summers of her youth, and the hard, cold winters. She recalled old friends that she had not thought about in years. Most of them were still living in Auxillac. Sometimes Camille did not know whether to laugh or cry when she thought of them now, so very far away.

Marcel Proust listened to every word, his eyes never leaving hers while she talked. Occasionally he would elicit an extra detail from her, but for the most part he remained silent. He wanted to know about Olivier's courtship, those long drives along the country lanes with the wind in her hair.

"Ah, youth is wasted on the young, Camille," he said softly.

He began to tell her stories about his own childhood. He recalled long-ago weekends spent at an uncle's house in Auteuil, summers at another uncle's house in Illiers. He recounted tales of the mischief that he and his brother, Robert, would get up to when out of sight of their parents. He told her of the dreadful trip to the Bois de Boulogne when he was nine years old, when there had been so much pollen in the air that he'd suffered his first asthma attack. "That was when everything changed, Camille," he said. "It's only when you have to fight for every breath that you realize how essential air is to life."

He spoke lovingly of his parents, especially his mother. "She was the greatest love of my life," he told her. "From the moment I was born, my world revolved around her, until she drew her last breath." He was silent for a moment. "I remember the day she died so clearly. I walked through the apartment one last time before they took her poor body away. There was a floorboard near her bedroom that creaked every time someone walked on it. Whenever my mother heard it she would make a little noise. It was her way of saying she wanted me to go and kiss her." He gave Camille a sad smile. "That day I stepped on the floorboard, and it creaked as usual. But there was no little noise from the bedroom. No kiss."

"But you still have your memories," said Camille.

"Memories, yes." He gestured around the room. "And all this helps, of course."

"All this?"

"Why do you think this apartment has so much furniture in it?"

"I've never really thought about it," lied Camille. Every day she had to navigate the forests of tables and chairs, keeping all the mahogany surfaces polished and free of dust, and had often wondered, somewhat irritably, what it was all doing there.

"These pieces all belonged to my parents," explained Proust. "When my mother died I couldn't bear the thought of parting with any of them. The idea of a stranger's clothes hanging in that armoire, of someone else sitting at that desk—" He waved a hand around the room and shuddered. "It was too much to contemplate. So I kept it all." He paused. "When I look at an empty armchair, it's not empty to me. I see my mother sitting in it, reading a book."

"I have nothing like that," said Camille.

Proust looked at her kindly. "Well, you don't really need such things, you know. The only place where you can regain lost paradises is in yourself."

One morning there was a knock on the apartment door. One of Olivier's sisters stood in the corridor, her face white and drawn. She was clutching a blue envelope tightly in her fist. Camille looked down at the telegram and her world collapsed messily in on itself. Her tongue felt thick inside her head. She croaked one hoarse word: "Olivier?"

A shake of the head.

Moments later Camille knocked on the door of Monsieur Proust's bedroom. He looked up from his work in surprise. She never disturbed him without being called for.

"*Oui*, Camille? What's the matter?"

"It's my mother, monsieur."

"Yes? What about her?"

"She's dead."

At once his work was forgotten. He gently took her hands in his. "Oh, my dear Camille. I'm so very sorry."

Camille said nothing. She was determined not to cry in front of him. She wanted him to think her strong.

"You must go back home at once, of course," said Proust. "Now is the time to be with your family."

But you are my family now, she thought. All she could think to say was: "Who will look after you if I am gone?"

"I shall manage very well, don't you worry about me. Go and see your mother one last time and say your good-byes. It would be too awful if you didn't."

And so later that day Camille was on a train headed south, staring out of the carriage window at the snow that covered the fields as far as she could see. Every mile closer to her childhood home was a mile farther away from Olivier on the front, and Marcel Proust in Paris. She had never felt so alone.

By the time she arrived in Auxillac, her mother was already buried. Camille stood in front of the freshly dug grave, staring numbly at the ground. The following day, she climbed back on board the train to Paris.

After that, her old home was forever out of reach. The trains still ran, but there was no returning to where she wanted to go.

Monsieur Proust continued to ask for tales from her childhood, and she continued to oblige him, but now she told those stories as much for herself as for him. Memories were all that remained now—both sweeter than before, and more painful. When she had finished, when the words had finally exhausted themselves and a sad, heavy silence took their place—then he would begin to speak, softly, slowly, telling stories of his own. Alone together in their strange cocoon, they shared more and more confidences. Marcel Proust told her things that he had never spoken of to anyone else.

"Ah, my dear Camille." He sighed. "Everyone thinks they know me, but nobody knows me like you do."

As their intimacy deepened, Marcel Proust began to ask her opinion about things. He wanted to know what she thought of the progress of the war, or whether he should attend this soirée or that. Camille would always demur, insisting that she knew nothing of such things. One evening, after she had refused to say which scarf went best with his hat, he lost his patience.

"I don't ask you these things to be polite, Camille," he said. "I ask you because I want to know what you think."

"But what does it matter what I think, monsieur? I'm just—"

"A country girl from the south, yes, yes, I know." Marcel Proust stood by the door to the apartment, a scarf in each hand. "For some reason you believe that means you shouldn't have an opinion about anything. But you're quite wrong. You should have an opinion about *everything*." He handed both scarves to Camille. "Wait here," he said, and disappeared into his bedroom. He returned with a sheaf of papers in his hand. "I want you to listen to this," he told her. "Tell me what you think."

Marcel Proust began to read. Camille stared at the floor, wishing, as devoutly as she had ever wished for anything, that he would stop. But he did not stop. He stood in the hallway with his coat still on and read and read. After what felt like an eternity, he finally looked up from the pages in his hand.

"*Et alors?*" he said. "What do you think?"

Camille let out a small moan.

"It's not a difficult question, Camille. Did you like it?"

"Oh yes, very much," she said at once.

"What did you like about it, exactly?"

She glanced at the clock. "Won't you be late for your rendezvous?"

"They can wait." He looked at her expectantly. "Tell me what you liked about it."

"It was very— interesting."

"Really," said Proust. "That's your opinion?"

She nodded. "That's my opinion," she said.

"Well, I thank you for that." He pointed at the two scarves she was still holding. "And now would you please choose a scarf for me to wear?"

One scarf was made of blue silk, the other of dark gray wool. After a moment's pause, she handed him the woolen one. "This is warmer, and it suits you better."

Proust took it from her. "Thank you," he said. He gave her his papers and began to tie the scarf around his neck.

"Your sentences are too long," blurted Camille.

He looked up. "Oh?"

"They just—they go on and on and on. Whoever is speaking gets halfway through a point, and then he starts talking about something else for an age, and then he finally gets back to the first thing he was talking about, but then he goes off on a different subject, and it took forever for him to say anything, and it was all very confusing." She paused. "And, well, it was boring, monsieur. Nothing really *happened*." She stared at him, her cheeks burning with mortification.

Marcel Proust turned and picked up his hat off the table in the hallway. He put it on. "There," he said with a small smile. "That wasn't so difficult, now, was it?"

And with that he walked out of the door.

In the summer of 1916 a telegram arrived with the news that Nicolas Cottin, the valet to whom Camille had curtsied so prettily on her first visit to Boulevard Haussmann, had died in a military hospital, and her anxiety about Olivier escalated. She awoke every morning terrified that another telegram would arrive—but it never did.

Olivier was finally discharged from service, and returned to Paris. Camille did not want to return to their old apartment in Levallois. Boulevard Haussmann was her home now. When Marcel Proust invited Olivier to move into the apartment, he gave a small shrug of acquiescence and carried his suitcases into the spare bedroom without another word.

Camille's relief at her husband's return did not last long. She wanted to ask him about the war, about everything he had seen at the front, but Olivier did not want to talk about that. He did not want to talk much at all. At night he moaned in his sleep, sometimes crying out in terror, unable to keep his memories at bay. He spent his days staring out of the window, alone with his thoughts. Whenever Monsieur Proust needed a driver, Olivier took him. These trips across the city would lift his spirits, but never for long. He began to complain about the peculiar hours his wife kept.

"We live in the same place but I never see you!" he told her. "You spend more time with him than me!"

"You are quite capable of looking after yourself, Olivier," answered Camille, although as she spoke the words she wondered if this was, in fact, true. "Monsieur Proust, on the other hand—"

"Oh, I know, I know," muttered her husband. "You're the only one who can make his coffee just how he likes it. And what could be more important than that?"

"Really, Olivier, must you be so ungrateful? Monsieur Proust has been so kind to us both! Think how lucky we are to stay in this apartment!"

"Yes, as long as we follow his rules!" hissed Olivier. "I'm walking around all day and night on my tiptoes, Camille, for fear of disturbing him! It's driving me to drink!"

Camille had become so accustomed to creeping through the apartment that she no longer noticed that she was doing it. "Is that really so difficult?" she asked.

Olivier sighed. "I spent years living at the front, Camille, up to my armpits in mud and shit. Now that I'm back, all I really want is to live in a place I can call my own. Somewhere I can stomp around and make as much noise as I want."

"A home, in other words," said Camille quietly.

"If you like, yes. A home."

They looked at each other for a moment. Within the tired, anxious man before her, Camille saw the ghost of the person she fell in love with, and her heart ached with loss.

"Perhaps we should start a family," she said.

The words hung between them.

"Really?" said Olivier.

Camille's mouth opened and closed a few times as she tried to formulate a sentence, a phrase, anything that might reel back in the words that had just escaped her. Then she saw the light that had appeared in her husband's eyes, and nodded.

"Really," she whispered.

It was the key that set him free. Olivier fell on the idea like a starving dog on a juicy bone. A family, yes, of course! At once he began to conjure up a whole new life for them, a spontaneously improvised nirvana of domestic contentment. Camille listened as he spun stories and hatched plans for the future. She was delighted by his excitement, but felt a shadow of apprehension that she could not ignore. She had shifted the axis of Olivier's world with a few whispered words. There was no going back now.

She was right to have worried. Every month they held their breath; every month they were devastated by fresh disappointment. Olivier suffered the most. Camille began to wish that she had never said a word. Her attempt to rescue her husband had left him more miserable than ever. Olivier became obsessed with the baby that they could not create. Month by month, he sank deeper and deeper into a private sadness, where Camille could not reach him.

When their daughter finally arrived in the spring of 1918, everything changed. Marie was a tornado, sweeping away everything that had gone before. There was of course no question that Monsieur Proust would ever tolerate a crying baby in the apartment, and so the new parents found somewhere else to live. Camille continued to keep the same, upside-down hours as before, which meant that Olivier was largely responsible for looking after their daughter. It was precisely the lifeline he needed: Marie rescued her father and brought him home. He no longer spent his days looking out of the window, lost in his memories of the war. Now, when Camille returned home, he regaled her with stories about everything he and Marie had done that day. Camille listened to these reports with a smile fixed firmly in place, trying to ignore the twinge of guilt that caught somewhere deep within her. She was a mother now. Shouldn't she be tending to her child, rather than to her ever-demanding employer?

As it was, Marcel Proust needed her more than ever. He was, in his way, just as helpless as an infant. He suffered from a procession of illnesses, infections, and diseases. Some were real, some were imagined, but he was convinced that each one spelled the end. His brother, Robert, a doctor, was frequently summoned to examine him and deliver his verdict on the latest symptoms. Robert listened to Marcel's litany of complaints and would then briskly inform his brother that he was perfectly fine. His fraternal duty performed, he would wink at Camille in a friendly way and let himself out while the patient seethed with impotent rage at these disappointing diagnoses.

Now that it was just Camille and her employer in the apartment again, they became closer than ever. Marcel Proust, propped up in his bed in his strange, cork-lined bedroom, became her confessor. She told him about Olivier's bad dreams, the weight of his sadness. She admitted her misgivings about leaving him with the baby, her jealousy when she saw Marie asleep in his arms.

"Ah, but what must I be thinking, to say such things to you!" she said with a sigh one day.

"To me?" said Proust. "What do you mean?"

She pointed to the sheets of paper that lay scattered over the bed, every one covered with his small, neat handwriting. "You're a writer, monsieur. All those stories you tell me when you return from your trips into the city. The gossip you hear at those parties. It all goes into your novel, doesn't it?"

"Some of it," he admitted.

"*Et alors*. I don't want to see the tales that *I* tell you in your book."

He looked hurt. "It's not the same thing at all, Camille. The things you tell me are quite different from the stories I hear at parties. Those are between the two of us. I would never betray a confidence. Not from you."

"All right, then," sniffed Camille.

"You believe me, don't you?"

"Yes, I believe you," she said. She picked up the tray on the bedside table and turned to leave.

He crossed his arms. "No, you don't."

She laughed. "*Tenez*, now you read minds, as well?"

"I know you too well, Camille," he said. "I can tell when you're lying to me."

Now it was her turn to be hurt. "I *do* believe you, monsieur," she said.

"Prove it!"

She shook her head in exasperation. "How am I supposed to do that?"

"Tell me something you've never told another soul."

"Oh, if only my life were that interesting! I have no such secrets."

A sardonic eyebrow. "*None*, Camille?"

She thought of the one secret that she had never told anyone. Her guts twisted anxiously at the thought of saying the words out loud.

"There *is* one thing," she said.

"I knew it," exclaimed Proust, triumphant.

"You promise you'll never tell a soul?"

He sat up in the bed. "I cross my heart."

She put the tray back down.

As the war progressed, German bombs fell daily on the city. During these aerial bombardments, the occupants of 102 Boulevard Haussmann retreated to the basement—all except Marcel Proust, who refused to stop working and remained in his bedroom, writing furiously while the rockets fell. Camille was terrified by the prospect of a direct hit on the building, and so always fled downstairs, each time wondering if she would ever see her employer again. The attacks reduced large parts of the city to rubble, and as the danger to civilians showed no signs of abating, hundreds of thousands of Parisians fled to the safety of the countryside. Camille longed to follow them out of the city, and when Monsieur Proust was offered the use of a villa in Nice, she was thrilled at the prospect of escaping the bombs and feeling the warmth of the southern sun on her face. Marcel Proust, though, thought only of his work, and decided that there would be too many distractions in the countryside—to say nothing of too much pollen. He decided to remain in Paris. Camille was disappointed, but there was no question that she would ever leave the city without him.

The streets were half empty. In addition to those who had left for the country, there were many soldiers still away at the front, and hundreds of thousands of men who had been killed. Death hung over Paris like a shroud. On the sidewalks Camille passed young widows dressed in black, often with fatherless children in tow. She looked away, ashamed of her own good fortune. Many of the men she passed in the street bore the scars of war. Some hauled themselves down the boulevards on crutches, others wore coats with empty sleeves rolled up and pinned at the shoulder. For some, the damage lay deeper, betrayed by their vacant stares.

Still, there were young and healthy men living in Paris, miraculously untouched by the war's devastation. Camille knew this because she would catch glimpses of some of them, late at night, as they closed the door of Marcel Proust's bedroom and crept down the corridor, tucking their shirts into their trousers as they went. Camille sat in the kitchen, hidden in the shadows. She watched every one of them come and every one of them go, and she never breathed a word to anyone.

She kept her employer's secrets, and he kept hers.

25

Overheard Memories

SOUREN CLIMBS THE STAIRS of the Métro station and steps into the sunshine. As the traffic streams along Quai Saint-Michel, he puts down his suitcases and gazes across the river at Notre-Dame. All across the city there are vast, imposing cathedrals, although none quite as magnificent as this one. He thinks of the small church in the village where he grew up. It had been a modest, functional building, without even stained glass in the windows. The simple black cross above the door was the only marker that it was a place of worship. Souren looks at the elaborately carved exterior of the cathedral. The French must have a lot on their collective conscience, he muses, to have built such a monumental testament to their own piety. A legion of stone gargoyles scream silently down from the cathedral's towers. Every monstrous, open maw is frozen in a rictus of jeering contempt. The view of Paris from up there must be spectacular, thinks Souren. He has never climbed to the top to find out for himself. His perspective on the city is circumscribed and unchanging, and resolutely earthbound.

On the bank of the river a line of men sit side by side, each one hunched over a fishing rod. Their caps are pulled down low over their faces. They do not talk, do not move. They are like lizards basking in the sun. A fine life that would be, thinks Souren, as he picks up his suitcases. He crosses the road and makes his way down Rue du Chat qui Pêche.

Men, cats—everyone in Paris is fishing.

He likes to walk through the Latin Quarter. It is the oldest part of the city, a labyrinth that meanders and intersects with itself without apparent design or purpose. The pace of life feels a little slower here. People linger a little longer at café tables as they watch the rest of the world amble by. One more sip of coffee, one more story in the newspaper. Souren prefers these streets to the grandiose thoroughfares north of the river. When his feet hit the ancient cobblestones, he feels a connection with the city that otherwise eludes him. Generations of stories inhabit every brick in every wall. He can almost see the ghosts.

He thinks about his conversation with Younis in the shop that morning. His friend was right: when Souren walks these streets, he is invisible. A ghost himself. Younis and his brothers will never have that luxury: everyone sees the color of their skin. Souren turns onto Rue de la Huchette, wondering what it must be like to be noticed everywhere you go, suspicious eyes always following you—and yet Younis is more at home here than Souren will ever be. Family can inoculate you against most things, he thinks.

Ahead of him, two men are shuffling down the sidewalk, their heads close together. Both are wearing hats and heavy coats, despite the warmth of the day. Souren is about to step into the road to skirt around them when familiar sounds snag the edges of his consciousness.

The two men are speaking Armenian.

At once he falls back into step behind them, no longer interested in navigating past the slow-moving pair.

"I don't know what to tell you," says the shorter of the men, who leans heavily on a cane as he walks. "Old age is a terrible thing. My poor Sirvat! She is so lost, so sad." He gestures at the street in front of him. "She thinks this is Diyarbakir. Every day she frets about going to visit her mother, who died thirty years ago, God rest her soul."

"And it never lets up?" asks the other man sympathetically.

"Not even for a moment." The first man shakes his head. "Perhaps I should be grateful. If she knew that we're living in France, she would be heartbroken. Although she was the one who insisted that we leave, you know. She could see the way the wind was blowing before anyone else. Me, like a fool, I wanted to stay. I was sure we would be safe." The man sighs. "Sirvat was right, as usual. And now she remembers none of it. As far as she's concerned, we never left."

The second man puts a consoling hand on his friend's shoulder. "Perhaps it's for the best," he says.

"Ach, who knows? These days she just stays in bed, the covers pulled up over her face. The outside world terrifies her now. She won't even look out of the window. She last left our apartment six months ago. We went for a little walk. She spent the whole time looking over her shoulder and asking why she couldn't understand a word anyone said." The man pauses. "She saved my life by getting us out of Anatolia before it was too late. Truly, she did. But now when she needs me to save hers, there's nothing I can do. My heart breaks for her every day."

Souren is now so close behind the two men that he can hear the soft fall of their shoes on the sidewalk. His heart balloons, despite the sadness of the man's words. This stranger's mournful elegy for his wife is the sweetest sound he can imagine. He has not heard another person speak his language since he arrived in France a decade ago. All at once he is drowning in a sea of old memories. He is sitting at the family dinner table, passing food, laughing with his father, fighting with his brother. He is streaking through the streets with Yervant, staring at the pretty girls, too scared to do anything but yell at them and run away as fast as he can. He is—

"Watch out!"

The man with the cane has stopped and is looking at Souren, furiously rubbing the back of his leg. "What's wrong with you?" he demands in French. "You hit me with your suitcase."

Souren blinks at him. He wants to talk to them in the language they share, but the man's anger catches the words in his throat. "Excuse me," he mutters, also in French.

"There's no need to walk so close to us," says the second man.

Oh, but there is, Souren wants to tell him.

The man with the walking stick stares at him for a moment longer, and then turns back to his companion. "Clumsy idiot," he mutters in Armenian.

The two men start walking again, each delivering one last, suspicious glare at Souren as they move away. He picks up his suitcases, not ready to let the men go just yet. This time he follows at a more discreet distance.

"You'd think the French would have worked out by now how not to step on each other as they walk down the street," complains the second man. "There's plenty of damn room."

"Such an arrogant bunch," says the man with the cane. "Their noses always stuck up in the air!"

The second man points over his shoulder toward Souren without looking back. "And half of them are imbeciles."

"This place. I won't be sorry to say good-bye."

"You're really going to leave?"

A nod. "Once Sirvat is gone I'll have no reason to stay."

"You don't think you're a little old to start a new life somewhere else?"

"Oh, probably so. But that apartment will have too many memories for me."

"So move to another apartment! You don't have to cross an ocean!"

The man with the cane wheezes in amusement. "The trouble with you, Grigor, is that you have no sense of adventure."

"And Sirvat suspects nothing? She hasn't asked why you have started bringing home all these books in English?"

"My sweet wife barely knows who I am anymore. She doesn't care what I'm reading."

"How is your English these days?"

"Getting better. The novels help, of course. But it's one thing to be able to read a language. Quite another to be able to go into a store and ask for a loaf of bread."

"Perhaps you won't need it much. There are plenty of Armenians in New York."

"Five of my cousins, for a start," agrees the first man. "I last saw them at the train station in Diyarbakir. We planned to leave together, but there wasn't enough room for all of us on one train—so they left first, and Sirvat and I waited for the next one. That was all it took to blow our family apart. Now there's an ocean between us." He pauses. "They live in a place called Queens. Queens! What do you think about *that*?"

"America," says his friend in wonder.

"You should come with me, Grigor. Keep me company on the boat."

The second man holds up his hand. "I'll stay here, thank you."

"Our countrymen are scattered across the globe now. You could go anywhere in the world and feel at home."

"Ah, my friend, now you're telling fairy tales." The man called Grigor shakes his head.

The pair walks in silence for several minutes. Souren continues to follow them. Consumed by the echoes of his youth, he has lost his bearings. Halfway down a street the men's pace slows.

"Here we are," says the man with the cane.

"What are you going to buy today?"

A shrug. "Something funny would be nice. There's a writer I like called Wodehouse. He writes about the English aristocracy. They're buffoons, every last one of them. It's a miracle the British Empire still exists." With that he pushes open the door to a shop and the two men disappear inside.

Souren puts down his suitcases. The language of his childhood has filled his ears and his heart, and now loneliness and regret threaten to overwhelm him. Ten years he's been waiting to speak Armenian with another person, and when the moment finally came, all he could do was to stammer two words in French. Of course, the two men had dismissed him as another clumsy Parisian, unworthy of their interest. He wants to follow them inside and make them understand their mistake. Souren looks at the building that the men entered moments earlier. He is standing in front of a large window, filled with books. No two titles on display are the same, and they are all in a language he does not understand.

That is when he sees the painting nestling in the lower right corner of the window.

The painting is of a small house, in the middle of a wood. On either side of the house erupts an army of trees, streaking upward into swirling knots of darkness, black stars of mordant energy. Ranks of lichen-wrapped trunks surge toward each other, a sinister labyrinth of shadows. There is no sky: the dark forest marauds across the canvas, annexing every square inch. There is a strip of lawn in front of the house. On the grass stands a solitary wooden chair. An owl is perched on the back of the chair. Its feathers are silver and purple. It is gazing off into the distance. A path leads to the house, but there is no door there, just a wall. The walls of the house are painted white. All the light gathers here, a radiant defiance against the encroaching shadows. But Souren cannot see what lies within the little cottage in the forest, because it has no windows. No windows, no door . . . but no, there *is* a door. It is a rich, deep blue, and it sits in the very center of the building's façade, suspended halfway between the ground and the roof. The door is the only way into the house.

Souren stares at the blue door. Is is beautiful and unreachable.

He can barely breathe.

This painting, Souren knows with absolute certainty, was created with him in mind. The artist has looked into Souren's soul and has painted what he saw there.

He cannot take his eyes off the canvas in the window. He steps forward until his nose is almost touching the glass. He is crucified with a yearning to be close to the artwork, to disappear into the artist's two-dimensional universe. Souren stares at the ridges left by each brushstroke. There are raised knots of color, straining to escape the canvas. Not quite two dimensions, then: the painting is a roiling landscape of tiny hillocks and fortifications, a choppy sea. It's marvelously, undeniably alive.

Souren feels as if someone has reached inside him and neatly filleted his heart into slices. Tears fill his eyes. A stranger has painted him from the inside out, and the truth is there for every passerby to see.

He knows what lies inside the little house. He knows what is on the other side of the blue door.

It is everything he has ever wanted. And it is forever out of reach.

The door opens and the two Armenians step back out onto the street. The man with the cane now holds a small brown paper bag. Seeing Souren, he stops abruptly and turns to his friend. "That's the fool who bumped into us earlier," he says in a low voice.

His companion nods. "He's been waiting for us."

"Have you ever seen him before?" asks the first man. He sounds worried.

"I don't think so." The two men turn away from Souren, their heads close together. "What could he want from us?"

"Don't worry," whispers the man with the cane. "We're safe enough. It's broad daylight. We're in the middle of the street. There's not much he can do to us here."

"And if he follows us home? We can't very well outrun him. He's young, and he looks as strong as an ox."

"What do you think is in those suitcases, Grigor?"

The two old men look at each other in silent apprehension. All these years after they were driven out of their homeland, the men are still terrified. Souren picks up his suitcases and walks over to the two men.

"Puppets," he tells them. *Tiknikner*.

The men are too surprised to respond.

"My suitcases are full of hand puppets," explains Souren gently, in Armenian. "They're perfectly harmless, I can assure you. You have nothing to fear."

He feels the astonished stares of his countrymen on him as he sets off down the street. He does not look back.

Souren enters the Jardin du Luxembourg at the northeast gate. He carries his suitcases to his usual spot beneath the regimented ranks of well-pruned chestnut trees, where he and his audience will be protected from the summer sun. He opens the larger of the two suitcases and begins to screw together the poles that make the skeleton of the puppet theater. As he works, his mind drifts back to the painting that he saw in the window of the bookshop. He wonders about the man who painted it. What has happened to him, that he can move strangers so profoundly with his art? Souren looks up at the passersby as they stroll up and down the pathways. He is dazzled by the idea that there is someone walking the streets of this city who understands him so precisely. The thought gives him comfort: he is not alone. Then he wonders if he's the only person so arrested by the little white house and all of the unreachable promise hiding within its walls. Perhaps there is a whole tribe of people like him in Paris! Suddenly he is consumed by an urgent, visceral need to lay eyes on the painting again. He resolves to return to the bookshop after his performance.

Once the poles of the tent have been erected, he stops to eat the first of the apples that he purchased from Younis that morning. His lunch finished, he pulls the sheath of striped fabric over the frame. It is a good, tight fit. There is a window in the front of the tent around which Souren attaches a wooden proscenium arch. Twelve inches behind the stage hangs a sheet, the backdrop that hides him from the audience while he performs. Beneath the stage is a shelf. Before each play Souren arranges the puppets he needs there, where they wait until he is ready for them.

Souren walks across the gravel path to a hut that stands near the gate by Rue de Vaugirard. Around the back of the building there is a metal bucket hidden behind a small bush, exactly where he left it. Souren fills the bucket with water from a spigot and carries it back to the puppet theater.

He is ready to begin.

26

A Fleeting Vision

GUILLAUME CLOSES THE DOOR of the gallery and sets off down Boulevard Raspail. He walks quickly, trying to outpace his despair. Emile Brataille has refused to lend him the money he needs, and so that is the end of that.

He crosses Rue d'Assas and steps through the gate of the Jardin du Luxembourg. He makes his way along the gravel path toward the center of the park. He would love to sit for a moment and watch the children play, but every bench is occupied on this beautiful afternoon. There are couples, holding hands and gazing into each other's eyes. There are solitary readers, immersed in their books. There are mothers, watching their children skitter carelessly between the trees.

As he walks, Guillaume considers his hastily improvised act of revenge. He does not feel particular satisfaction at the prospect of Brataille unwittingly provoking the ire of the violently inclined pimps who work at Le Chat Blanc. Justice will be delivered. Whatever happens will be no more than the art dealer deserves.

The sun is warm on Guillaume's back. He feels thirsty, and remembers a small bar on Boulevard Saint-Michel that he likes. It will be as good a place as any for a final, valedictory drink. He exits through the gates on the east side of the park, the grand dome of the Panthéon ahead of him, and turns toward the river.

The bar is quiet at this time of day. Two old men are playing cards at a table in the corner. A waiter stands behind the *zinc*, reading a newspaper. Guillaume sits down at a table near the front of the room, with a view of the street. The waiter carefully folds his newspaper and glides over to him, an inquisitive eyebrow raised. Guillaume orders a glass of pastis and settles moodily back in his chair to watch the passersby. He downs his drink and orders another one, considering his ever-dwindling options. The only sensible thing to do is to leave the city before Le Miroir and his thugs find him. He should go directly to Gare Montparnasse and wait for the next train to La Rochelle. He thinks about his beloved apartment, and the empty wall where Suzanne's painting used to be. At least it will be easier to leave Paris without it there.

Suddenly he is flattened by a riptide of bittersweet regret. Gertrude Stein bought his painting! Perhaps Brataille was right, he thinks ruefully. Perhaps everything was about to change for him. Even now the little cottage in the woods might be up on her wall in the apartment on Rue de Fleurus, next to all those Cézannes and Matisses. He sips his drink. He imagines Pablo Picasso admiring the painting, insisting that his hostess reveal the name of the artist. He can almost hear the knock on the studio door—and there is the famous Spaniard, marching into the room, grabbing the younger man's hand and pumping it enthusiastically, proclaiming his genius. Guillaume will tell Picasso about looking for him at the Cirque Medrano all those years before. He'll explain about the acrobats, about Suzanne. Picasso will be enchanted by this story. They will become firm friends. Under the Spaniard's mentorship, Guillaume's rise will be stratospheric, legendary. He will move to Montparnasse. Emile Brataille will beg to sell his paintings in his gallery, and he will refuse. Collectors will fight over his work. He will be rich beyond his dreams—and finally he will knock on Suzanne's door.

Except none of this will happen, not now. As soon as he finishes his drink he's going to the train station and will leave Paris for good.

That is when he remembers that Gertrude Stein's six hundred francs is still in the studio, hidden beneath his mattress.

One of the old men at the back of the room says something in a low voice, which provokes wheezy cackles of laughter from his friend.

Just then Suzanne walks past the window.

She is holding her daughter's hand. The young girl is skipping, laughing and talking nonstop, just as she always does. Guillaume stares at the pair of them, thunderstruck. They should not be here. They are on the wrong side of the city. For a moment Guillaume wonders if they're ghosts, hallucinations summoned by his regret—but no, he's not imagining them. This is no creation of wistful longing on his part. He has watched them from a distance for so many years that he would recognize them both at a hundred paces. He looks through the window at their retreating backs, paralyzed. They're walking in the direction of the Jardin du Luxembourg.

Guillaume is not a religious man, but he recognizes a sign when he sees one. There's a reason Suzanne has materialized in front of him, here, on today of all days: he has to say good-bye.

He picks up his glass and finishes his drink in one long swallow. With fumbling fingers he throws some coins onto the table and gets to his feet. He pushes open the door of the bar and turns quickly to follow Suzanne and her daughter down Boulevard Saint-Michel. He walks a few steps and then stops, scanning the street in front of him. He can no longer see them. He starts to move through the crowd. People are dawdling along the sidewalk. Guillaume dodges and weaves between them as fast as he can. He is looking for Suzanne's hair glowing in the sunlight, but he does not see her. He pushes on until he reaches the corner of Rue Soufflot. There he stops, hands on hips, breathing hard.

They have disappeared.

Lost in a sea of ambling pedestrians, Guillaume's last soupçon of hope is brutally rubbed away. This feels like the cruelest twist of all, a final reminder of everything that he has lost and is about to lose. If only he had been faster on his feet! He closes his eyes and sees Suzanne's painting, but to his horror it has begun to change: the forest is inching forward. The knotted tree limbs stretch and unfurl, slowly wrapping the little house in their sinister embrace. Their black tendrils swarm across the whitewashed walls. The blue door in the middle of the wall is disappearing. Soon the house will be swallowed by the dark and hungry woods, its light forever extinguished.

Guillaume turns and walks toward the river, furious with himself for taking so long to run after her. Only once he has crossed the Île de la Cité does he slow his pace a little. At Châtelet he passes beneath a signpost for Les Halles, and an old memory returns, of his first weeks in Paris, back when he explored the whole city on foot, sketchbook in hand. Guillaume used to wander the corridors of the food market for hours. He loved the fare on display at the fishmongers' stalls, a silvery rainbow of glistening promise— sea bass, snapper, monkfish—but it was the people who captivated him most: the housewives, the merchants bellowing encouragement to shoppers, and the beggars who lingered in the shadows. He drew them all.

A sharp pang of nostalgia. The market is not far away from where he is standing. Minutes later he is making his way into the huge pavilions of iron and glass. His stomach growls as he walks through the meat hall, past the marbled steaks and fat chains of glistening sausage, and the golden rotisserie chickens crackling on their slow-turning spits. Next come the vegetables, stacked high in vast pyramids of color. The vivid orange of freshly harvested carrots. A violet wall of eggplant, shining darkly beneath the soaring skylights. Baskets of yellow onions. A forest of bright green lettuce, a white hill of cauliflower. Rainbows of precariously stacked peppers. The angry purple blush of radishes.

All this food has made him unbearably hungry, and he realizes that he has eaten nothing all day. He reaches into his pocket and finds a coin. At the next *boulangerie* he buys a fresh baguette. The bread is still warm from the oven. He tears off a piece and begins to chew. It is delicious, but his last meal in Paris is hardly the one he would have chosen for himself. He reluctantly leaves the market and starts to walk back to Montmartre. He finishes the baguette as he goes, but he can no longer taste it. He does not want to return to his studio, but he cannot afford to leave Gertrude Stein's money underneath the mattress.

Guillaume turns the corner onto his street. To his relief, the sidewalk outside his building is empty. He steps quickly through the front door. The hallway is deserted. Madame Cuillasse is nowhere to be seen. Guillaume is glad. The old concierge has never shown him the slightest bit of affection, but he'll miss her cantankerous ways, and the last thing he needs now is to be assailed by more regret. He climbs the stairs. Perhaps La Rochelle won't be so bad, he thinks. A change of scene might even do him some good. By the time he reaches the final flight of stairs, he has almost convinced himself that he will be happy to see his parents again.

There is nobody waiting for him in the corridor. He is whistling as he reaches into his pocket for his key. That is when he sees that the door is slightly ajar.

The tune dies on his lips.

27

The Jardin du Luxembourg

JEAN-PAUL STEPS OUT of the bookshop and limps down Rue de l'Odéon. A few minutes later he walks through the gates of the Jardin du Luxembourg and makes his way to the large octagonal pond in the middle of the park.

He liked Sylvia Beach hugely. She was funny, modest, and kind. She told him many stories about some of the city's famous expatriates. He asked her about Hemingway and Josephine Baker. I'm sure I don't know anything about *that*, she said. But Ernest often comes in and stays for hours. He's always looking for things to distract him from his writing. And I imagine, she said archly, that Miss Baker would be quite a distraction.

The pond is quite still, undisturbed but for two small ducks that bob nearby, emitting plaintive quacks at each other. Their gently rocking bellies send ripples across the surface of the water. They remind Jean-Paul of a pair of regal swans that used to live on the river that ran through his grandparents' pear orchard in Péchabou. When he was nine years old, his grandfather caught him lobbing pebbles at the beautiful birds. He still remembers the sting of the old man's belt that afternoon. *Why would you ever hurt a swan?* his grandfather demanded, again and again, as the leather strap swung. But Jean-Paul wasn't trying to hurt the swans. He loved them fiercely. They were so elegant, so perfect, so not of his world: he had just wanted them to notice him, to respond in some small way to his existence. What hurt more than the beating itself was the quickness of his grandfather's disappointment, his readiness to assume the worst. It was only after Elodie was born that Jean-Paul understood that it was the ferocity of the old man's love for him that had prompted such severe retribution. Love like that raises the stakes.

One of the ducks takes off in a typhoon of splashing water, leaving its companion sitting alone on the pond. As Jean-Paul limps along the pristine pathways toward the turreted, fairy-tale splendor of the Palais du Luxembourg, a swell of laughter floats by on the faint afternoon breeze. Curious, he turns in the direction of the noise. In the shade of the chestnut trees, close to Rue de Vaugirard, he sees a crowd of young children and their parents clustered around a tall, narrow tent with a striped awning and proscenium arch that has been painted gold.

A puppet show.

Most of the children are sitting cross-legged on the grass, their heads tilted up at the stage like sunflowers leaning toward the sun. Jean-Paul watches as the puppets chase each other back and forth, a frenetic whirlwind of motion. He tries to follow the story, but cannot work out what is going on. He walks a little closer, and realizes that the puppets are not talking in French. He listens, intrigued. Perhaps, he thinks, it is not a language at all, but some improvised argot, a deliberately nonsensical canvas of sound onto which the children can paint whatever story they choose. The puppets' words have a strange poetry, incanted spells whose opaque mystery is its own kind of beauty. Jean-Paul watches the faces of the young audience. One thing seems clear: the children know exactly what is going on. They are laughing in delight one minute, yelling worried warnings the next.

On the stage, a princess in a pink satin dress is confronting a fierce-looking knight, who is waving a long sword threateningly at her. The princess is clasping her tiny wooden hands together. She appears to be begging the knight for something—mercy, Jean-Paul guesses, or perhaps his heart.

The knight responds gruffly, each time moving a little closer toward the princess, until the two figures are almost touching. The nearer the knight gets, the more the children cry out. The princess is oblivious to their yells. She continues to plead with him. Jean-Paul waits for the knight to put down his sword and sweep the princess into his arms.

The children know better.

As the audience's cries reach a crescendo, the knight plunges his sword deep into the princess's chest, driving the blade clean through her body and out the other side. Suddenly there is complete silence. All eyes are on the princess and the sword that gruesomely skewers her. The puppet staggers backward and lets out a terrible moan. The knight watches her impassively.

Every child is agog.

The princess takes some time to die. She mutters and gasps, her little hands flapping helplessly at the handle of the sword that is now sticking out of her chest. She turns this way and that, but nothing will save her. Finally, she stops moving and begins to sing a slow, lilting song in that strange language. She completes two verses before finally dropping dead. The puppet falls forward dramatically, her wooden head hitting the frame of the proscenium with a doleful thump.

There is a moment's silence, then enthusiastic applause.

The puppets are quickly pulled back out of sight, and a moment later a young man appears from behind the tent. He has a thick black beard and wears a hat, which he removes as he bows awkwardly to the crowd. He does not smile, does not say a word. He hands his hat to a little girl sitting in the front row. The puppeteer stares at his shoes as the hat is passed among the audience. Jean-Paul likes his quiet dignity. Once the hat is returned to him, he bows in thanks and disappears again behind the striped awning. Children reluctantly allow themselves to be pulled away by their parents, and new arrivals take their place.

Jean-Paul checks his watch. He has time to watch one more play.

28

Paris, 1919: The First Betrayal

TO THE LEFT OF MONSIEUR Proust's bedroom door there was a small Oriental cabinet, upon which were arranged old photographs of the author and his brother when they were children. Next to the cabinet there was a large rosewood chest. Stacked in a neat pile on top of the chest were thirty-two notebooks.

These thirty-two books contained the kernel of Marcel Proust's masterwork. Between their covers he had already constructed the framework of the narrative. The heart of his fictional world was already beating within those pages; now he was fleshing out the body and creating the spirit of the thing. He was slowly bringing his story to life.

Proust knew the contents of every notebook by heart, but he liked to keep them close while he worked. Sometimes he asked Camille to fetch a particular book so that he could check a detail. He would flick to the page he needed, review the text, and then hand it back to her. Camille was comforted by the notebooks on top of the rosewood chest. If Monsieur Proust's fears about dying before he finished the book were realized, at least they would remain.

So it was a profound shock when one evening her employer summoned her to the bedroom and issued a most unexpected request. He lay, as usual, propped up in his bed, surrounded by pillows and paper. A small gaslight was flickering by his side, which barely illuminated his face.

"Ah, Camille," he said, smiling at her through the half-light. "There's something I need you to do for me. It's of the utmost importance."

"Of course, monsieur," she said. Everything he asked her to do was described in similar terms, no matter how trivial.

"I want you to burn my notebooks."

Camille stood quite still, unsure she had heard correctly. "Pardon?" she said.

"The notebooks." He pointed at the rosewood chest. "I want you to burn them."

Camille stood there, stunned. "Are you quite sure?" she asked.

"Of course I'm sure," said Proust.

"But why do you want to burn them, monsieur?"

"It's not your place to question such things, Camille."

"It's just that you are always worrying about what will happen if you die before you finish the book!"

He looked at her through those limpid eyes. "And?"

"Well, if you *do* die, without the notebooks nobody will know how the story ends!"

"But that's exactly the point. I've had some new ideas, you see." Proust sighed. "The war has changed everything, and now the notebooks are out-of-date. That's why I need you to burn them. I know every single one of them inside and out, anyway."

"But, monsieur—"

"Camille, please."

The words hung in the air between them. She remained uncertainly by the door.

"I have no wish to discuss this further," he said after a moment, as softly as ever. "Please burn the books in the kitchen grate, and then kindly come back and tell me when it is done."

. . .

An hour later, Camille knelt down in front of the kitchen hearth and set a fire. The notebooks were stacked in piles on the floor. She watched as the thin yellow tongues of flame flickered up and down the stack of kindling.

It was wrong to burn the notebooks. It was wrong to reduce all those years of work to ashes. But it was Monsieur Proust's wish. The notebooks belonged to him, and nobody else. Camille knew that nothing she could say would change his mind. She took the top notebook off the stack and opened it. She gazed at the familiar handwriting. Her eyes drifted down those well-ordered lines. Such clarity of thought, such unerring precision! She would be the last person ever to see these words.

The flames were growing higher. Camille put the notebook into the grate. For a moment the fire was trapped beneath its heft, but then the flames crept around its edges. The black leather curled into crescents, and smoke began to escape from between the pages as they browned and warped in the heat. She watched as the words were swallowed by the fire, reduced to ashes.

She reached for another notebook.

After that she began to work more quickly, throwing books onto the flames in twos and threes, numbly watching the growing conflagration. With every incinerated volume came the sensation of unbearable loss. Each time her fingers released another notebook into the fire's embrace, it was one more senseless eradication, terrible in its irreversibility.

In the end, her betrayal was an act of self-defense.

Just as Camille threw the final notebook onto the fire, she knew—as surely as she had ever known anything—that she could not let it burn. Instinctively she reached back into the flames. The black leather was already hot to the touch. She forced her fingers to close around the spine of the notebook, and pulled it out of the fire. She let go of it at once, her fingers scalded. The notebook landed on the flagstones. She had been quick. The edges of the paper had not even been singed.

Camille stared down at the rescued book, stupefied by what she had

done. Not once had she disobeyed Monsieur Proust in even the smallest
way.

She ran a finger across the cover, a thin straight line through the soft
ash.

After she had cleaned the kitchen grate, Camille hid the rescued notebook
in her handbag. She was stunned by her own betrayal. All those years of
faithful service, undone in a stroke.

She knocked on the bedroom door.

"Ah, Camille." Marcel Proust looked up at her. As usual, he lay in his
bed, surrounded by paper. "I smelled the burning from down the corridor.
You did as I asked?"

"*Oui*, monsieur."

"All the notebooks are destroyed?"

She looked down. "*Oui*, monsieur."

"Thank you."

"*Oui*, monsieur."

She closed the door and walked back to the kitchen.

Camille went home and hid the rescued notebook at the bottom of an old
trunk, beneath piles of neatly folded clothes and linens, where Olivier
would never find it. In the weeks and months that followed, she did her
best to act as if nothing had happened. She tried to pretend that the notebook was not there. There was no furtive rummaging to retrieve it when
she was alone in the apartment. To read the words that Monsieur Proust
had wanted to be burned would have compounded her guilt still further.
The notebook lay at the bottom of her trunk, unseen and unread. Camille
was appalled by what she had done, but she was unable to bring herself to
destroy what she had stolen. The notebook was hers, now, hers alone, and
she was determined not to give it up for anything: she would always have
it to remember him by.

She didn't tell Olivier, fearful that her husband would make her confess everything. Brick by careful brick, she hid her crime behind walls of ashamed silence. But too late, she saw that it was not just the stolen note-book that lay hidden within the catacomb that she had built. Camille herself was trapped in there, along with her secret. There was to be no escaping what she had done.

29

Performance

IN FRONT OF HIM, the puppets dance.

Souren watches the stories unfold at the ends of his arms. His hands move swiftly to the left and right, dropping out of sight as he swaps one puppet for another. He gives each of them a different voice, from the booming bass of the corpulent king to the shrill falsetto of the young dairy-maid. One by one, his family comes to life beneath his fingers. Now all those sightless eyes can see.

The crowd is a good one. Families stop and watch the show, grateful for a moment's stillness in the afternoon's humidity. A faint breeze rustles the leaves of the chestnut trees above him, but inside the tent it is hotter than an oven. Soon his shirt is soaked through with perspiration and clings to his back like a second skin. At the end of each play, he steps into the sunshine to accept the audience's applause, and silently passes his hat around the spectators. He never watches to see who contributes and who does not. When the hat is returned to him, it is always full.

Souren thinks about the pianist downstairs, playing the same song again and again, those beautiful notes offering charmed protection against some greater ill. These puppets and stories are Souren's own armor. His hands weave back and forth, his lips murmur incantations. He is casting a spell.

When Souren performs, he speaks only in Armenian.

He thinks of Amandine Nouvel, his first audience, and wonders what stories the children are telling themselves as they watch the puppets skitter across the stage. Most of them sit in haphazard rows in front of the tent, as close as possible to the puppets. But there are always some who stand on the edge of the crowd, clutching a parent's hand and ready to make a quick escape if the story doesn't turn out the way it should.

How do they know? Souren wonders when he sees the faces of these anxious children.

He performs folk tales and fairy tales for his audience—familiar stories for the most part, centuries old. But fairy tales are empty comforts to be whispered into the ears of children as they drift toward their dreams. Souren, though, needs to tell the truth, and so:

The wolf eats the woodcutter.

The evil witch has the last laugh.

The princess does not wake up.

The story never turns out the way it should.

Yes, on occasion he is confronted by an angry parent—always accompanied by a loudly sobbing child. But for the most part the cries of the audience betray not fear, but excitement. There are no happy endings to be had for Souren's puppets, and this is precisely why the children cannot look away.

They are bored with fairy tales.

Souren thinks about the old Armenian, leaning on his cane as he hobbled along the sidewalk, clutching his newly purchased book. He is learning English and making plans to be reunited with his cousins in America. Despite all he has suffered, he has not given up. He, at least, is still hoping for a happy ending.

All that lies between the old man and his family is the Atlantic Ocean. Such distances can be navigated easily enough. But there is no ticket that Souren can ever purchase that will reunite him with those he has lost.

Suddenly he is drowning in remorse. What moved him about the conversation between his elderly countrymen, he understands, was not hearing his native language spoken, but hearing it *understood*. That sense of connection is what he misses so badly.

Souren speaks Armenian when he performs, but it doesn't matter what he says. The children hear what they want to hear.

To be understood—that was the thing. As Souren left Younis's shop with his two apples that morning, Bechir stirred in his chair and said something to his eldest son. It sounded to Souren like no more than a string of low, guttural sounds—scarcely a language at all. Younis laughed and responded in kind. Lucky Younis, thinks Souren now. He can still speak his native language, even if only to scold his siblings and joke with his father. People might stare suspiciously at him when he walks down the street, but at least he is not alone.

On the puppets go.

Souren's performance becomes increasingly frenetic as he tries to edge out from beneath the weight of his sadness. A mawkish self-pity descends on him. How absurd he is, performing these plays that nobody understands! Even his delight at the discovery of the beautiful painting in the bookshop window dissipates. The little white house in the woods no longer offers comfort, only regret. What good does it do, he thinks bitterly, to be moved by the art of a stranger? What good does it do, to be one of a tribe whose other members you will never know?

Arielle. Her mother. Younis. Thérèse, when he could afford her.

His world is so small.

This is why he performs. The pianist from downstairs plays only for himself, but Souren *needs* an audience. He tells his stories to communicate, to connect with others. That is why he returns to the Jardin du Luxembourg every day. The gasps from the audience, the cries of alarm, the applause—this is how he knows he is alive.

It is time for the final play.

Souren moves the bucket of water in front of his feet. He places a small candle on the shelf beneath the stage and lights it with a match. The wick flares and then burns with a steady flame. He pulls a glove onto his right hand, then the puppet of Hector, the cherry-cheeked little boy. It is a snug fit. Souren takes a small tin of kerosene from his pocket and douses the tunic that he made in the early hours of that morning. The sharp smell hits the back of his nose, igniting old memories.

He is ready.

His hands begin to tell the story.

Here is Hector. Here is the Turk.

30

The Cost of Six Hundred Francs

GUILLAUME PUSHES THE DOOR open. There are three people in the room. He recognizes one of them—the small, rat-faced man he met in the café is sitting on the bed. But it is the other two occupants who draw most of his attention. One of them is a giant, so tall that the top of his head nearly scrapes the ceiling, and so broad that he blocks out most of the light from the window. His fists are the size of ham hocks.

The other man is holding a knife.

"There you are," says the rat-faced man. "Close the door behind you."

Guillaume does as he is told. As the door closes the man with the knife moves in front of it.

"You know why we're here," says the rat-faced man.

Guillaume nods. "I have money for you," he says.

"All of it?"

"Not quite."

"How much?"

Guillaume crosses the room, reaches under the mattress, and retrieves Gertrude Stein's money. Trying to stop his hands from shaking too much, he counts out the banknotes. Three unblinking pairs of eyes watch him. There is a long silence when he deals the last note onto the bed.

"That's six hundred francs," says the rat-faced man. "You owe me twelve."

Guillaume swallows. "I can get you the——"

"Did you not hear me say that we need every last *sou* repaid today?" interrupts the man. "Did you not understand? Or did you just not believe me?"

"This was all I could get," says Guillaume desperately. "I need more time for the rest." He thinks of Gertrude Stein and Emile Brataille. Neither of them would have missed the six hundred francs he needs. Guillaume glances at the man by the door. The blade of his knife glints in the afternoon sunlight.

"You don't *have* any more time." The man picks up the money from the bed and counts it again. "You've given me half of what you owe. *Half.*"

The man with the knife steps toward him and pushes the knife into Guillaume's side. The sharp point of the blade presses through the fabric of his shirt. "Big mistake, *mon gars*," he whispers.

"I can get you the rest of the money!" cries Guillaume.

"That'll do, Claude," says the rat-faced man. The man with the knife reluctantly steps back.

"How?" asks the man on the bed.

A glimmer of hope.

"See all these paintings?" asks Guillaume. The man nods. "A famous collector is coming to view them this afternoon. She's already bought one of my works. She says she's anxious to see more."

The paintings are still arranged around the room for the morning's viewing. The man looks at them, dubious. "How much will you get for them?"

"A lot more than six hundred francs, you can be sure of that."

"What's the name of this famous collector?" asks the man called Claude. The knife is twitching in his hand.

"She's called Gertrude Stein," replies Guillaume. "She's an American."

"The writer?"

The giant speaks for the first time. The other three men look at him in surprise.

Guillaume nods. "That's right. She's a writer."

The giant's face lights up. "Oh, she's wonderful," he says.

"You've read her stuff?" asks the rat-faced man.

"Oh yes. She's a genius." The giant pauses. "A bit strange, but a genius."

"You're such a pretentious ponce, Arnaud," sneers the man with the knife.

"It wouldn't kill you to open a book sometimes, Claude," says the giant mildly.

The man on the bed waves at them to be quiet. He is thinking. "So this American is coming by later today?" he says.

Guillaume nods.

"How do I know you're telling the truth?"

Guillaume walks over to the mantelpiece. There is Gertrude Stein's card, exactly where he left it this morning. He hands it to the rat-faced man, who examines it closely.

"You say this person is a *writer?*"

"Yes."

"Is she rich?"

"Rich enough."

The man stands up and begins pacing the room, weighing his options. "And you'll have the rest of the money by tonight."

Guillaume nods and points to the wall where Suzanne's painting used to hang. "She's already bought the one that was here. That's where the six hundred francs came from."

"He's lying," growls Claude. "I say we follow our—"

"Would you shut up?" snaps the rat-faced man angrily. "If waiting a little longer is going to give us the full amount owed and one less body to dispose of, I'm going to consider it."

Claude spits on the floorboards. "You're swallowing his story about this rich American?"

"Let me remind you of something, Claude," hisses the man. "My job is to make decisions. *Your* job," he continues, poking an angry finger at him, "is to follow my orders."

Guillaume sees Claude's knuckles whiten around the handle of the knife. Perhaps, he thinks, they'll all kill each other and he'll be able to escape.

The rat-faced man paces for a few more moments and then stops. He looks at Guillaume. "All right," he says. "One more chance."

"*Putain*," mutters Claude.

"Thank you," breathes Guillaume.

"When is this American supposed to be coming by?"

Guillaume shrugs. "She didn't say."

A sharp look. "But today?"

"Oh yes. Definitely today."

The man points at Claude. "He's going to be waiting outside, watching the door. Don't even think about trying to escape. He's good with that knife. He'll fillet you into ten pieces before your feet even touch the sidewalk."

"Why do *I* have to wait?" whines Claude.

"Because I said so," says the man, his face thunderous.

"I'll do it," says Arnaud.

The other two men turn to look at him. "Why?" says the leader.

Arnaud puts up his huge hands. "Gertrude Stein," he says simply.

"*Mon dieu*, all right then."

Guillaume swallows. He points to the six hundred francs on the bed. "So is that sufficient for the moment, then?" he asks.

"No, *mon ami*, it's not sufficient at all," says the rat-faced man. Then without warning he throws a strong, low punch into Guillaume's gut. Guillaume doubles over, and as he goes down his attacker takes a step forward and drives a ferocious knee into his face. Guillaume's nose erupts in blinding pain. He falls to his knees.

The man bends down so that his mouth is right next to Guillaume's ear. "You're getting one last chance," he says. "But all that means is that you're not quite dead yet."

Guillaume clutches at the smashed cartilage in the middle of his face. His fingers are slippery with what he supposes must be his own blood.

31

Verdun, 1916: Passacaille II

THE CROWD IN FRONT of Jean-Paul settles down for the next puppet play, still with expectation.

A boy is alone outside his family's house. He climbs a tree, he spins a wooden top. He is quiet and content, until the peace is shattered by the arrival of a scowling warrior, who wears a purple turban and has a grotesquely hooked nose—a Turk, Jean-Paul supposes. The warrior shakes the boy roughly and yells at him in the same, unintelligible language as before. The boy, clearly terrified, replies in a high-pitched voice, but his answer just makes the Turk angry. He starts to hit the boy with a long stick. The boy collapses under the blows. Some of the children are yelling, urging the boy to escape. The warrior waves the stick over his head, bellowing in fury. The children boo and hiss as he leaps across the stage. Finally the Turk puts down the stick and ties the boy's hands behind his back. The boy is shaking in terror. His assailant waves his arms, and lets out a murderous cry. At this, the boy appears to burst into flames, and the audience gives a collective gasp. Jean-Paul can't help but be impressed. As gory as the puppet show is, the effects are very realistic. Then he sees wisps of black smoke spiraling upward into the canopy of trees overhead. He looks more closely, and realizes that this is not a trick. The flames are real. The puppet is actually burning. The boy remains quite still in the middle of the stage as the fire engulfs him. He does not make a sound. His head finally slumps forward, and the next moment he vanishes behind the tent's striped awning. The stage is empty.

This time there is no applause. The audience waits to see what will happen next. All eyes are fixed on the empty stage. Just then a child begins to cry. Jean-Paul turns toward the sound. Not far away from him, a young girl is sobbing. Her face is buried in the folds of the skirt of the woman standing next to her.

"Ah, *maman!*" the girl weeps. "That poor little boy!"

The woman holds her daughter close. "Don't cry, *chérie*," she says. "It's just a puppet show."

Except it's not, thinks Jean-Paul. This is more than just a puppet show. The burning boy is more than just another gruesome story. He looks back toward the stage. The puppeteer has not reemerged to pass the hat. This time he has remained behind the striped awning. The girl's tears have broken the spell cast by the burning puppet. Parents are collecting their children and pulling them away. In a matter of minutes the grassy area in front of the theater is nearly empty. Still the puppeteer remains inside the tent. What is he waiting for? Jean-Paul wonders. Why did he not pass the hat?

The crying girl and her mother have not moved. The woman is stroking her daughter's hair, trying to calm her tears. The girl's shoulders are shaking. Her face is still hidden in her mother's skirt.

"Hush now," says the woman. "It's over."

But the girl cannot stop crying. After a moment, her mother begins to sing a gentle, wordless melody. Her voice is slightly breathless, and beautiful. The tune is sweet and sad. Jean-Paul closes his eyes and listens. The music catches somewhere deep within him.

In this day full of memories, another falls into place.

After the explosion, the first thing he noticed was the absence of sound.

When Infantryman Jean-Paul Maillard of the French army's 203rd Regiment opened his eyes, the devastation in front of him was accompanied by a terrible silence. As the smoke cleared, he saw five bodies lying in the middle of the road. Not one of them moved. A helmet lay in front of him on the tarmac. Next to it there was a crooked bayonet, its blade warped by the blast. Not far beyond that, a single boot.

From the corner of his eye, he sensed movement. He turned his head and saw Grasset staggering toward him. Grasset's mouth was open. He was yelling, but Jean-Paul could hear nothing.

It had been Grasset's nineteenth birthday the day before. General Pétain himself made a surprise visit to the front, shook the boy's hand and gave him a medal. The other members of the platoon had cheered and slapped their young colleague on the back. That evening Grasset had proudly sewn the medal onto his uniform with a blunt needle and some old black thread. Now, as Grasset stumbled through the smoke, Jean-Paul saw the bloodied stump of the boy's upper arm protruding from his uniform. Grasset did not appear to have noticed that his right arm had been blown off. Instead he was clutching at his chest with his remaining hand, his mouth contorted into a silent scream of fury.

The medal was no longer there.

Suddenly a hole appeared in the middle of Grasset's forehead, and his body crumpled to the ground.

A sniper, mopping up survivors after the mortar attack.

Jean-Paul thought of Anaïs, his new bride. They were married two days before he shipped out to the front, not knowing if they would ever see each other again. Every morning he woke up to the sound of German shells screaming overhead, and wondered if that day would be his last. Verdun, the bloodiest battle ever fought. Soldiers on both sides were being massacred, the scale of daily human destruction beyond comprehension. There were mountains of slain bodies everywhere, pushed to one side to allow those troops who had not yet perished to keep fighting. There was no time to bury the dead. For months Jean-Paul had marched past the corpses of his countrymen, numb to the horror of it all. He was waiting for the grenade explosion that would be the final thing he heard, the last crack of the sniper's gun. Within a week of arriving at the front he had stopped daring to hope that he might make it out alive. But as he looked at Grasset's inert body lying in the middle of the road, a ferocious instinct for survival surged through him. He was not ready to give up, not yet.

He knew that the sniper would be watching for the slightest movement. He closed his eyes and pretended to be dead. As he lay there, wondering when it would be safe to move, he became aware that something was wrong with his leg. Terrible pain was radiating up his thigh. He could feel his toes pressing against the hardened leather of his boots, which meant that his foot hadn't been blown off. There was still hope, he told himself, just before he passed out from the pain.

When Jean-Paul regained consciousness, the sun had dipped behind the line of trees to the west. Several hours must have passed. Through half-closed eyes he scanned the scene. Nothing had moved. The pain in his leg was worse than ever. For the first time he dared to look down. A piece of twisted metal was sticking out of his right calf. He struggled into a sitting position and unhooked his combat knife. He hacked away his fatigues and examined the wound. The shrapnel emerged from his flesh at a grotesque angle, bloody and incongruous. When he tried to bend his knee, the pain was excruciating. If he wanted to move, he would have to pull the metal out of his leg.

Now Jean-Paul wished he had been more careful when he cut away his uniform. He needed a good length of strong material for a tourniquet. He looked around him. To his left he saw something on the ground. It looked both familiar and yet entirely alien. He stared at it for a moment before he realized that he was looking at Grasset's arm. With a monumental effort he stretched out and grasped the bloodied fringe of the fabric. Grimacing, he shook the material until the dead boy's pale limb fell out. Jean-Paul did not give it a second glance. With his knife he sliced Grasset's sleeve into two long strips. He pulled the first around his leg, just above the shrapnel's entry point, and knotted it as tightly as he could. He had yawned his way through the mandatory first-aid lessons when he'd enlisted, but he was grateful for them now. The tourniquet would reduce the blood flow to the lower part of his leg, which in turn should reduce blood loss. He looked down with dread at the twisted piece of shrapnel. He gripped the metal, took three deep breaths, and then pulled as hard as he could.

A terrible scream escaped his lips. The blood glistening on the metal marked how deeply it had been buried in his flesh. While the shrapnel was in his leg it had acted as a plug; now the wound became a dark geyser. Gasping, Jean-Paul reached for the second strip of Grasset's sleeve and wrapped it around the lacerated flesh to stem the flow of blood. Within moments the material was sodden, but now he could bend his knee without the whole world exploding.

Just then he heard the sound of a vehicle. It was the first sign of human life he had seen since Grasset was felled by the sniper's bullet. Night was approaching; there was no way of knowing when another vehicle would come this way. Jean-Paul understood that this was his only chance of survival. He clambered unsteadily to his feet, stunned by the pain. He staggered toward the noise, moving blindly past the dead bodies of his companions. A truck was approaching. In the fading light Jean-Paul could not tell whether the vehicle was French or German, but he no longer cared. The Germans might shoot him, but that would be preferable to bleeding slowly to death overnight. He stepped into the middle of the road and waved his arms above his head.

The truck slowed to a halt a few yards ahead of him. It was in bad shape. The windshield was cracked, the wheels were poorly aligned, and the sides were dented and scratched. There were no markings on its exterior, but Jean-Paul felt safe now. The Germans would never have employed such a decrepit vehicle near the front. The engine shuddered to a halt with a rattling sigh. A short man in well-pressed army fatigues climbed out. He was wearing a helmet several sizes too big. Jean-Paul called out his name and platoon number. The truck driver saluted.

"Mortar attack?" he guessed. Jean-Paul nodded. The driver looked around. "Any other survivors?"

"I don't think so," replied Jean-Paul.

"Well, one is better than nothing."

Jean-Paul pointed to his leg. "I took some shrapnel. It hurts like hell."

"I have morphine," said the driver.

"You do?"

The man nodded and patted the side of the truck. "Believe it or not, this lovely old pile of junk is an ambulance." He fetched a box of medical supplies from the back of the vehicle, and removed a syringe and a small bottle. His fingers were nimble, and he worked quickly.

"Thank you," breathed Jean-Paul a moment later.

"That should help until we get you back to the field hospital," said the driver.

Jean-Paul nodded, rubbing the flesh where the needle went in, wanting to hurry the medicine along his veins. He climbed into the cab of the truck and watched through the windshield as the driver moved among the corpses, looking for signs of life. He bent down next to each soldier, usually for no more than a couple of seconds. It didn't take long to check for a pulse, and sometimes even that wasn't necessary.

"You were lucky," said the driver when he climbed back into his seat. He gunned the engine.

"Are you going to leave them there?" asked Jean-Paul.

"The bodies will be recovered in the morning." The man executed a deft three-point turn. "My job is to tend to survivors." He extended his hand. "Maurice."

"Jean-Paul." They shook.

"This damned war, eh?"

Jean-Paul thought of Grasset lying in the mud with a hole in the middle of his forehead and said nothing.

"How long have you been at the front?" asked the driver.

"An eternity, it feels like."

The driver grunted. "I wanted to be a pilot," he said, "but they wouldn't take me."

Jean-Paul tried to concentrate on what the man was saying, hoping it would distract him from the pain in his leg. "Why not?"

"They said I was too old." He shifted gears as he took a sharp corner, and the engine growled in protest. "But I wanted to do something for the war effort. So they put me in this ambulance. I'm proud to do what I can for France. You make the best of the cards you're dealt, *non*?"

"I suppose so."

They drove in silence for a while. The sun had disappeared and twilight was edging into darkness. Jean-Paul leaned his head against the window of the truck. "Where are we?" he asked.

"That is an excellent question."

"You don't know?"

Before the man could answer, a fireball erupted just to one side of them and the windshield exploded into a million tiny shards of glass. A tornado of earth and mud ripped through the night sky. Rather than slow down or stop, the driver put his foot on the gas pedal and accelerated through the inferno. He pulled down hard on the steering wheel, and the truck veered sharply to the right. The engine screeched in complaint. The vehicle stuttered unevenly for a few more yards, its progress marked by a rainbow of sparks from the undercarriage. Finally they came to a halt. There was a glittering mosaic of shattered glass across Jean-Paul's lap.

"What the hell was that?" he gasped.

"A land mine. We were lucky. We only caught the edge of it. Wait there." The driver opened his door and hurried around the front of the truck to inspect the damage.

"How bad is it?" asked Jean-Paul.

"The wheel's all but destroyed."

"Do you have a spare?"

"I did, but one of the rear tires blew out last week. They never issued me with a replacement."

"So what do we do now?"

"Well, the first thing is to get out of sight." The driver climbed back into the cab of the truck and turned the ignition. There was a shower of sparks as the vehicle lurched forward. The metal of the ruined front wheel scraped against the road, making a terrible noise. They limped along for fifty yards or so. "Hold on tight," said the driver. The truck swerved across the verge into an opening between the trees that lined the side of the road. They edged forward a few yards and came to a stop. The driver grimaced, put the truck in low gear, and tried to ease it further forward. The three good wheels spun but could not gain traction on the soft, uneven ground.

"This is hopeless," he muttered.

"My leg hurts," Jean-Paul whispered.

"I'm afraid we're going to have to walk," said the driver.

"Through the forest?"

"Unless you have a better plan."

"Can you give me some more morphine?"

"I'll bring some with me, but I need you conscious until we find shelter for the night. You're twice my size. I couldn't carry you ten yards."

Jean-Paul nodded and opened the door of the truck. When he put weight on his damaged leg, the pain took his breath away.

"Here." The driver handed him a thick branch. Jean-Paul leaned heavily on the makeshift walking stick and started to hobble into the trees. He followed the driver, who was holding his medical bag in one hand, his service revolver in the other. The only sound was the snap of twigs underfoot. Jean-Paul had to pause every few steps to regain his breath.

"Sorry I'm so slow," he muttered through gritted teeth.

"Hardly your fault," said the driver. "I'm the one who should be apologizing. My job was to get you to safety, not to take you on a hike through the countryside."

The pain obliterated everything else after that. Every step felt as if it would be his last, as if there was no way for him to move another inch, but then he closed his eyes and somehow took one more. Time and distance had no meaning. All he could do was keep moving forward.

Night had fallen now. The two men stumbled through the darkness of the woods, moving slowly over the uneven terrain. There was no more talking.

After what felt like hours, they reached the far edge of the forest. As they emerged from the trees, they passed from darkness into light—a gibbous moon hung above them, high and pale in the night sky. There was an open field in front of them. Beyond it lay the dark outline of a cluster of buildings.

"There's a village," said the driver.

As soon as they began to make their way across the field, Jean-Paul longed for the safety of the forest they had just left behind. The moon illuminated the scene more clearly than a searchlight. Two dark figures moving slowly over an open field: they must have been visible for miles. He leaned heavily on his stick and pushed on. At least the ground was firmer now.

By the time they reached the village, both men were breathing heavily. "Let's find some shelter," said the driver.

"Can't we just knock on the nearest door and ask for help?" asked Jean-Paul.

The driver shook his head. "This place is deserted."

"How do you know?"

"There are villages like this all along the front. Ghost towns. Abandoned. People just locked up their homes and left."

"Where did they all go?" wondered Jean-Paul.

"As far away as possible, until the fighting is over. This is what war does, *mon ami*. The whole world is holding its breath, waiting for life to begin again."

Jean-Paul thought of Anaïs. While he was in a convoy being driven toward the Western front, she had taken a train to Montpellier to stay with her parents. The war had put the whole country between them.

"What's your plan, then?" he asked.

"There's one place in every village that's always open. Follow me."

They continued down the narrow streets until they reached a small square, deserted but for some empty wooden benches around its periphery. Jean-Paul had a fleeting vision of a bustling market, bursting with color and noise, farmers selling their wares and shouting out to the passing shoppers.

There was a church on the far side of the square. The driver led Jean-Paul toward it. He grabbed the iron handle on the large wooden door and gave it a twist. The door opened.

Once inside, the driver switched on his flashlight. He trotted toward the altar and disappeared into a side room. A moment later he emerged and shone the beam of his flashlight directly into Jean-Paul's face. "I found some candles," he said.

The candles were short and thick. The driver placed them in a circle at the front of the church and lit each one with a box of matches he had found in the vestry. The flames flickered, casting long shadows up the dark walls. Jean-Paul lay down on the front pew, utterly exhausted and weak from pain. The wood was hard and unforgiving, but he did not care. He had stopped moving; that was all that mattered. The altar was covered in a heavy white sheet. The driver pulled it off, folded it, and lay it over his patient's shivering body.

"I need that morphine," whispered Jean-Paul.

The driver knelt down beside him and opened his medical bag. He quickly prepared the syringe and pushed the needle into Jean-Paul's arm. "I'm going to clean that wound in your leg," he said.

But Jean-Paul was already drifting away.

How long he slept he did not know. His rest was deep and dreamless.

It was the music that pulled him back to consciousness.

A piano.

The first theme emerged quietly from the depths of the keyboard, no more than a whisper. Jean-Paul heard a heavy melancholy in the stately procession of low, single notes. What had the driver lived through, he wondered, to draw such sadness out of himself?

And then, through the dark clouds, a shaft of brilliant sunlight. A new melody emerged, high and clear and heartbreaking. The tune cleaved the gathering shadows and wrapped itself brightly around Jean-Paul's heart.

Those first brooding tones retreated, but they did not vanish. Now the music was two intertwined melodic lines, one low, one high, one sad, one full of hope. They met and diverged, echoing each other, dual counterpoints of darkness and light. Sometimes they came together in sweet harmony; sometimes not.

Finally the music resolved back to its first theme, that simple, forlorn elegy. The driver's left hand stretched down the keyboard into ever-lower registers, until there were no more keys to be pressed, no more notes to be played.

Silence crowded in.

Jean-Paul opened his eyes. All the candles had burnt out. He twisted his head to one side. He could make out the silhouette of the window behind the altar, early dawn light creeping at its edges. He heard the driver clear his throat, and then the low, mournful melody began again. Jean-Paul lay still, bewitched by the beauty of the music. He closed his eyes and allowed the notes to wash over him. The driver played the piece two more times. Jean-Paul listened, finding his way through the complex thicket of harmonies. Finally, after the notes faded away for the third time, he called out.

There was a scraping of a piano stool against the cold flagstones of the church floor, and then the driver was by his side. "How is the leg?" he asked.

"It hurts like thunder," replied Jean-Paul.

"I would imagine. I cleaned it up as best I could last night, but the wound is deep." He knelt down and started to unwrap the bandages. "I'm going to see how things look and apply a fresh dressing. You need to keep the weight off your leg. I'm going to leave you here and go and find help." He paused. "This is going to hurt. You passed out last night, so you didn't notice."

"All right," said Jean-Paul. He gasped as the driver swabbed his leg with a pad soaked in alcohol. How could it be, he wondered, that the same fingers that conjured such beauty from the piano keys one minute could cause such excruciating pain the next? "I liked that piece you were playing," he said. "It's sad, but beautiful. It made me think of my wife."

"Is she sad and beautiful, too?"

Jean-Paul shook his head. "Just beautiful."

"Ah, then you are a lucky man."

"Who wrote it?"

The driver smiled at him. "I did."

Jean-Paul stands in the Jardin du Luxembourg, his eyes closed. He knows every note of the wordless tune that the woman sings to calm her daughter. It is the same melody that the diminutive ambulance driver played in the abandoned church in northern France all those years ago.

He will never escape Verdun—every damaged step he takes reminds him of the tangle of metal he pulled from his leg that day. But the memory of this melody casts a different spell. The low, sad notes pull him back: he can smell the damp inside of the church, he can feel the hard, wooden pew at his back. The driver—the pianist—is there by his side, that small smile on his face.

The man had saved his life. If he hadn't appeared in that decrepit truck, Jean-Paul would have bled to death on the battlefield along with the rest of his platoon, and Anaïs would have been another young French widow.

If he had died, she would have stayed in Montpellier with her parents, and met someone else. If he had died, she would not have been singing at the Good Friday Mass in the Église Saint-Gervais when the German bomb fell.

If he had died, she would have lived.

"Monsieur?"

Jean-Paul opens his eyes.

The little girl has stopped crying. She has taken her face out of the folds of her mother's skirt and is looking at him. And there, as if conjured up by the music, her gray eyes resting steadily on him, stands Elodie.

32

An Unanticipated Development

ON PLACE SAINT-SULPICE, Camille passes in front of a café. There is a cluster of tables on the sidewalk. Every one is occupied. People talk and argue with each other as they watch the world go by and enjoy an *aperitif*. Camille realizes that she has not eaten anything all day. She turns abruptly through the door, sits down at the nearest table and orders a sandwich, and, after a moment's hesitation, a glass of white wine.

She settles back in her chair and glances at the clock on the wall. The afternoon is nearly gone. She has lost count of how many people she has spoken to today. She has met with pompous antiquarian booksellers in their expensive shops. She has interrogated dozens of *bouquinistes*, the shifty-eyed, weather-beaten men who sell old books out of the wooden stalls that line both banks of the Seine. By now she has perfected her pitch. Her delivery is all wry exasperation, amused tolerance at her husband's well-meaning mistake. This was all an innocent misunderstanding, marital crossed wires; it happens to us all from time to time, *n'est-ce pas?* And would you happen to have . . . ?

The money that she took from the safe that morning remains in her handbag. All day she's been getting blank looks and lectures about the futility of her mission. Such a notebook does not exist, she has been told, again and again. Inquiries as to where else she might look elicited baffled shrugs.

Camille sighs. After a day traveling across the city, she's back in her own neighborhood and almost ready to admit defeat, to return to the hotel and tell Olivier what was in the notebook. Then she remembers that there is a bookshop near here, on Rue de l'Odéon. It will be, she decides, her last stop of the day.

She looks out of the window. A woman walks past, hand in hand with her young son. They are making slow progress. The little boy stops to examine everything he sees—a bird pecking at the sidewalk, a discarded newspaper wrapped around the base of a tree—with a rapt expression on his face. Each time they stop, the woman crouches down next to him and talks softly in his ear. She is explaining the world to her child. Camille wistfully remembers similar expeditions with Marie, short walks around the neighborhood to nowhere in particular, and how the most mundane sights were transformed into things of wonder through her daughter's young eyes. Watching the two of them, she is overwhelmed with the desire to run back to the hotel and hold Marie tight, but she knows that such indulgence would provoke nothing but awkward squirming and complaints. These days it's all Camille can do to steal quick hugs, before her quarry wriggles away.

When Marie was a baby, Camille had drowned in a delicious ocean of human touch. Her tiny body had to be cleaned, dressed, inspected, cared for. Skin was always on skin, a blissful, dazzling communion. She never imagined that such happiness might end. She watches as the woman runs her fingers through the little boy's curly hair. Enjoy it while you can, she thinks. Time travels in one direction only. There is no going back.

The wine is so cold that by the time it arrives at the table the glass is beaded with tiny drops of condensation. Camille takes an unladylike swallow, and then attacks her sandwich. She contemplates her return to the hotel as she eats, wondering how Olivier will react when she tells him what's in the notebook. She realizes that she does not especially care anymore. She's come a long way since she climbed off the train as a newlywed at Gare de Lyon all those years ago. Back then she depended on her husband for everything. They had both proceeded on the assumption that she was always wrong and he was always right. Camille's life was one of meek capitulation and uxorial obedience. But those intimate conversations with Marcel Proust at all hours of the day and night changed all that. Beneath the warm sun of her employer's attention, her confidence took root and began to grow. It did not take long for her newfound self-belief to manifest itself on the domestic front, too. Like Marcel Proust, Olivier was delighted with Camille's growing independence. Unlike Marcel Proust, his delight had its limits. Having a confident, free-thinking wife was a fine thing, but only up to a point.

Olivier, too, had learned that there was no going back.

She takes another swig of wine. Perhaps that was Monsieur Proust's most enduring gift, she thinks. It wasn't her fond memories of their time together, or the wretched notebook. The most valuable thing he gave her was her independence. That, at least, is something that cannot be bought or sold at any price.

When Camille pushes open the door of the bookshop, the place is empty except for a young woman sitting at a desk, her head bent low over a leather-bound ledger. Camille looks at the volumes on display, and contemplates turning around and leaving, because all the books in the shop are in English.

There is a small cough from the far end of the room. The woman behind the desk is looking up at her, smiling. "Good afternoon, madame," she says. "Can I help you?"

"I don't think so," replies Camille. "But thank you."

"Are you looking for something in particular?"

She may as well ask. "Do you buy books, as well as sell them?"

"It depends on the books, madame."

The woman has a kind face. Camille suddenly feels very tired. "I'm looking for a notebook," she says. "My husband sold it." She looks down at her shoes. "We had a misunderstanding. It wasn't his to sell."

"Did this notebook belong to Marcel Proust, by any chance?"

Camille's head snaps back up. "Yes!"

"You're Camille Clermont," says the woman behind the desk.

She can barely breathe. "Was Olivier here?" she whispers.

An outstretched hand. "Sylvia Beach." Her grip is strong. "Yes, your husband came into the shop yesterday. He told me that Monsieur Proust gave you the notebook years ago. He said that you'd asked him to sell it."

"That was a lie!" says Camille hotly.

"Yes, I rather wondered," says Sylvia Beach. "He couldn't quite look me in the eye when he said it."

Camille sighs. "So you didn't buy it from him, then."

"Of course I bought it!" says Sylvia Beach. "Your husband was asking for a fraction of what it's worth. I'd have been a fool to let him walk out with such a treasure!"

Camille tries to hide her elation. "Did you happen to *read* any of it, by any chance?" she asks anxiously.

Sylvia Beach laughs. "Oh no, madame. I'm too busy to read the books I sell."

Camille reaches into her handbag for the banknotes that she took from the hotel safe that morning. "I'd like to buy it back," she says. "I have the money, every franc of it. As I said, it wasn't my husband's to sell. I'm sure you understand."

"I'm very sorry," says Sylvia Beach, "but you can't have it."

Of course. The shopkeeper knows how much the notebook is worth. She stands to make a huge profit.

"What if I paid you double what you gave for it?" asks Camille.

"Oh, it's not about the money, Madame Clermont." Sylvia Beach gives her a sympathetic smile. "I'm sorry about what's happened. One more reason, if I may say so, why I'm glad I'll never have to worry about a husband."

Camille's head feels a little thick. She is regretting that glass of wine. "Then why can't I have it?"

"Because I've already sold it."

She stares at Sylvia Beach, aghast. "Who did you sell it to?"

"I'm not sure I should tell you."

"Oh please, you absolutely must. I *have* to get the notebook back. It's a matter of life or death."

Sylvia Beach considers this. "You understand that even if I give you his name, he's under no obligation to sell it back to you? He purchased it in good faith. The thing is legally his."

Camille nods. The thought of the notebook beneath a stranger's fingers makes her feel sick. "But I have to try."

Sylvia Beach picks up the pen that lies next to the ledger. She pulls a piece of paper from one of the desk drawers, and starts to write. "He's a writer. An American. This is the address of his apartment," she says. "It's not far from here. Perhaps you'll find him there."

"Thank you," says Camille. It is all she can do not to burst into tears. She turns and hurries out of the shop.

33

Eastern Anatolia, 1915: Hector

IT BEGAN WITH AN URGENT knock on the door. It was the sound that announced the end of everything good, and Souren Balakian can still hear it now, that frightened fist on wood echoing across the years.

His best friend, Yervant, was standing there, breathing heavily.

"You need to come," he said. "All of you."

"Come where?" asked Souren. Hector stood just behind his older brother. Souren was only seventeen years old, but ever since their father disappeared he had been the man of the house.

"To the square. Your mother, too."

Souren shook his head. "My mother is sick."

"But they want the whole village!"

"They?"

"*Kasab taburu*," said Yervant.

The two boys looked at each other in silence for a long moment. Souren glanced back toward Hector. "What if we don't go?"

"They'll find you, you know they will. It's better to go now than to be discovered later. Haven't you heard the stories?"

Souren had heard the stories. They all had.

"I'm not scared of them," cried Hector. "We should go and tell the stupid Turks what we think of them."

"We'll go," said Souren, "but Mother stays here." He tousled his brother's hair. "But Hector, listen. We're not going to cause trouble, do you understand? We're going because it's the safest thing to do. The Turks are dangerous."

Hector was too excited to listen to his brother. "Let's go!" he shouted, and started to run down the street toward the main square. Souren and Yervant followed him. A dry wind blew through the village, whipping up small tornados of yellow dust. The narrow streets were baking in the hot afternoon sun.

Word of the arrival of the *kasab taburu* had spread quickly. By the time the boys arrived in the market square, most of the village had already assembled. People clustered together in small groups, terror on their faces. After Cevdet Bey's posse descended on Bitlis, fifteen miles to the east, the trees on the outskirts of town had hung heavy with gruesome new fruit— the mutilated corpses of Armenian men.

But there were no Armenian men in the village, not anymore—at least, none of fighting age. They had all been conscripted into the Ottoman army months ago, carted off without warning one night to fight on the Eastern Front. Souren's father was one of the men taken away. They had not heard from him since.

The crowd that gathered, then, consisted mainly of women and children. Souren held Hector's hand, but as they approached the group his brother slipped free from his fingers and ran into the mass of bodies, disappearing from view. Moments later a group of warriors on horseback thundered into the square. The men came to a stop in front of the church and dismounted. Only one man remained in his saddle. He wore a black turban and filthy combat fatigues. His cheeks were scarred by deep pockmarks. There was a small armory strapped to his back—two revolvers, a sword, a Mauser rifle, and two long ammunition belts, fattened with cartridges.

"My name is Kamil Ömer," shouted the man. "I come on the authority of your new *vali*, the honorable Cevdet Bey."

Yervant stood next to Souren, his arms crossed. He nodded at the warlord astride his mount. "Look at the smile on his ugly face. He'll happily kill us all, and he'll be paid well for his trouble." Kamil Ömer had been serving time in jail in Artamid for multiple murders until the new governor had released him to carry out his dirty work with his gang of thugs.

"He won't kill us *all*," said Souren.

Yervant spat on the ground. "We'll see."

Kamil Ömer was walking his horse up and down in front of the crowd. "I come with new instructions from the *vali*," he cried. "It is my duty to ensure that they are carried out to the letter. The smallest failure to comply is an act of treason against the empire, and the perpetrators will be punished accordingly. Do you understand?"

The villagers nodded. If all they had to do was follow instructions in order to survive, there was hope for them yet.

Ömer looked satisfied. "Very well," he declared. "First, effective immediately, every household must surrender all weapons."

Yervant nudged Souren. "Easier to massacre us if we have nothing to fight back with," he whispered.

"Second, my men are hungry. They need food. We have authority from the *vali* to requisition any supplies from this village as we deem necessary for our continued defense of the empire against its enemies." The Turk cast his eyes across the worried faces in front of him. "We will come into your houses this afternoon and take what we need. If you try to hide so much as a morsel of food for yourselves, you and your family will be punished without mercy. When you are dismissed from here, you will return to your homes and wait for my—"

Kamil Ömer stopped in midsentence. He clutched his jaw, a look of surprise on his face, which quickly turned to fury. Slowly he lowered his hand, revealing a dark red gash in his cheek. He climbed off his horse and picked up a rock that was lying on the ground. "Who threw this?" he screamed.

The villagers stared at him in terrified silence.

The warrior drew the long curved sword from the scabbard strapped to his back. "I am not a man who asks a question twice," he snarled. He strode to the edge of the crowd and grabbed a young girl. She could not have been more than six years old. He dragged her out of the crowd, ignoring the screams of her mother. The Turk roughly pulled the girl's long hair backward, exposing her neck. The look on his face was one of vicious delight. "A child will die every ten minutes until the person who threw that rock steps forward," he shouted.

"Wait," said a voice.

Souren's blood turned to ice in his veins.

Kamil Ömer released the girl, who ran sobbing back into her mother's arms. He turned his attention to Hector, who had stepped out of the crowd and stood defiantly before the Turk, his arms folded across his chest. He was twelve years old, and small for his age, but he confronted the heavily armed warrior without the faintest shadow of fear. Just as Souren began to move to his brother's defense, he felt Yervant's hand on his shoulder.

"Stay where you are," hissed his friend.

"I can't just——"

"Souren, listen." Yervant's words were low and urgent. "That man is a murderer, and he's armed to the teeth. You have no weapons, and you've never thrown a punch in your life. If you try to intervene, he'll kill you. You understand that, don't you? He's *looking* for reasons to slaughter us all."

Souren stared at Kamil Ömer, who was circling his brother with a predatory look on his face.

"So I'm supposed to just stand here?" said Souren.

"Think of your mother," whispered Yervant. "If you act the hero, she'll have two dead sons instead of one. Who will care for her then?"

Kamil Ömer continued to pace around Hector. There were so many ways to kill a young boy. Souren watched those small eyes as they made their calculations. The Turk was deciding how to make the most of this opportunity—how best to show the villagers that he was not a man who made empty threats. He spoke to one of his lieutenants. The man nodded and ran into the church. He returned a moment later carrying a wooden chair and a length of rope. Ömer looked at Hector and pointed to the chair. Hector sat on it.

"I'm not afraid of you," he shouted.

Ömer issued more instructions to his lieutenant, who began to wrap the rope around Hector's body, securing the boy's arms by his sides.

Yervant's hand was heavy on Souren's shoulder, holding him in place. "*Your mother*," he said again.

Souren closed his eyes. He knew Yervant was right.

Once Hector was trussed to the chair, Ömer's lieutenant went back into the church and emerged a minute later carrying a large metal canister. He placed it on the ground next to Hector and unscrewed the lid. Hector's look of defiance vanished immediately and was replaced with naked terror. The man began to tip the canister's clear liquid across Hector's back and shoulders. He kept pouring until the boy's shirt was completely soaked, front and back, then he did the same to his trousers. By then tears were streaming down Hector's cheeks, but still he made no sound. Some of the women began a high, keening wail. The soldiers stepped forward, rifles cocked, ready to quell any disturbance.

Kamil Ömer stood to one side and watched proceedings, idly smoking a cigarette. At his command, the man stopped pouring. Souren could smell the pungent aroma of kerosene. The Turk stepped forward and addressed the crowd.

"Let there be no misunderstanding," he shouted. "I require total obedience from every person in this village, man and woman, no matter how old or how young. Nothing less will be tolerated." He looked down at Hector. "You, boy, are going to help everyone learn this lesson." He almost put a hand on Hector's wet shoulder, and then thought better of it. Instead he took a long drag on his cigarette, so that its tip was burning brightly, and then he dropped it onto Hector's lap.

34

A Priest's Advice

GUILLAUME LIES PROSTRATE in the middle of the studio. He listens to the retreating footsteps of the three men, who are bickering with each other as they walk down the staircase. He rolls over and slowly pushes himself up onto his knees. A string of blood and saliva falls from one side of his mouth and pools on the floor. He crawls across the room toward his bed. Once on the mattress, he stares up at the ceiling. The middle of his face is a white-hot supernova of pain.

The corridor is silent. The men have gone for the moment —although presumably Arnaud, the giant, will be on sentry duty outside the building, keeping a hopeful eye out for Gertrude Stein.

Guillaume twists his head and gazes forlornly at the faded rectangle of wallpaper where Suzanne's painting used to be. For more than ten years the little house in the woods has given him the strength to face every new morning, but today it has literally saved his life. Without Gertrude Stein's six hundred francs to offer them, Guillaume would already be dead. His earlier regret dissolves and reassembles itself into a bitter kind of gratitude.

With a sigh, Guillaume crosses the studio to the small sink in the corner of the room. He gingerly washes the blood off his face and examines himself in the small mirror on the wall. His nose has been flattened by the rat-faced man's knee, and there are matching dark purple crescents beneath both of his eyes.

When Gertrude Stein fails to appear, Le Miroir's men will be back to finish the job. There's no way of knowing how long their patience will last. Guillaume knows he must escape while he still can. He strips off his bloodied shirt and puts on a clean one. He looks at the paintings strewn across the room. He must leave all this behind. To his surprise he feels no great regret. Survival is all that matters now.

He walks over to the window and peers out at the rooftops and chimney pots. He unfastens the latch and opens the window. The sounds of the city below rise up from the streets to meet him. Grunting with the effort, Guillaume hauls himself through the window. He looks back into the studio one last time and then lowers himself onto the slate roof. After a moment to get his bearings, he sets off, picking his way across the unfamiliar terrain, navigating from one roof to the next. By the time he sees what he is looking for, he is several buildings away. The top of the iron ladder pokes up over the edge of the rear of the roof. Guillaume approaches it with trepidation, his stomach churning. He has never had a head for heights. Slowly he begins to climb down, rung by cautious rung.

Finally, the ground. He is in a small, paved courtyard. A scrawny cat eyes him from behind a potted rosebush. At the far end of the courtyard there is a gate. Guillaume opens it and steps into a deserted alley, barely wide enough for a man to walk down. At the end of the alley he can see pedestrians marching by. He catches his breath for a moment, exhausted and enervated by his escape, and then starts to walk toward the street.

Among the crowd of Parisians, he feels safer. He tacks through the throng, averting his gaze from passersby, aware that the bruises on his face are attracting some curious glances. As he goes he watches for men who might be watching for him.

His nose is in agony. He must get to Gare Montparnasse, but all he wants to do is to stop moving.

Ahead of him he sees a small church. On impulse he pushes open the door. Pale shafts of light fall through the tall, narrow windows. He sits down in the back pew and closes his eyes.

"Can I help you?"

At the end of the pew stands a priest. He is a small man, neatly put together, precise and compact. He wears wire-rimmed spectacles. A pair of shiny black shoes pokes out from beneath the hem of his cassock.

"Forgive me, father," mutters Guillaume. "I just need to rest for a little while."

"Your nose looks sore," says the priest.

"It's felt better," admits Guillaume.

"Do you need a doctor?"

"I don't think so. I daresay I'll live. Besides, I don't have time for a doctor. I need to get to Montparnasse."

"Why?"

"I have a train to catch."

"Oh yes? Where is this train going?"

"Home."

"And where is home?"

"A long way from here. Somewhere I won't be found."

The priest points at Guillaume's broken nose. "Are you running from the person who did that?"

A nod. "They've promised me they can do worse. Much worse."

"What did you do to deserve it?"

"I didn't repay a debt."

"That sounds like a bad business." The priest sits down. "Do you really have no choice about leaving?"

"I would stay if I could, believe me. But I have no other options. They made that pretty clear."

"Have you tried praying?"

Guillaume snorts. "For what?"

"Guidance? A miracle?"

"It's a little late for either, I fear."

"Oh, it's never too late."

"I admire your optimism," says Guillaume.

The priest shrugs. "You call it optimism. I call it faith."

The men sit in silence for a moment.

"Do you have family in Paris?" asks the priest. "Will you be leaving anyone behind?"

The smallest pause. "I have a daughter."

"She's not going with you?"

Guillaume closes his eyes. "She doesn't know I exist."

"How can that be?"

And so Guillaume tells the priest about the Cirque Medrano, the acrobats, and Suzanne Mauriac. He explains how he has stood on Rue Nicolet every morning for ten years, how he watches them from a distance. The priest listens quietly. As Guillaume speaks, he feels a warmth running through him. He has never told anyone about Suzanne, but hearing the words spoken aloud, to another, gladdens his heart.

"What's your daughter's name?" asks the priest when he is finished.

"I don't know," confesses Guillaume.

"Then may I offer you some advice?"

"Please."

"Before you catch your train, go and see her."

"But I've never spoken to her!"

"All the more reason to do so now."

"What would I say, after all this time?" wonders Guillaume.

"It doesn't matter. Tell her you like her dress, anything. Just speak to her. Look her in the eye, and say a few words. Ask her what her name is, if nothing else." The priest pauses. "Don't do it for her, though. Do it for yourself. You're her father."

The idea of speaking to his daughter fills Guillaume with both elation and dread. He sits back, lost in thought. "I don't know," he says.

"You'll regret it if you don't," says the priest.

Guillaume touches his chest. "I've ten years of regret stored up in here already. Every morning when I watch them walk away from me, I collect a little more."

The priest nods at this. "I have a theory. It's not especially popular around here, but I believe it anyway." He pauses. "I believe that God wants us to be happy."

Guillaume grunts. "Isn't it more important to be good, rather than happy?"

"Some people think so," agrees the priest. "But I don't believe that God put us on this earth so we could be miserable. We only get so many chances at happiness. I think we should take every single one of them."

"But what if they want nothing to do with me? I might be much *less* happy."

The priest looks at him. "Less happy than you are now?"

Guillaume is silent. He is thinking about the sight of Suzanne and his daughter earlier that afternoon, as they walked hand in hand along Boulevard Saint-Michel. He remembers his regret when they disappeared into the crowd, his opportunity to bid a final farewell lost.

The priest is right. Perhaps he has one last chance.

"Listen," says the priest. "Every once in a while you have to make a leap into the unknown. To do that, it helps if you have a little faith. Or hope, if you prefer." He stands up. "Spend as long as you need here. But, please, go and see your daughter before you leave. Just knock on her door and see what happens. At least find out her name, for the love of God." He pauses. "Besides, what have you got to lose?"

To this question, Guillaume has no response.

35

A Reconfigured Heart

"MONSIEUR? ARE YOU ALL RIGHT?"

It is not Elodie who is speaking, but the woman standing behind her. Jean-Paul feels a delirious tumbling within him. He cannot look away from his daughter. He knows those eyes so well. He has been waiting a long time to see them again. Every day he has searched the streets of Paris, hoping for this blood-deep connection, an unbreakable bond across generations. Now that it has come, he almost forgets how to breathe.

"Monsieur? *Tout va bien?*"

He drags his eyes away from Elodie. The woman is staring at him, a concerned look on her face. Her arms are wrapped protectively around the girl's shoulders.

"I beg your pardon?" he says, his throat dry.

"Are you feeling quite well? You look as if you've seen a ghost."

Jean-Paul blinks. "That tune you were singing," he says. "It brought back some memories, that's all."

The woman smiles. "Good ones, I hope."

"Old ones." He allows his gaze to fall back onto his daughter. "What's your name?" he asks her. Three small words, but enough to make his voice crack.

"Arielle," the girl tells him.

No, he wants to say. No, no, it's not.

"That's a pretty name," he manages.

"We were watching the puppet show," says the woman. "But that last scene, with the little boy—" She pulls the girl closer to her.

Jean-Paul nods in sympathy. Of course Elodie would be upset by it. Anaïs hated anything violent. "It's just a story," he tells her gently. "There's no need to be sad about it."

"Ah, but she feels everything strongly, this one," says the woman, stroking the girl's hair. "Such an imagination! Even fairy tales are real to you, *n'est-ce pas?*"

Elodie looks at her shoes and nods.

The woman casts an eye toward the puppet theater. There has been no sign of the bearded puppeteer, and the grass in front of the tent is empty now. "It looks as if the show is over, Arielle."

Don't go, Jean-Paul thinks. Don't ever go.

"Perhaps we should go and find a slice of cake for you," says the woman. "That will cheer you up, won't it?"

At this the girl turns her head toward the woman and delivers a smile so full of joy, so beautiful, that Jean-Paul can do nothing but stare. The woman grins back at her—and just like that, his dream is shattered.

The crinkle at the edges of the eyes, the delighted twitch of the lips, the upturned corners of their mouths—each smile is a perfect facsimile of the other.

These two beauties are mother and daughter.

Jean-Paul feels the color rush to his face. What a fool he is! He has been bewitched by old memories. The melody that echoed across the years— from shadowed church to sunlit park, from invisible piano to a stranger's lips—has hoodwinked him. It has lured him down a chasm of impossible longing, whispering fantasies he desperately wants to be true. He looks down at the girl, this child who is not his daughter after all. His heart breaks into a million tiny pieces and then puts itself back together, reconfigured, a little larger than before.

"You should have chocolate cake," he advises her solemnly. She laughs at this.

The woman takes her daughter's hand. "*Alors*, chocolate cake it is!" she declares. She smiles at Jean-Paul. "Never underestimate your memories, monsieur," she tells him. "They can be ferocious if left unguarded."

The candles flickering in the abandoned church. His baby daughter in his arms.

"Very true," he agrees. He crouches down so that his face is level with Arielle's. "Have an extra-large slice of cake, young lady," he tells her. "Possibly two."

"I shall!" She giggles.

"Enjoy the rest of your afternoon," says her mother as they turn to leave.

"*Vous aussi*." Jean-Paul inclines his head toward her. She gives him one last smile as they turn and walk away. He watches them go. The little girl, animated by the prospect of cake, is gesticulating excitedly to her mother as they make their way toward the park exit. The woman, he notices, walks with a slight limp. She leans in, caught in her daughter's orbit. Her whole body tilts toward the girl as they walk. She edges closer and closer, unable to help herself. There's a physical pull that she cannot resist, just as a compass needle has no choice but to point north. Love skews the body, a gorgeous twisting. Adoration made manifest. Jean-Paul thinks that it is the loveliest thing he has ever seen.

The afternoon sun has begun its slow descent through the cloudless sky.

36

Paris, 1922:
The Second Betrayal

NOT LONG AFTER THE WAR ended, Marcel Proust's great-aunt sold the building on Boulevard Haussman to a bank, and—appalled at the prospect of a never-ending parade of noisy customers trooping in and out of the place, disturbing his peace—Camille's employer moved into a smaller apartment on Rue Hamelin.

By then Proust was working with increasing intensity, forgoing almost all social engagements as he feverishly wrote and edited his manuscript. He lay in his bed, surrounded by paper, working frantically. The bell rang incessantly as Camille was summoned for fresh hot water bottles and cups of *café au lait*.

The fireplaces in the new apartment were narrow and poorly built. Every time Camille set a fire, smoke would billow into the room, causing Monsieur Proust to cough uncontrollably. And so there were no more fires. During the winter of 1921, the apartment was bone-chillingly cold. Proust suffered from a raging fever that didn't leave him for weeks on end. Camille brought him sweaters that he draped over his shoulders as he worked. Sometimes he was so weak that he could barely hold a pen.

Marcel Proust was sure that he was dying, and he was desperate to finish his book before the end came. He would not rest, would not eat. Camille begged him to see a doctor, but he refused, chiding her that he no longer had time to waste on such trivialities. He struggled for breath while he worked, pale and shivering with cold.

And then, one day that spring, Camille walked into his bedroom and was surprised to find him sitting up straight in bed, with a twinkle in his eye that she had not seen for months.

"There you are," he said with a smile. "Come over here and see what I've just written."

She went over to the bed. Proust showed her the piece of paper he was holding. There she saw a single word: *Fin*.

Camille gasped. "You've finished, monsieur? Can it be true?"

"Well, there's still much to be done." He pointed at the mass of paper on the bed. "Corrections, edits, amendments." He smiled wanly at her. "Paul Valéry once said that poems are never really finished, only abandoned. I think the same principle applies to novels."

Sure enough, the following day Proust began correcting proofs of the manuscript at a pace even more frenzied than before.

The trees outside the apartment caused a certain dampness that made his asthma intolerable; still he worked, coughing and wheezing beneath a mountain of paper. On one cold October night he caught a chill, and within days his body was racked with fever.

That was when he finally agreed to see his old physician, Doctor Bize.

The diagnosis: pneumonia. Doctor Bize administered an injection in an attempt to revive the patient. Soon after the doctor left, Monsieur Proust rang his bell. He was lying in his bed, his body turned toward the wall, and he did not move when Camille entered the bedroom. "You must promise me something of the utmost importance," he began, his voice muffled by the pillow.

"Of course, monsieur."

"You must never, under any circumstances, let anyone put another needle in me. Do you understand?"

"But if it's what the doctor thinks is for the——"

"Camille." The single word hung in the air, reproachful and desperate. "Will you promise me this one thing?" he asked softly. "Can I trust you?"

"You know you can trust me, monsieur," she replied. Then she remembered the notebook lying hidden at the bottom of her trunk. She was relieved that he was not looking at her. He had always been able to see exactly what she was thinking.

"Yes, Camille," murmured Marcel Proust, "I know I can trust you. I just wanted to hear you say it."

She felt sick with guilt. "No more injections," she said.

"Thank you." He shuddered. "Those needles! I would prefer to suffer anything than go through that again."

"And the other medicines?" asked Camille. The doctor had given her a long list of prescriptions on his way out.

"By all means go and fetch them, and then we'll see."

But Monsieur Proust did not take the medicines that Camille brought back from the pharmacy, and no amount of pleading could get him to change his mind.

His health continued to deteriorate. His face became sallow and gaunt and he continued to starve himself, existing on almost nothing except for coffee. In desperation, Camille begged Monsieur Proust's brother to come and try and talk sense into the patient. Robert Proust arrived later the same day, barging into his brother's bedroom and conducting a brief but thorough examination, ignoring the stream of rich and colorful threats that Camille heard through the bedroom door.

Soon afterward Robert came to see Camille in the kitchen. He sat down heavily in a chair and placed his hat on the table in front of him.

"*Et alors?*" said Camille.

"It doesn't look good. He's having great difficulty breathing. The pneumonia has led to an aggravated inflammation of the bronchial passages." Robert Proust was silent for a moment, staring at the table. "Marcel has gone untreated for so long that secondary infections have taken hold. There's an abscess on his lung that I think has given him septicemia." He looked directly at her. "I fear we have left it too late."

After that Robert and Camille cared for the sick man together. Proust continued to work on his manuscript, half delirious with the fever that would not relinquish its grip. By the middle of November it was clear that the end would come before long. Camille called Doctor Bize again. Proust lay unconscious, hidden beneath a mound of blankets but for one swollen arm, deathly white, that hung limply down by the side of the bed. The doctor asked Camille if he might administer an injection of camphorated oil.

She turned to look down at the bed. Her beloved employer was dying, she knew that. All she wanted to do was to ease his pain, but he had begged her, implored her, never to allow another needle near him.

Will you promise me this one thing?

You know you can trust me, monsieur.

She turned to the doctor. "Will it help?" she asked.

"*Bien entendu,*" nodded Doctor Bize.

Marcel Proust's dying body was motionless beneath the bedsheets.

Will you promise me this one thing?

Camille loved him. She wanted to honor his wishes. But more than that, she wanted to stop his pain.

"Madame Clermont?" said the doctor. "Should I give him the injection?"

She tried to speak but the words would not come. Finally she gave the smallest of nods.

The room was silent as the doctor prepared the treatment. Camille watched as he flicked his fingers against the side of the syringe. The needle was long and glinted in the half-light of the bedroom.

Camille pulled up the bedsheets and looked away as Bize injected the dose into Marcel Proust's thigh. After a moment the patient rolled over and looked directly at her. He reached out and grabbed her arm. "Oh, Camille," he whispered. Then, not taking his eyes off her, he pinched her wrist.

His brittle fingers on her skin.

She wanted him to twist viciously. Instead he relinquished his grip, his arm dropping weakly to his side. They looked at each other without speaking. After all the words that had passed between them, there was no more to be said.

A few minutes later Camille showed Doctor Bize out of the apartment. When she returned to the bedroom, Robert Proust was leaning over the bed speaking softly to his brother.

Marcel Proust lay back in the bed and stared at Robert and Camille as they stood side by side next to the bed. His face was spectral, half hidden by a thick, dark beard. His eyes never left them for a moment.

No more words were spoken.

And then Robert Proust stepped forward. He reached out and gently closed his brother's eyes.

"Is he dead?" she whispered.

"Yes, Camille. It's over."

The days after Marcel Proust's death were made tolerable only by the numbing weight of duty. Camille was too busy to grieve. She and Robert welcomed a procession of mourners into the apartment to pay their last respects to the great man. Haughty aristocrats and eminent men of letters stood by his bedside and wept. Renowned artists sketched the dead man's face. Man Ray took photographs of the body. From dawn to dusk the apartment was full of visitors clamoring for the chance to say a last good-bye. Camille knew that Monsieur Proust would have been appalled at the chaotic spectacle of it all. All he had ever wanted was peace and quiet, and time to write. In rare moments of calm she sat quietly beside her employer's body. His face was serene, finally at rest.

She helped Robert with the funeral arrangements, and traveled with him in the front car of the funeral procession. The small cross of flowers that she had chosen was placed in the middle of the coffin.

Several days after the funeral Camille walked past a bookshop on Rue Hamelin. The shop's window was lit up, casting a bright glow into the cold gloom of the winter's day. Every book Marcel Proust had written was on display, each one arranged in groups of three. Camille stood and stared at this act of tribute, and wept.

That evening, she waited for Olivier's snores to fall into their familiar rhythm, and then crept out of their bed. Her trunk was packed away in a cupboard at the far end of the corridor from their bedroom. As quietly as she could, she pulled it out, praying that she would not wake her husband or daughter. She opened the latches and reached beneath the sheets and blankets that had kept her secret hidden for so long.

She pulled the notebook out of its hiding place and stared at it. She opened the covers and leaned into the musty pages, sniffing deeply. The smell of old paper immediately transported her back to the strange, cluttered apartment on Boulevard Haussmann.

Fingers clumsy with guilt, Camille finally opened the notebook. The handwriting was more familiar than her own. She knew the anxious topography of each letter, every sinewy loop and jagged dash. Words tilted forward on the page, as if eager to discover how each sentence would end.

The corridor was lit by a single, dimly glowing lightbulb. She sat down and began to read. Every sentence was a small resurrection, quietly conjuring up those conversations that took place at all hours of the day and night. As she turned the first page, a single tear fell onto the stiff paper, washing the words beneath it into gentle oblivion, lost forever to her sorrow.

Each evening Camille waited for Olivier to fall asleep and then escaped back to the past. She never allowed herself to read more than a few pages every night. She wanted to stretch out the pleasure of reading his words for as long as she could. She could never escape a small twist of guilt every time she opened the notebook. She imagined Marcel Proust staring down at her from the heavens, a disappointed frown on that affable, moon-shaped face, and her heart quietly folded in on itself. Still, she never regretted rescuing the notebook from the flames in the kitchen grate. All she wanted was a little piece of her old friend and employer, just for herself. His words became a refuge: when her sorrow became too much to bear, she retreated to the warmth of old memories.

And then one night, she read:

Camille told me an interesting story this evening.

And there it was on the page in front of her: her secret. The one he had begged her to tell him. The one he had promised he would never breathe a word of to another living soul.

Two neat paragraphs, with not a single detail left out.

She let out a low, choking gasp of horror.

He was a thief, a pirate. He plundered other people's lives for his own ends. *I would never betray a confidence. Not from you.*

Camille had believed him.

First came disbelief, then sorrow, then anger.

Then terror.

It was bad enough to see her darkest secret written in the pages of a private notebook. But if Marcel Proust had included it in his novel, then it would live on for the whole world to see. People would read it and wonder. Someone might call for an investigation. Camille could already hear the heavy knock on the door.

There were three volumes of *À la recherche du temps perdu* that had still not been published when Marcel Proust died. His brother had taken the remaining manuscripts from Rue Hamelin and was overseeing their publication. Camille had been living in close proximity to all that paper for years, but she had never thought much about the words on the pages that spread so chaotically across her employer's bed. Now she cursed herself for not paying more attention. She had no choice but to wait. When each new volume was published she tore through the pages, searching for the treacherous words that would condemn her. But there was nothing.

Only those two paragraphs remained.

Camille knew that she should destroy the last remaining evidence, but she could not bring herself to part with the notebook. It contained too many fond memories. Besides, nobody knew that it even existed.

Her secret was safe.

37

Penance or Remembrance?

IT HAS TAKEN SOUREN YEARS to perfect the finale to his puppet show.

The hardest part is creating fire while both of his hands are inside the puppets. An extra strip of material, invisible to the audience and soaked in kerosene, hangs down the back of the boy's tunic. Souren just has to bring the puppet in alignment with the candle that sits hidden beneath the stage. When the material touches the flame, the conflagration is immediate.

Through a long process of trial and error, he has learned precisely how long he can keep the burning puppet on his hand. The glove he wears gives him precious extra seconds. When he can bear the heat no longer, he drops the puppet into the bucket of water at his feet. By then the tunic has been charred to cinders.

Thanks to daily repetition and practice—he never ends his performances any other way—Souren always executes his final stunt with flawless precision. Everything is timed to the second. The fire that consumes Hector so ferociously is contained and controlled.

All these years later, there is no danger, no risk.

. . .

Souren watches the flames as they engulf his fist. Thin tendrils of black smoke spiral upward. He stares at the burning puppet. For whom does he kill his brother, over and over again? Is this daily ritual an act of penance, or remembrance? The flames that consume Hector day after day cauterize his own wounds, numb his pain, and keep that constellation of sorrow and longing trapped within him for a little longer.

The puppet burns, and he can still hear the cries of the villagers, still taste the acrid smoke at the back of his throat, still feel Yervant's hand on his shoulder. He does not want to forget. His memories are all that he has left.

But this afternoon he also hears Younis: *I'd die for my brothers in a heart-beat.*

The words lurk, quiet assassins.

Souren did not die for Hector. Millions of heartbeats later, he is still here. Penance or remembrance? Perhaps it doesn't matter now. He watches the burning puppet.

What kind of a brother is he, to have stood by while Hector burned to death? What kind of a man?

His day crowds in. The old Armenians, staring at him in fear. The painting in the bookshop window. His puppets, speaking words that nobody understands.

Missed connections at every step.

He cannot breathe.

His hand is growing hot. The fire has destroyed the tunic, and now Hector's wooden head is burning. Souren should have already dropped the puppet into the bucket of water at his feet, but he cannot move. His forefinger—the finger inside the burning puppet's head—is growing hotter. The heat is spreading over his palm and across the back of his hand. All at once there is astonishing pain: his glove has caught fire. His hand is a blazing sheath of searing, impossible heat. No: this is more than just heat. Souren's skin is burning. The flames are eating into his flesh. The pain screams down his arm and through the rest of his body, but still Souren does not move. The fire bites deeper and deeper into his hand, through to the muscles that lie beneath his charred skin. A thought edges past the agony: *this*, he thinks, is penance.

Finally, the instinct for self-preservation overrides his paralysis. Souren's hand, at last, is moving, plunging into the bucket that waits at his feet. What is left of the puppet melts away in a cloud of falling ash. The fire is immediately extinguished—a quiet hiss, and then silence. The remains of the glove dissolve in the water and then float to the surface, a fragmented, blackened cloud.

Outside, the crowd is dispersing. Soon enough the afternoon's show will fade from the audience's memory and become no more than a tiny fleck in the tapestry of their lives.

Souren thinks of his brother, tries to imagine the agony in his hand across his entire body, and finds that he cannot. Many times over the years he has wondered how much Hector suffered before he died. Now he understands that he will never, ever know. He plunges his hand back into the water, and this offers a small measure of relief from the pain, but only for a moment. Every decimated nerve and tendon is a pulsating sun. He breathes through gritted teeth as he moves his hand in and out of the water, trying to contain the agony. Souren stares down at his hand. His fingers are blackened sentinels, ravaged by the flames.

He does not know how long he stays hidden inside the puppet theater. Time passes, its edges dissolved by the scrim of his pain. Air becomes the enemy. Out of the water, his charred flesh screams.

Clumsily, he tears the costume off the nearest puppet and wraps it tightly around his hand. The fabric acts as a makeshift skin. He grabs another puppet and applies a second layer, then a third. The material stings like murder, but anything is better than having his wounds exposed to the flaying air. With his one good hand he puts the puppets back into their suitcase. He does not bother with Hector's charred remains. With difficulty he dismantles the booth, unscrewing the poles and folding the fabric as best he can. Then a new problem presents itself. He cannot carry both suitcases. After a moment's thought he picks up the case containing the tent and takes it to the hut at the entrance to the gardens, where he hides it next to the bucket. It will be safe enough there until tomorrow.

He will not abandon the puppets.

Souren closes the smaller suitcase. The pain in his hand is getting worse. He knows he must see a doctor, but there is a more immediate way to numb the agony. He stumbles out of the park toward Rue de Vaugirard. The first bar he sees is a quiet place with a handful of occupied tables. The evening rush has not yet begun. He sits down and places his suitcase on the chair next to him. Along with the puppets, inside there is a cloth bag full of coins. The audience has been generous today. He puts the bag on the table in front of him.

A waiter approaches. Souren keeps his damaged hand by his side, out of sight. He pushes the bag across the table.

"Brandy," he whispers.

The waiter brings glass after glass of cognac, and then reaches into the cloth bag to remove the correct number of coins before returning to the zinc. The two men do not exchange another word.

Souren is a quiet drunk. He keeps his ruined hand hidden. He broods as he nurses each fresh glass. His pickled introspection does not bother the tables of convivial patrons who fill up the tables all around him. Over the next few hours he drinks himself into a silent stupor.

The brandy has numbed some of the pain in Souren's hand, but also it unshackles him, robbing him of any instinct for self-preservation. And so, helplessly, he returns to Anatolia, to the memories that lacerate him more ruthlessly than his ravaged hand ever will. He remembers his father, before he was dragged away to fight—hauled from his bed at the point of a bayonet in the middle of the night. He remembers his mother taking off her dirt-stained dress and pulling it over his head, urging him to flee. And he remembers his brother's silent scream, his terrified face half-hidden behind a wall of fire.

Souren's guilt eviscerates him. A bilious well of loathing erupts from somewhere deep within him, and a bitter hiss escapes his lips. Souren

Balakian, master of puppets! Entertainer of the well-fed burghers of Paris! His fairy tales mean nothing to the audiences who idly interrupt their afternoon strolls to enjoy a little distraction. The children shout and applaud, but then they return to their comfortable lives, and the warnings of the puppets go unheeded.

The French know nothing, he realizes. Suddenly he hates them all, every last one of them. Souren looks up from his glass and surveys the drinkers around him. What unimaginable luck to be born here, and not one of them recognizes his good fortune! He remembers the stench of the corpses piled high along the banks of the Euphrates, and envy riots in his gut. When a Frenchman dies, he is dressed in his best suit and buried in a fine coffin, with a polished tombstone to mark the spot. Souren does not know where or when or how either of his parents died. There is no marker for them, or for Hector, except for the ones buried deep within him.

Souren cannot stay another minute surrounded by these affable men as they nurse their drinks and lean in toward each other, deep in contented conversation. He needs to escape. He is suddenly consumed by a need to talk to Younis, who understands what it is to be a stranger in this place. But it is late; the shop is closed for the evening. Younis will be at home, patiently corralling his brothers and sisters and taking care of his father. Souren imagines his friend standing in a kitchen somewhere in Belleville, scolding and cajoling and making order. Younis may be hundreds of miles from Tunis, but he is warm in the heart of his family, and that is sovereign territory all of its own.

He needs someone to tend to his hand, to ease the pain, but there is nobody to turn to. He wonders if he could ask Arielle's mother for help, but then he remembers that she is going out to listen to some jazz tonight. He closes his eyes, and then he thinks: Thérèse.

Perhaps her body would be a welcome distraction from his burns.

Souren makes a decision. He puts the bag of coins, lighter now, back into the suitcase. He stands up and weaves unsteadily between the tables, back out onto the street.

38

Arielle

WHAT DOES HE HAVE TO LOSE?

Guillaume Blanc sits in the pew at the back of the church, waiting for an answer to the priest's question. None comes. What's the worst that could happen? The game is up. He is leaving for La Rochelle. There is nothing left for him here.

He makes a decision. He will go and see his daughter.

Just a few words to take with him, that's all he wants.

That, and a name.

Guillaume has never felt so tired in his life. Wearily he gets to his feet and shuffles toward the door of the church.

Outside, the evening is cruelly perfect.

Paris looks too beautiful for words. The cobblestones of Montmartre glow golden in the fading sunlight. The shadows of the buildings grow long across the streets. Children swarm up and down the sidewalks, laughing and shouting. Guillaume imagines his daughter skipping along the streets with her friends, and the last ten years rush up in ambush. Half her childhood, already gone. Helplessly he begins to mourn the millions of moments that he has missed, and the millions more still to come. He wilts beneath the weight of his regret.

Finally Guillaume reaches Rue Nicolet, but rather than assuming his usual post on the opposite side of the street, he walks up to the front door of Suzanne's apartment building. He inspects the list of names alongside the column of polished brass buzzers. There it is: *Mauriac*. He does not dare press the button, fearful that he will not be allowed in if he announces himself. Instead he waits. Finally he hears the latch click, and a young couple steps out onto the street. Guillaume slips inside before the door closes. He crosses the hallway and slowly climbs the staircase. Suzanne's apartment is at the far end of the corridor. He stands outside the door, listening, but all he can hear is his heart clattering against his rib cage, as loud as the klaxon on a fire truck.

He knocks.

At first he hears nothing. Then, the soft fall of footsteps approaching. The door opens, and standing in the doorway is the girl. She smiles at Guillaume.

"Hello," she says.

Guillaume looks down at her. After all these years of watching his daughter from afar, it's all he can do not to stare at her, drink her in. He wants to examine every bit of her. He is catching up for lost time, and it's a race he already knows he will never win. "Hello," he says. "What's your name?"

"Arielle," says the girl.

Arielle!

"What happened to your face?" she asks.

"My face? Oh." Guillaume has forgotten about his broken nose. "I fell down some stairs." He beams at her. "It's nothing."

"What's your name?"

"Guillaume." The girl has Suzanne's gray eyes. He clears his throat. "I'm a friend of your mother's. Is she home?"

"No," says Arielle.

A momentary pang.

"You're here all on your own?"

"Oh no. Well, yes. I'm going downstairs in a moment to eat dinner with Madame Leloup. She's the concierge. Sometimes she looks after me when *maman* goes out." Arielle looks at him, weighing him up. "I don't really want to go," she confides in a low voice.

"Why not?" asks Guillaume.

"Because she's a *terrible* cook," whispers Arielle.

Guillaume puts his hand up to his mouth in pretend horror. "I promise I won't tell anyone," he whispers back. He looks down at his daughter, and worries that his heart will stop beating for good, drawn to exquisite stillness by overwhelming love for this little girl. He wants to know everything about her. "What's your favorite thing to eat?" he asks.

Arielle bites her lip as she considers her answer. "I had some chocolate cake this afternoon, and it was *delicious*," she tells him. "So probably that."

"I love chocolate cake, too," says Guillaume.

She beams at him. "We went to see a puppet show this afternoon. My friend Souren was doing it. He's very good at puppets."

"Ah, puppets, what fun!" exclaims Guillaume.

"Only a little boy died in the last play and that made me cry and that was why I was allowed to eat the chocolate cake." Arielle pauses. "I don't usually get to eat chocolate cake," she adds sadly.

Guillaume peers over her head. "When will your mother—" he begins, and then the words freeze on his lips.

He stares into the apartment, unable to formulate another thought.

In a frame on the hallway wall are his sketches of stone angels.

Guillaume can scarcely breathe. All this time, he thinks, stunned. She's been looking at my drawings *all this time*.

"Monsieur?" says Arielle. "Are you all right?"

Guillaume tries his best to refocus his attention on the girl. He does his best to remain composed while his brain is feverishly recalibrating everything it has ever known.

"Do you know when your mother will be home?" he asks.

Arielle shakes her head. "She said she was going to watch a famous musician play music with his band. His instrument is the saxophone."

The sight of the stone angels has set Guillaume's brain spinning in a million improbable directions.

All this time, he thinks.

Is that hope he feels?

Suddenly he is no longer so concerned about the rat-faced man and his minions.

Perhaps this is one of the priest's miracles.

"Do you know the name of the place where she's gone this evening?" he asks.

Arielle nods. "She wrote down the name and address for me." She disappears for a moment, and when she returns she is holding a piece of paper, which she presents for Guillaume's inspection. "Here," she says. "It's called Le Chat Blanc."

Guillaume's smile slips, just a little.

39

‿◡‿

Hope, Rekindled

JEAN-PAUL MAILLARD PUSHES OPEN the heavy wooden door of his building, and steps inside. In the hallway he waits for the door to close behind him. As the latch clicks into place, the frenzied brouhaha of the *quartier* retreats. The harried whine of passing automobiles, the yells of marauding children, the slow, rhythmic clang of an invisible workman's hammer—now these are no more than a muffled collage of noise, suddenly a world away. Jean-Paul loves this moment. He relishes the quiet grace that lies in the transition between the city outside and his private life within these walls. Paris is always there, waiting for him on the other side of the door. But how sweet it is to turn away from all that, to come home.

He climbs the stairs to his apartment. He hangs up his coat in the hallway. At the far end of the living room is his desk. A photograph of Anaïs and Elodie hangs on the wall. Anaïs is leaning forward, laughing, kissing the baby on her nose. Elodie's tiny fingers are reaching out toward her mother. The photograph gathered dust in a cupboard for years, when he was unable to look at all that he had lost. These days he hungrily devours every detail of the picture: these two beloved faces stir up a quiet wonder within him now.

Jean-Paul thinks of the young girl in the Jardin du Luxembourg. What was her name? Arielle. He closes his eyes.

Arielle, yes. Not Elodie.

He'd been caught unawares, blindsided by memory, longing, and hope. For a dizzying moment time had stopped as he stared into those gray eyes, the last ten years erased in an instant. His world had been briefly reconfigured beyond all hope, all comprehension—and then mother and daughter smiled their identical smiles, and his dreams evaporated as quickly as they had come. He remembers watching the pair as they walked away from him, off in search of chocolate cake, each wholly absorbed in the other's existence. He remembers the mother's body, exquisitely, unconsciously skewed toward the little girl. A new understanding dawns: wherever Elodie is, she is not alone. There will be someone next to her who cannot quite walk in a straight line either, pulled off kilter by helpless love.

He quietly hums the lovely melody that transported him back to the deserted church near Verdun. *Never underestimate your memories, monsieur*, Arielle's mother told him. There's no danger of that: memories are all he has. He reaches out and touches the photograph. Where is his daughter now?

His fingertips leave the faintest trace on the glass.

His typewriter awaits. Jean-Paul sits down at his desk and feeds a fresh sheet of paper into the blackened maw of the machine. He turns to his notes of the interview with Josephine Baker. There's some hastily scribbled description of the apartment itself—the opulent mess, the gaudy flourishes, the parakeets. He begins to type.

Some hours later, the floor around his desk is a landscape of discarded paper. Jean-Paul stares at the single, desultory paragraph on the page in front of him, and then pulls it out of the typewriter. He mashes the paper into a ball and drops it on the floor to join the others. He cannot find his way into the piece. Josephine Baker's story has everything—impoverished beginnings, triumph over adversity, talent, and beauty. He thinks about her, surrounded by expensive trinkets and pursued by men whose names she does not remember. Those red roses, so carelessly given away. He sighs. She perched on the edge of that huge sofa and smiled at him, and he was as smitten as everyone else. All he knows about her is exactly what she wanted him to know. She is the most famous person in Paris, but her celebrity is a mask. That dazzling smile was a suit of armor, hiding her from view.

He stands up and walks across the room to the gramophone player. A moment later, the familiar clarinet fills the room. As Gershwin's music gallops majestically forward, Jean-Paul thinks about another George— the invisible composer from New Jersey who lives above Shakespeare and Company, making that terrible noise on the piano. *He never would have written such a thing in Trenton, you can be sure of that*, said Sylvia Beach.

All these Americans in Paris! Josephine Baker he understands—and Sidney Bechet, and Lloyd Waters. France has liberated them from the color of their skin. But what about all the other Americans in Paris? What are they escaping?

Everyone is running toward somewhere, he told Josephine Baker that morning. Perhaps it's as simple as that, he thinks. We're always gazing toward the horizon, searching for the next adventure. And those who are trapped still dream helplessly, obsessively: *Rhapsody in Blue* still fills his heart with longing for New York.

His notebook is lying on the table, as usual. Elodie's story is always within reach. Jean-Paul remembers Josephine Baker's offer to mention it to Ernest Hemingway. That morning he dismissed the idea—the story is his, and his alone. But now he begins to wonder.

What if he were to ask for Hemingway's help? Suddenly his imagination hurtles forward, and he cannot resist.

He'll give Hemingway his novel. Then, a few days later, he'll receive an enthusiastic note from the American, inviting him to lunch. Over steak and oysters, he'll listen modestly as the famous writer tells him what a masterpiece he has written. With this enthusiastic endorsement, publishers will fight for his book. There will be meetings with editors, legal contracts. Money, he supposes, although he does not much care about that.

Jean-Paul imagines a mountain of books, Elodie's life bursting from between the covers of every one. His daughter, resurrected a thousand, ten thousand times!

And then.

Perhaps one day Elodie will pick up the book.

Perhaps she will read it, and see herself in those pages.

Perhaps he will no longer have to look for her.

Perhaps she will come looking for him.

40

A Woman Scorned

CAMILLE HURRIES DOWN Rue de l'Odéon, clutching the piece of paper that Sylvia Beach has given her. The address is a short walk away from the bookshop, and she sees no reason to waste any time.

She unfolds the paper. It reads:

ERNEST HEMINGWAY
6 RUE FÉROU

A writer, said Sylvia Beach. Camille has never heard of him. To her horror, she feels a tear run down her cheek.

Ernest Hemingway's apartment is just around the corner from Rue des Canettes, where her husband is probably wondering if she is ever going to return.

All Camille really wants is to see Marie and hold her close.

The door at 6 Rue Férou is slightly ajar. Camille steps into the cool, dark interior. On the other side of the hall is a staircase. She crosses the room and climbs the stairs.

In front of Hemingway's apartment she pauses for a moment. She takes a deep breath, and then knocks. Does he even speak French? she wonders.

If not, she realizes, he won't have been able to read the words she is so frightened of. Camille's English is passable—most of the hotel's guests do not even try and speak French and just assume that they'll be understood if they shout loud enough—but still her stomach knots tightly in apprehension.

The door is opened by a woman. She is holding a cigarette in one hand and a glass of red wine in the other. She wears long, flared trousers and a silk blouse, both dazzlingly white, and no shoes. Her dark hair is cut very short, almost like a boy's, with a thick fringe swept across her forehead. This gives her a masculine air, despite the elegance of her clothes. She leans languidly against the doorframe and takes a long drag of her cigarette.

"*Oui?*"

Camille glances at the hand that is holding the wineglass, and sees a wedding band. "Madame Hemingway?"

The woman acknowledges this with a slow tilt of the head. She does not take her eyes off Camille. "Do you speak English?" she asks.

Camille nods. "A little, yes."

The woman's eyes are dark and flat and cool. Camille is suddenly aware of how tightly she is clutching her handbag. "How can I help you?"

"My name is Camille Clermont." Camille beams. "I would like to speak to your husband."

At this, the woman emits a short, bitter laugh. "So would I, madame. I've not seen him since he stumbled out of here this morning."

Camille's smile slips. "He's not here?"

"Alas, no."

"Is he writing somewhere?"

"I sincerely doubt it."

"Do you know where I might find him, Madame Hemingway?"

"Call me Pauline," says the woman. She takes another drink. "I'm afraid I don't know where my husband is. We only arrived back from our honeymoon a few weeks ago, but I hardly see him anymore. He says he missed his friends while he was away, and so he's been busy catching up." She pauses. "Very busy."

"Do you know when he'll be back?"

"If the last few nights are any indication, it won't be until very late, and when he does, he'll be roaring drunk."

Camille stares at her in horror.

"John Dos Passos is in town," continues Pauline Hemingway. "My husband tells me that when writers get together they need their space, their freedom. No women to bother them, you understand."

Camille nods, although she does not understand. She has never heard of John Dos Passos.

"Perhaps I shouldn't complain." Pauline sighs. "I'm probably better off on my own, anyway. Ernest has been in a *foul* mood ever since we got back from our honeymoon and he realized that he'd missed Lindbergh's arrival at Le Bourget. He thought he should have been there. A witness to history, or some such nonsense." She leans forward conspiratorially and cracks a small, lopsided grin. "He can't stand the fact that Lindbergh is younger than he is, and more handsome, *and* a million times more famous. He's as mad as a wet hen about it. And apparently it's all my fault. As if I held a gun to his head and made him whisk me off to the south of France!" The woman laughs her short, bitter laugh again. "So here I am, abandoned by my new husband and left to fend for myself, with nothing but a couple of bottles of middling Burgundy for company." She holds up her glass of wine and scrutinizes it closely.

"I really do need to find your husband," says Camille.

Pauline looks at her. "What do you want with him?"

"He was at Shakespeare and Company earlier today. Mademoiselle Beach sold him something of mine by mistake. I came to ask for it back."

"Ah, the lovely Sylvia. It was a book, I assume?"

"A notebook. Just a little thing. But it's important to me."

"I'm sorry I can't help you. He could be anywhere. For Ernest, Paris is a giant playground." Pauline makes an unsteady sweep of her hand to indicate the city that lies beyond the apartment walls. "So many delights around every corner, and he doesn't see why he should deprive himself of a single one of them."

"Could you tell me some of the places he likes to go?" asks Camille.

"You could try any of the bars in Montparnasse."

Camille's heart sinks. There must be a thousand of them. "Thank you," she says, and turns to go.

"Wait. I've just remembered. Do you know Le Chat Blanc?"

Camille shakes her head.

"It's a jazz club in Montmartre. Sidney Bechet is playing there this week. Ernest said he might go tonight, with John." The last of the wine disappears down her throat. "I heard Bechet play once, in Aix. I loved him. But do you think it occurred to my husband to ask his new bride if she would like to go and see him again? Do you think he thought to include me in his evening's plans?"

Camille does not answer.

The newly minted Mrs. Hemingway looks at her wineglass for a long moment. "Anyway, yes. Le Chat Blanc," she says. "Just look for the two loudest Americans in the room."

"You've been most helpful," murmurs Camille.

"I hope you get your little book back."

"Thank you." Camille turns and walks back toward the stairs. She can feel Pauline Hemingway's gaze on her back as she hurries down the corridor.

"If you find my husband," calls the American from the door of the apartment, "tell him to drink up and come home."

41

Le Chat Blanc

FINALLY, RUE DES ABBESSES.

Souren Balakian staggers along the street, clutching his suitcase. His improvised bandages protect his ruined hand from the lacerating night air, and the brandy has helped, but the pain still stuns him. He should be at a hospital, he knows, but no doctor can attend to his regret, or mend his broken heart.

It is a warm night. The streetlamps are on, casting small pools of light up and down the road. The sidewalks are thick with people, but Souren does not see them. He moves forward, thinking only of Thérèse. In the bar on Rue de Vaugirard he imagined her body, but those cravings have dissipated. Now all he wants is comfort and kindness.

He does not know whether such things can be bought, or what they might cost.

His pace quickens as he approaches Le Chat Blanc. There is a crowd gathered outside the entrance to the club. A few steps away women are leaning up against a wall, half in and half out of the shadows. Souren puts down his suitcase and scans their faces.

After a moment, Thérèse steps forward. "Are you looking for me, *chéri?*" Her smile disappears when she sees the stricken look on his face. "What's wrong?" she asks.

Souren holds up his hand, still wrapped in the puppets' tunics. "I burned my hand," he says.

Thérèse frowns. "Why have you come here?"

Souren knows that somewhere in the darkness a man is watching them.

"I need you," he says.

"No, you need a hospital."

Out of the corner of his eye Souren sees a dark shifting in the shadows. "Please," he whispers. "Let's go upstairs. Will you take me upstairs? Just for a little while?"

Thérèse puts her hand on his arm. "I'm no doctor."

"I don't need a doctor," he tells her.

She looks at him for a long moment. "You have money?"

He nods.

"All right." She sighs. "Let's go."

The music is heavenly. Jean-Paul sits at a table near the front of the low-ceilinged room. In the center of the stage stands Sidney Bechet, resplendent in a tan double-breasted suit, eyes closed, horn raised to the sky. Beads of sweat glisten on his brow as his fingers fly across the silver keys of his instrument. He weaves syncopated spells, bewitching concatenations of rhythm, melody, and swing. The saxophone's fat, honeyed tone fills the room. Behind him, the band plays their hearts out. The bass rumbles. The high hat snaps in crisp time. The trombone delivers a sweet countermelody. All move as one. They're playing "Muskrat Ramble," a jaunty tune full of sass and vinegar.

Jean-Paul takes a sip of his drink. It has been a long day. He glances at his watch, and wonders where Josephine Baker is. A vague unease flutters down. Perhaps she has forgotten her invitation. Perhaps she just wanted to say something kind.

The song ends, and the room fills with applause. Sidney Bechet holds his saxophone aloft to acknowledge the crowd, his face cracked into a wide, mischievous grin. His eyes roam around the room, his hungry gaze lingering longest on the beautiful women. Jean-Paul watches him. The bandleader is a man of notoriously prodigious appetites. He looks completely at ease in front of a roomful of strangers. He is doing precisely what he was put on this earth to do, and he is enjoying every moment of it. Bechet says something to the band. Then he turns to the audience and announces, "Salty Dog Blues." The band breaks into the new tune, a raucous dirge, heavy with longing and regret. The audience cannot take their eyes off the saxophonist—except, Jean-Paul notices, for one woman, a few tables away, who sits alone, a half-drunk glass of white wine in front of her. She is not looking at Sidney Bechet. In fact she hardly seems to notice the music at all. She sits bolt upright, her head turned away from the stage. She is staring at something, or someone, on the far side of the room.

The band is building up steam. The pianist pounds out gutbucket despair. The trombone shimmers. The saxophone wails. The crowd, enraptured, breathes into the music. They don't want to miss a note. Jean-Paul glances again at the woman. She has resumed her gaze across the room. He follows the trajectory of her stare.

On the far side of the club, sitting with another man, he sees Ernest Hemingway.

Guillaume Blanc stands in line outside the club. Every time the door opens to admit another customer, he hears a blast of music. His heart is clattering as loudly as the drums on the stage.

As he shuffles forward, a low counterpoint of bittersweet regret has begun to rumble within him. His tombstone angels have been on Suzanne Mauriac's wall for all these years! He has already begun to mourn each day that he has stayed away with an ache that is seeping into his bones. He is tormented by the thought of an alternative universe, one where he had not waited so long.

He cannot leave Paris without seeing her first.

Ahead of him a man and a woman are leaning into each other, their faces nearly touching, laughing softly at something. They are holding hands.

A terrible thought strikes Guillaume—so terrible that he momentarily forgets to breathe.

What if Suzanne is here with someone else?

A rush of nausea. Guillaume remembers Arielle's beautiful face, and thinks of the priest's words: *We only get so many chances at happiness.*

He can't leave now. If Suzanne is not alone, he'll just turn around and walk out again.

The line moves forward slowly. Guillaume glances at the small group of prostitutes standing in the nearby shadows. The tips of their cigarettes glow as they watch the crowd. He does not see Thérèse in her usual spot.

A shiver of apprehension. He wishes Suzanne were anywhere but here. Guillaume is now regretting sending Brataille into the unforgiving hands of Léon and his thugs. He has no wish to witness the art dealer's come-uppance himself.

Finally he is at the front of the line. He pays the admission fee with the last of the coins in his pocket and steps inside. At the far end of the room the band is in full flight. In front of the stage there is a dance floor, bordered by a sea of small tables. There's a single candle on each table: the place is more shadow than light. Guillaume needs to see the faces in the audience, so he walks closer to the stage to look out across the tables.

And there, near the back of the room, Suzanne sits with her eyes shut. She is swaying, ever so gently, in time to the music. There is a small smile on her face.

She is alone.

Ernest Hemingway wraps an arm around his friend's back and shouts something into his ear, trying to make himself heard over the music. The other man picks up the notebook that is sitting on the table in front of him. He flicks through it idly. Camille watches the stranger's fingers on the pages, unable to pull her eyes away. The music is no more than an echo on the fringes of her consciousness.

She has been sitting here for half a lifetime.

Thanks to Pauline Hemingway's advice to look for the two loudest

Americans in the room, Camille identified her quarry even before she sat down. The pair would have been impossible to miss in any event. Their laughter is long and loud and is attracting looks of irritation from people at nearby tables. Neither man cares in the slightest. Camille thinks of Hemingway's new wife, marooned in the apartment on Rue Férou and drinking herself into a lonely stupor. She wants to stride across the room and tell him to go home. Instead she is frozen in her seat, unable to move. She watches as the two men toss the notebook back and forth, trying to summon up the courage to approach them. Camille looks down at the glass of wine in front of her, no longer sure whether it is her second or her third. Her head has begun to swim alarmingly.

She picks up her glass and empties it in one swallow.

Still carrying his suitcase, Souren follows Thérèse up the staircase at the back of the club. When they reach the second floor they turn down a long corridor. Numbered doors line both walls. The sounds of the band from the club below waft up through the floorboards. Thérèse stops in front of number 8. She opens the door and Souren follows her inside. The room is small, with a long mirror on one wall, a chest of drawers, a rug, and a bed. Embers of a dying fire glow in the grate. On the wooden mantelpiece there is a large brass lamp. Thick drapes cover the walls.

He has been here many times before. He sits down on the bed and watches as Thérèse moves around the room, lighting candles. When she is finished, she sits down next to him.

"Can I see?" she asks, reaching out to touch his hand.

Souren nods, and with that Thérèse carefully starts to unwind the outermost bandage. He does not want to look.

"Ah, *mon dieu,*" breathes Thérèse. "What have you done?"

"There was a fire," whispers Souren. "My hand——"

"Hush, now, don't talk." Thérèse stands up. She opens the chest of drawers and begins to rummage through it. "You need a fresh dressing, for a start." After a moment she produces a red silk scarf. "Here. This will have to do." She sits down next to him on the bed and pulls his hand toward her.

She examines it closely. "There's not a lot I can do for you, *chéri*," she tells him. "You need a doctor."

But Thérèse is giving him something more valuable than the most expert medical attention. The last time someone looked at him with such kindness, he'd been no more than a boy: Françoise, sitting by her dead son's bed, feeding him and teaching him French. Ever since he crept out of that house and escaped into the moonlit night, the world has been an unbearably lonely place.

She holds him gently by the wrist and begins to wrap the scarf around his fingers. She pulls the silk tightly to his ravaged skin. As she works, she starts to sing. Her voice is gentle, full of light.

Souren Balakian starts to weep.

Jean-Paul watches Ernest Hemingway and his companion from across the room. On the table in front of the two men is a black leather-bound book. Every so often one of them picks it up, opens it, and reads a little. They keep the waiters busy, beckoning at them from behind clouds of cigarette smoke and calling for more drinks.

The band is playing a raucous up-tempo piece now. The trombone player has taken center stage and is playing a lively solo. Sidney Bechet stands to one side, stamping his foot in time to the music and nodding his head in approval. Jean-Paul looks back to the other side of the room. A tall black man has joined Hemingway and his companion at their table. He stands between them, a giant hand on each man's shoulder, laughing at something Hemingway has said. Jean-Paul guesses that this must be Lloyd Waters, the war hero who stayed in France when the fighting was over. The three men are shouting to make themselves heard above the music. If Americans behave with such self-satisfied entitlement when they are thousands of miles from home, how on earth do they behave in their own country? Jean-Paul checks his watch, wondering when Josephine Baker will appear.

There is nothing to do but wait.

· · ·

"Good evening," says Guillaume, the words barely escaping his lips. Somehow his feet have carried him between the tables and now he is here, standing in front of Suzanne. She looks up at him. There is no flicker of recognition on her face.

"You don't remember me," he says.

She tilts her head to one side and looks at him with those gray eyes he has dreamed of for so long. "You *do* look familiar," she says.

"We met a long time ago," says Guillaume. "I painted your portrait."

"Yes." A smile. "You actually painted a house."

She remembers! "That's right," he says, stunned.

"I liked that painting very much, I remember." She looks at him, curious. "What are you doing here?"

"Oh, well." He points toward the stage. "I just *love* jazz." The band is so loud it's making his ears hurt. The noise is a terrible caterwauling, a screeching calamity of wrong notes.

Suzanne takes a sip of her drink. "The music is wonderful, isn't it?"

"It's unbelievable," he answers, honestly enough.

"Did you break your nose?"

He waves her words away. "A small accident. Nothing serious. Would you mind if I joined you?"

Suzanne hesitates. "I suppose that would be fine."

Guillaume sits down before she can change her mind. "Quite a coincidence, seeing you after all this time!" he says.

"Tell me your name again," says Suzanne.

"Guillaume. Guillaume Blanc."

"Yes. Guillaume." She pauses. "You gave me a sketch of some statues. Stone angels from the Montmartre cemetery. Do you remember?"

He pretends to think about this. "No," he says, "I don't think I do."

"I love those statues. I look at them every day."

Before Guillaume can respond, he is horrified to see Emile Brataille weaving between the tables. The art dealer is determinedly making his way toward the far side of the room, and quickly disappears behind a full-length velvet curtain. Guillaume looks around, hoping to see Léon in hot pursuit, but nobody seems to be following him.

The band ends its song with a terrible flurry of squawks and honks. It sounds as if a dozen swans are being brutally murdered. As the noise mercifully subsides, the audience bursts into applause. Suzanne claps enthusiastically, and so Guillaume joins in.

The saxophonist waves for quiet. "A dear friend of mine has just arrived in the house," he announces in English. He looks over the heads of the crowd and smiles at someone in the back of the room. "Please welcome the most beautiful woman in all of Paris," he says. "Ladies and gentlemen, Mademoiselle Josephine Baker!"

A low murmur of excitement sweeps through the crowd.

Along with everyone else, Camille turns and watches as the city's most famous resident floats across the room, smiling and waving at the audience as she goes. She is wearing a dazzling silver dress that clings to every curve of her body. Her beautiful skin glows. She moves with effortless grace.

The audience is applauding wildly. She blows kisses to the men and waves at the women as she shimmers between the tables. The band has stopped playing. They know they cannot compete with such a spectacle. She walks up to the stage. Sidney Bechet takes her hand and kisses it twice, ostentatiously. She laughs, curtsies, and gives him a peck on the cheek.

As Josephine Baker bathes in the approval of these strangers, Camille thinks of Monsieur Proust, alone in his bedroom with just his pen and a flickering candle for company. He was always so modest, and so very private. He enjoyed a grand party, but liked to stay on the outside, looking in. She watches Josephine Baker as she finally relinquishes the spotlight and walks over to a nearby table. A man sits there alone. He gets stiffly to his feet to greet her. All eyes in the room are still on her, and she knows it.

The band begins to play again. Josephine Baker and her companion are deep in conversation. Camille looks back toward the tables where the loud Americans are sitting. Ernest Hemingway has vanished. The other man sits there alone, smoking a cigarette and listening to the music. The notebook sits on the table in front of him, forgotten.

This is her chance.

Camille stands up.

There is a ferocious banging on the door.

"Ignore it," whispers Thérèse to Souren. "Whoever that is, they won't—"

"Thérèse!" comes a shout from the corridor. "Thérèse!"

She does not take her hand off his. "I know that voice," she says, frowning.

Souren stares blankly at her. He just wants her to keep singing.

"Thérèse!" The door handle rattles. "You shouldn't be working! Let me in." More thumps on the door.

"Go away!" she calls. "I'm busy!"

"But it's Emile, *chérie*. From the art gallery. I've come to take you away."

At this Thérèse closes her eyes. "Ah, *non*." She stands up and walks across the room. At once Souren longs to feel her touch again. "What do you want?" she hisses through the door.

There is a pause.

"Didn't Guillaume come and see you today?" asks the voice.

"Guillaume Blanc? Yes, I saw him this morning."

"And he talked about me?"

"Well, we talked about your little *cacahuète*," says Thérèse. "Now go away and leave me alone."

There is silence. Thérèse turns back to the bed. "I'm sorry, *chéri*," she says to Souren. She sits back down next to him and takes his hand in hers once more. "Now where were we?"

Just then there is a loud crack of splintering wood and the door flies open. Souren turns to see a man standing there, his frame silhouetted against the light from the corridor. He is breathing heavily. The candles next to the bed flicker.

"You're supposed to be coming with me!" shouts the man.

"I'm not going anywhere with you," says Thérèse.

"But you don't understand," cries the man. "I want to take you away from here! I want you to live the life you deserve. With me, in Montparnasse!"

Souren Balakian stands up. He does not know who this man is. All he knows is that Thérèse, who has treated him with care and kindness, is not treating him with care and kindness anymore. She has stopped singing her beautiful song. She is not even looking at him. And it's all because of this man. Souren takes a step toward the intruder. "Leave," he growls.

"Thérèse," pleads the man. "Be a good girl and come with me."

A white-hot anger is rising within Souren. All he wants, all he cares about in the world, is for Thérèse to keep holding his hand. He steps forward and shoves the intruder as hard as he can. The man staggers back a few steps before he regains his balance. He looks at Souren for the first time.

"Who the hell are you?" he demands.

Josephine Baker kisses Jean-Paul on the cheek as if they're old friends. She slides into the seat next to his. "I hope you haven't been waiting too long," she says.

"I've been enjoying the music. How was the show this evening?"

"*Comme ci, comme ça*. I danced. The audience clapped. You know how it goes." A waiter materializes at her side. "Champagne," she declares. "Bring several glasses."

Jean-Paul raises an eyebrow. "Several?"

"I'm going to introduce you to some people, remember?" She points toward the stage. "Sidney, of course. And Lloyd Waters. And Ernest, if he's here."

"Oh, he's here," says Jean-Paul.

"Did you bring your book?"

Jean-Paul pats his jacket pocket. "I did."

"Who's this?" asks a voice.

Josephine lets out a small cry of delight, and stands to kiss Ernest Hemingway on both cheeks. "Come and join us," she says. "Champagne is on its way."

Hemingway looks down at Jean-Paul. "Who's this?" he asks again.

"Ernest, this is Jean-Paul. Jean-Paul, this is Ernest."

The American nods at Jean-Paul and turns his attention back to Josephine. "Look, do you want to dance?" he asks.

"I've only just arrived," she replies. "I haven't even had a drink yet. Perhaps you've forgotten that I've been dancing all night."

"Just a quick one," he pleads.

The waiter arrives with a bottle of champagne and glasses. "At least let me have a drink first," says Josephine.

Hemingway pulls out a chair and sits down, watching her keenly.

"Both of you are writers, you know," says Josephine as the waiter pours the champagne. "Jean-Paul has written a book, too, haven't you?"

Jean-Paul pulls Elodie's book out of his pocket and puts it on the table.

Hemingway looks at it suspiciously.

"We were hoping that you might be able to help Jean-Paul find a publisher for it," says Josephine. She winks at Jean-Paul.

The American looks pained, but he desperately wants to dance with Josephine Baker, so he picks up the book. "It's in French," he complains a moment later, as he flicks through the pages.

Jean-Paul performs his most Gallic shrug. "*Et oui.*"

Ernest Hemingway puts the book down and empties his glass of champagne in one swallow. "All right, so we had a drink. Won't you dance with me now?"

She rolls her eyes at Jean-Paul. "Would you mind?"

"Not in the slightest," he says. Josephine stands up and touches him gently on the shoulder. "I'll be back," she promises.

Hemingway nods at Jean-Paul before turning away, his arm around her waist as he leads her to the dance floor.

He leaves the book on the table.

. . .

Guillaume and Suzanne watch as Josephine Baker glides across the room. The man she is with has a handsome but glowering face. She says something in his ear, but this just makes the man's frown even deeper.

"She looks divine," says Suzanne. "I wonder who that is with her?"

"Whoever it is, he doesn't seem very happy," says Guillaume. His gaze drifts back to the velvet curtain that Brataille disappeared through. He guesses that it leads to the rooms where the prostitutes ply their trade. With each minute that passes he feels a growing sense of unease.

Guillaume watches Suzanne's radiant face as she listens to the music, and his heart slips, just a little. The band is playing a blues, as hot and as sultry as a New Orleans night. Josephine Baker and her companion have started to dance. They push their bodies against each other in time to the pulse of the music. The man is holding Josephine Baker very tight. Not a sliver of light escapes between their bodies.

"I've been watching you," says Guillaume suddenly.

Suzanne looks at him. "Watching me?"

He clears his throat. "After we were together, you became pregnant." He pauses. "Since then I've watched your daughter grow." He takes a deep breath. "Our daughter."

There is a moment's silence.

"You're not Arielle's father, Guillaume," says Suzanne gently.

"Of course I am."

"I was already pregnant when I met you."

He shakes his head. "That can't be."

"It's true."

"But I worked it out," he says. "I looked at the calendar. I did the calculations. She was a few weeks early, but—"

"She was born two weeks *late*."

Guillaume is silent then. Arielle has been the sun around which he has been devotedly orbiting for years, but now he's been cut loose. Suddenly he's streaking away into nothingness.

. . .

"Good evening," says Camille.

The sole occupant of the table looks up. He has been staring disconsolately at the empty glass in front of him while a forgotten cigarette smolders between his fingers. "How do you like that?" he says in English, gesturing toward the couple on the dance floor. "A fellow asks you out for a drink and then leaves you high and dry while he goes off to chase tail." He pauses. "Exquisite tail, I'll grant you," he concedes, "but still. Bad form all around." He looks up at Camille. "Do I know you?"

She finds it hard to decipher the American's slurred delivery. She points toward the dance floor. "Is that man Ernest Hemingway?"

The man sighs. "Yes, that's him."

"My name is Camille Clermont," she says.

"Camille—?"

"Clermont." She points at the stage, then at her ear. "The music is very loud."

The man grunts in agreement. The notebook is sitting by his right elbow, forgotten. The ash from his cigarette hangs in a precarious arc over the black leather. Camille wants to grab the notebook and make a run for it, but she is not going to act like a common thief.

"I suppose you want to talk to him, do you?" says the man. He glances toward the dancing couple. Josephine Baker has thrown her head back and is laughing at something Hemingway has said.

Camille shakes her head. "Actually, monsieur, I wanted to talk to you."

He looks astonished. "To me?"

She points at the table. "It's about that notebook."

"What about it?"

"It belongs to me."

The man shakes his head. "I'm afraid you're mistaken. Ernest purchased it earlier today. He brought it along to show it to me. He's very proud of it."

Too late, Camille understands her mistake. There's no reason for this man to believe a word she says. She has no way of proving her story.

She should have asked Sylvia Beach to write a note, explaining what has happened. She turns and looks toward the dance floor. More people are dancing now. In the throng, Ernest Hemingway and Josephine Baker have disappeared.

Souren does not take his eyes off the intruder. "Who are you?" asks the man for a second time. Souren does not reply.

"You need to leave!" cries Thérèse.

The man shakes his head. "I'm not going anywhere without you, *mon amour.*"

Thérèse folds her arms across her chest. "I'm not going anywhere."

"This isn't the time to change your mind."

"What do you mean, change my mind?"

"Guillaume told me everything, *chérie*. He said that you wanted me to come and rescue you from this awful place." The man smiles. "And here I am."

"But I told him that I never wanted to see you again," says Thérèse.

"Is that so." The man closes his eyes for a moment. When he opens them again, they are dark with fury. In two swift paces he crosses the room and punches Thérèse hard in the face. As she falls to the ground, Souren steps forward and swings his undamaged fist into the man's jaw with all the strength he can muster. The man's head flies sideways under the force of the blow and he crashes into the table next to the bed, sending the candles flying. Blinded by fury, Souren throws another punch, then another. Without thinking, he hits the man with his damaged hand. Stunned by the pain, he stops just long enough for his opponent to hurl himself at Souren's legs. Caught off guard, Souren lands heavily on the floor, and then the man is on him, his fists flying. He lands a punch on Souren's cheek, another on his chin. He drives a knee between Souren's legs. The pain of the blows barely registers; all Souren feels is the agony of his burned hand.

Thérèse shrieks, and this causes his assailant to pause for just a second, and Souren smashes his forehead into the man's nose. There is a terrible howl. Souren pushes the man off him and gets to his feet. He sees the reason for Thérèse's cry of alarm: the drapes next to the overturned table are slick with flames, ignited by the candles that the men have knocked over during their fight. The fire is spreading quickly across the room, leaping from one piece of fabric to the next. Within moments all the walls are burning. Thérèse is standing in front of Souren. Her nose has been broken by the man's punch. There is blood splattered across her face. She is screaming at him, but he cannot hear the words coming out of her ruby-red mouth. Smoke fills his nostrils, his mouth, his throat.

Just then the man stumbles into view. He is holding something in his hands, something large and heavy. It is the brass lamp that was sitting on the mantelpiece, realizes Souren, half a second before it smashes into the left side of his head.

Jean-Paul pours himself more of Josephine Baker's champagne. It is first-rate. He takes a long swallow. If he's going to sit here alone while she is dancing, he may as well enjoy himself. He watches the two Americans. Hemingway is an arrogant fool, he thinks. Then he looks down at the note-book on the table in front of him. Ah, Jean-Paul, he chides himself. Perhaps it's you who is the arrogant one.

Just then there is a loud crash from somewhere overhead, and the band jitters to an uneasy stop in the middle of its song. Sidney Bechet stands with his saxophone in one hand, looking up at the ceiling. A low murmur spreads across the room. Without the music to cement their bodies together, Hemingway and Josephine Baker have pulled away from each other. He still has his arm around her, as if he cannot quite bear to let her go, and is whispering something in her ear. She puts a hand on his shoulder and says something in response. At once Hemingway drops his arm from her waist and storms back to his own table. Josephine watches him go, and then saunters back to where Jean-Paul is sitting. She sits down and picks up her glass of champagne.

"Is everything all right?" asks Jean-Paul.

"Oh yes," she replies.

Jean-Paul looks at Ernest Hemingway's empty champagne flute. "Your friend looked a little unhappy just now."

"Oh, he often is. He may be a famous writer and everything, but he acts like a big baby sometimes."

"He forgot my book," says Jean-Paul.

"That's very rude of him," says Josephine.

"I think he was a little distracted."

"You should take it over to him."

Jean-Paul looks at her. "Do you really think I should?"

Slowly, that famous smile appears on her face.

The crash that interrupts the band feels as if it was immediately over their table. Guillaume looks up in alarm. Moments later there is a swish of the velvet curtain and Brataille appears, roughly pulling Thérèse along behind him. The art dealer is barely recognizable from the dapper suitor who vanished upstairs earlier. He has lost his jacket. His shirt is untucked and torn along one arm. His usually impeccable hair is an unruly riot. Thérèse does not look up. She is clutching her face. Her top is stained with blood. The band has not started playing again, and so every pair of eyes in the room stares at the couple. Brataille glares right back. Guillaume shrinks back into the shadows. All around him people are murmuring and pointing. Brataille yanks on Thérèse's arm and starts to pull her toward the exit. Thérèse follows him in silence, casting a single glance up to the ceiling as she goes. Guillaume watches them, paralyzed.

What in God's name has he done?

"Who are you?"

Ernest Hemingway is looking at Camille suspiciously. His breath is heavy after his exertions on the dance floor.

"My name is Camille Clermont, monsieur." She points to the table. "I spoke with Sylvia Beach this afternoon. She told me that she sold you that notebook."

"What of it?"

"I was Marcel Proust's maid," she says. The words make her feel stronger. "The notebook belongs to me. My husband took it without my permission and sold it to Mademoiselle Beach, but it wasn't his to sell."

Hemingway sits down and takes a drink. "I don't see what any of that has to do with me," he says.

"The notebook is mine, monsieur."

The American shakes his head. "I bought that notebook fair and square, madame. I paid decent money for it. It's not my problem if you can't keep control of your husband."

Camille thinks of Pauline Hemingway alone in her apartment.

"I have money," she says.

"I don't want your money," says Hemingway.

Just then another man approaches the table. He appears to be limping. Hemingway does not look happy to see him. "What do *you* want?" he demands.

The man is unperturbed by the American's rudeness. He turns to Camille and gives her a polite nod.

"You forgot my novel," replies the man. He puts a book down on the table. "I didn't want you to leave without it."

"I didn't forget it," says Hemingway. "I left it there on purpose."

"But it was a gift," says the man.

"Since Mademoiselle Baker is so keen to spend time with you," says Hemingway icily, "perhaps you should give it to *her*."

"Is everything all right over here?" The club owner has appeared.

"Everything's fine, Lloyd," answers Hemingway, leaning back and lighting a cigarette. He points at the man standing next to her. "This fellow is just about to leave."

Just then Camille notices the unmistakable smell of something burning.

Souren opens his eyes to a wall of flame. With an immense effort he props himself up on one shoulder. His eyeballs are hot, stinging with smoke. Everything is burning now. The side of his head, where the brass lamp stunned him, throbs viciously. He begins to cough. Covering his mouth with his sleeve, he tries to get to his feet, but he cannot. Where is Thérèse? He calls her name, but his voice is swallowed by the roar of the flames. He looks around him. He is alone in the burning room. A blazing beam has fallen from the ceiling and is blocking his route to the door.

He goes back, one last time, to the dusty village square.

Hector is roped to the chair.

The glowing tip of Kamil Ömer's cigarette falls into his brother's lap.

The conflagration is instant. Flames spread quickly up and down the boy's arms and legs, and within seconds he disappears beneath a blanket of fire. A woman screams. The crowd emits a disbelieving moan. Hector's fuel-soaked clothes burn fiercely. Clouds of thick black smoke billow angrily into the air, obscuring his face.

He does not yell out. He does not struggle.

Souren watches his brother burn.

Ernest Hemingway is staring at Jean-Paul, his cheeks flushed with anger and whiskey. This is nothing to do with his book, Jean-Paul understands—the American is just angry that Josephine Baker ended their dance together so she could return to her table and speak with him.

The famous writer is jealous of him.

An involuntary grin cracks his face.

"What are you smiling about?" splutters Hemingway.

Before Jean-Paul can reply, there is a yell from the other side of the room.

"Fire!"

Mayhem and terror.

People are getting to their feet, staring around them in fear, and then they start to hurry toward the exit. The acrid tang of smoke hits Guillaume's nostrils. Where is the fire? He looks toward the door. Already there is chaos as the crowd tries to push its way to the safety of the street. There are yells of alarm as guests shove the people in front of them, desperate to escape. The bottleneck at the door worsens. A woman screams. Staff are trying to calm the crowd, to usher them out in an orderly fashion, but there is no marshaling the people's panic. They push and push; they cannot help themselves. On the stage the musicians are packing up their instruments. There must be a back exit, thinks Guillaume.

"What should we do?" asks Suzanne.

"Follow me," he says. He leads her away from the yelling, surging crowd. A small procession of scantily clad prostitutes is emerging from behind the velvet curtain, each one accompanied by a sheepish client. Guillaume's heart is hammering in his chest. If Thérèse was already upstairs with another man when Brataille arrived, where is that man now? He remembers Thérèse's anxious glance at the ceiling as Brataille dragged her away. There is a loud crack from somewhere above them.

The band is scuttling toward the back of the club, their instruments tucked under their arms. This is all his fault, Guillaume realizes. He is the one who sent Brataille here tonight.

Is there a man still in Thérèse's room?

He points at the disappearing musicians. "Follow them," he tells Suzanne.

"You're not coming?"

"In a moment. There's something I have to do first."

"Where are you going?"

"Upstairs."

She looks confused. "Why?"

"It's a long story." He tries a smile. "If you wait for me outside, I'll explain everything, I promise." The smoke is getting thicker. "You should go," he says. Without another word, Suzanne turns and walks quickly away. Guillaume pulls the cloth off the closest table and wraps it around his face to cover his nose and mouth. Then he pulls back the velvet curtain and runs up the stairs.

The enormous hand of Lloyd Waters is at Camille's back, pushing her forward. He is shouting instructions over his shoulder to his staff. He knows the game is up.

When the warning cry went up, Lloyd Waters pushed Hemingway and his companion toward the exit without ceremony. Then he took her arm. "Those two can fend for themselves," he told Camille, "but you need to stay with me, madame." Now he is guiding her through the anxious crowd, easing her passage through the throng of bodies, his bulk shielding her from the crush.

All around her people are panicking, but with every step Camille feels a sense of peace descend.

When the two Americans hurried away to save themselves, they forgot the notebook, and Lloyd Waters pulled her away before she could grab it herself.

It is sitting on the table behind them, waiting for the fire.

The heat is impossible now. Souren's breath is ragged, choked.

The fire is hungry. It pulls everything into its vortex of brilliant destruction. It's not just objects that warp and disappear in the flames' embrace: the inferno devours everything. Short distances become infinite. Time vanishes. There are no more minutes or seconds, just an eternal present. Nothing is as it was.

Souren peers across the blazing room. The fallen beam lies across the door.

There is no way out.

He is so thirsty. He looks down at his injured hand, and remembers Thérèse's careful touch as she changed the dressing. How kind she was! The smoke is thick and black now. It sits deep and malignant within his lungs. On the floor by the bed Souren sees his suitcase. He crawls toward it and tugs at the brass clasps. Familiar faces greet him when he opens the lid. The policeman, the cook, the princess. He smiles. His family. He puts his hand into the suitcase, pulling out the puppets. He is looking for one in particular. Hector. Where is Hector?

Then he remembers, and he begins to weep.

"Don't cry, Souren."

He looks up. There is his brother, walking toward him through the flames.

"Why are you crying?" asks Hector.

"I was looking for you," answers Souren, "but you weren't there."

Hector gives him a small, sad smile. "Well, I'm here now." He crouches down next to his brother and puts his hand on his shoulder. "I've been waiting for you," he whispers. "Come on."

The cries of panic are growing louder. Jean-Paul shuffles along with the rest of the crowd toward the exit, bumped and jostled at every step. He clutches his book tightly in front of him. The smell of smoke is becoming stronger. In the distance he can hear the wail of a fire truck's klaxon. Behind him a woman is weeping while her husband nudges him constantly in the back, as if this could make him move any faster. In the scramble for the door he has lost sight of Hemingway and his friend, and the woman who was arguing with them. He turns and looks back toward the stage. Josephine Baker is speaking with Sidney Bechet. The saxophonist has his hand on her arm and is gesturing behind him. Neither of them seems especially alarmed. There must be another way out.

Another shove in the back. "*Hurry up*," snarls a voice behind him.

For people like Josephine, thinks Jean-Paul, there's always another way out.

Behind the velvet curtain, the smoke is thicker, more toxic. It is hotter, too: by the time Guillaume is halfway up the stairs he has begun to sweat. He pulls the tablecloth more tightly over his nose and mouth.

The second floor corridor belches clouds of black smoke. The wooden doorframes along each wall are ablaze. Guillaume takes a cautious step forward, then another. He stops in front of the first door and squints inside. Everything is burning. The fire is all that there is. There can be no survivors here.

He makes his way down the corridor, looking into each room. Who was with Thérèse when Brataille appeared, and where is he now? Every room is an inferno. Halfway along he finds a closed door, a silver number 8 glinting in the light of the flames. The frame has been smashed where the lock is, but when Guillaume puts his shoulder against the door and shoves, it just opens a fraction, and then hits something heavy. He pushes as hard as he can, but it will not yield further. He peers through the crack. This room, too, is ablaze. All of the other doors have been left open, hastily abandoned by their occupants as they fled.

"Hello?" yells Guillaume into the smoke and flames. "Hello?"

There is no response.

He stumbles to the end of the corridor. The other rooms are all empty. By now the fire is all around him. He runs back toward the stairs, as quickly as his straining lungs will allow. As he pounds down the staircase, one of the steps disintegrates beneath his weight. His foot is swallowed by the wood, and he loses his balance. He tumbles the rest of the way down, falling through the velvet curtain and landing in a heap on the floor of the club. He can see figures moving on the far side of the room. The smoke is deep inside his body now, filling his lungs, acrid and poisonous. He heads toward the stage, looking for the exit.

Sure enough, behind the stage there is an open door. He tears through it, his chest bursting, and gratefully gulps down the fresh night air. Around him, the musicians are milling about, shaking their heads, watching the building burn.

He scans the crowd for Suzanne.

She is not there.

The crowd spills out into the street, and finally Camille is on Rue des Abbesses. A metal sign swings in the night breeze above the entrance to the club: a white cat standing on a rooftop in the moonlight, its back arched in a languorous feline stretch. A fire truck arrives, and a posse of men hurries into the building. She looks up. The fire is clearly visible from the second-floor windows. There is now a sizable crowd in the street—not just the refugees from the club, but also residents who have emerged from their homes to watch the conflagration.

Let it burn, thinks Camille.

Finally, the notebook will be incinerated, just like its thirty-one brothers and sisters, and just as Monsieur Proust intended all along.

Camille takes her scarf out of her bag and pulls it over her head.

At last her secret is safe.

All around him people are coughing, crying, and clutching each other in relief. Jean-Paul limps through the crowd and looks up into the sky.

He is tired. He is leg is hurting, and he wants to go home. He should have known better than to come here, he thinks ruefully. These Americans only ever look out for themselves. What a fool, to imagine that Ernest Hemingway might help him! Jean-Paul does not need his story published, anyway. He wrote it for himself, and nobody else. He looks down fondly at his notebook, and then he stops walking.

Something is not quite right.

He opens the black leather covers and stares down at the neat lines that span the page. He flicks through the notebook, baffled. The words are not his. The handwriting is not his. It's as if someone has performed an elaborate conjuring trick. Where has his story gone? Where is Elodie? He turns and looks back at the burning building, and is baptized by fresh sorrow.

At the front of the notebook there is a loose sheet of paper. It's a piece of hotel stationery. Jean-Paul examines it in the dim light of a nearby streetlamp.

The hotel is on Rue des Canettes.

Guillaume walks the streets. There are small groups of people huddled on each corner, reluctant to return to their beds after such excitement. He looks at each person, but does not see the face he is hoping to see.

Suzanne has not waited for him.

He looks at his watch. Le Miroir's goons will have discovered his escape hours ago. He imagines the rat-faced man's fury, and Claude's silent gloating. Arnaud the giant will be trying to hide his disappointment that he won't be meeting Gertrude Stein, after all.

They will be watching for him now.

Guillaume plunges his hands into his pockets. There will be no trains to the west coast until the morning. He has the rest of the night ahead of him. He turns up the collar on his coat, and sets off across the city. He is going to walk to the train station.

He shakes his head. Montparnasse at last.

Camille Clermont walks away from Le Chat Blanc. The night air is cool on her face. She wanders along the narrow cobbled streets of Montmartre, lost in a memory.

That evening, nine years ago, after the Easter service at the Église Saint-Gervais.

After the bomb fell.

Olivier was in the choir.

He appeared at the door of the kitchen, covered in dust and debris, his face streaked with dirt. He held a baby in his arms.

I found her in the rubble, he said.

For two days they fed her, rocked her, sang her to sleep. They agreed that they would return her to the authorities after the Easter weekend.

Monday came, then Tuesday, then Wednesday.

Camille could not tear her eyes away from the child. Olivier watched his wife as she stared down at the baby, her body stilled by longing.

Thursday, Friday.

They called her Marie.

42

Morning

"MARIE!"

Camille stands in the lobby of the hotel, hands on hips. Moments later she hears footsteps patter down the staircase. She sees her daughter, pretty in a dark green pinafore, and her heart performs a small somersault.

"*Oui, maman?*"

"We have work to do," says Camille. The breakfast service is well under way in the dining room. Berthe is pouring coffee and taking orders. Some guests have already eaten and are getting ready to leave for the day. Camille looks around the place with a critical eye. She takes one day off, and there is dust everywhere. She points to the reception desk. "Why don't you sit there? I'll bring you the silver we never got around to cleaning yesterday. You can work on that, and you can take people's room keys when they leave. You remember how to hang them up on the hooks?"

Marie nods. She likes to watch the hotel guests come and go. She fetches two extra cushions, so she'll be able to see everything that's going on. She clambers up onto the chair.

"Ah, look at you, Marie! All ready for business, I see!" Olivier walks in, a big smile on his face. "She's a natural, eh, Camille? Before we know it she'll be running this place."

Camille takes her husband's hand and gives it a squeeze. He looks down at her and grins. He does not understand how much she has to be grateful for, and with luck, he never will.

She has not told Olivier what happened at Le Chat Blanc last night. She has not told him that she found the notebook, or that it has now finally been destroyed. She can see no good reason to enlighten him. He need never know how close they have sailed to disaster.

When she returned to the hotel, Olivier was both magnanimous and smug, and still not remotely apologetic about what he had done. Camille was too relieved to feel especially irritated. She climbed into their bed and they held each other close. Marie was fast asleep in the next room. My family, she thought.

Now she places a drawer full of knives and forks on the reception desk in front of her daughter. Marie sits up straight. She enjoys polishing the silver. She likes how the tarnish vanishes beneath the rub of the cloth, leaving everything looking perfectly new. Camille watches as she sets to work. She looks so prim and proper, perched behind the desk. Marie looks up and grins at her mother.

The notebook has gone for good, thinks Camille.

Everything looks perfectly new.

Jean-Paul Maillard suppresses a yawn as he walks slowly along Rue Saint-Sulpice. He has not slept well. The night was spent tossing and turning, restless with regret.

He does not understand how he left Le Chat Blanc with the wrong notebook under his arm.

His own will be ashes now.

Elodie has disappeared for good.

He nearly threw the other notebook away when he realized what had happened, but his own loss gave him pause. The hotel stationery he found tucked inside its pages is the only clue he has as to its provenance. Perhaps the management will be able to find its rightful owner. He has not read a word of it. He does not care whose pen has filled its pages.

It's another beautiful day in Paris. Jean-Paul turns onto Rue des Canettes. He pauses for a moment in front of the hotel to check he has the
right address.

He pushes open the front door and steps inside.

Acknowledgments

When *A Good American* was published in 2012, I used to tell a story about how a hotshot editor in New York read an early draft of the manuscript and rejected it. A year later, after I had rewritten half the novel, my agent somehow persuaded the same hotshot editor to read the book again, at which point she bought it. Then she made me rewrite the *other* half. This story will come as no surprise to anyone who knows Amy Einhorn. She sends me back to my desk to revise and rework, time and time again, until things are exactly right. For such editors, writers should be eternally grateful; I know I am. It has been a joy to move to Flatiron Books and work with Amy again on *The Paris Hours*. And, once again, she has pushed and prodded and inspired me to make the best of this book, and I could not be more grateful to her. My thanks to everyone else on the brilliant team at Flatiron, including Marlena Bittner, Cristina Gilbert, Bob Miller, Conor Mintzer, Caroline Bleeke, Amelia Possanza, Nancy Trypuc, Katherine Turro, and Julianna Lee.

As always, Emma Sweeney in New York and Andrew Gordon in London have advised and guided me with skill and assurance.

I'm eternally grateful to my oh-so-smart and generous early readers:

Pamela Klinger-Horn, Bibi Prival, Allison Smythe, Alexandra Socarides, and Stephanie Williams.

Only now that I've become a bookseller myself have I really begun to understand the devotion and smarts that are needed to succeed at what is simultaneously a quixotic and utterly necessary undertaking. Make no mistake, booksellers are superheroes. Every last one of them deserves a cape and their own Marvel franchise, and I thank and celebrate all of them. I am so proud and happy to have joined their ranks. In particular, I'm grateful to my business partner, Carrie Koepke. I never would have dreamed of opening Skylark Bookshop without her. Thank you for all of it, Carrie. And thanks and love to our amazing team at Skylark: Becky Reed, Carol Putnam, Beth Shapiro, Faramola Shonekan, Erin Regneri, and Chris Talley.

P. G. Wodehouse once dedicated a book to his daughter, Leonora, "without whose never-failing sympathy and encouragement this book would have been finished in half the time." Families can be like that sometimes, and thank heavens. To Alexandra Socarides and our children—Hallam, Catherine, Archer, and Nate—I offer up all my love and thanks. I could not wish for a better distraction.

Author's Note

One of the joys of writing novels is all the travel. Not actual travel, mind you, but the journeys you get to take in your imagination. While I was writing my last book, *Setting Free the Kites,* I spent countless hours on the coast of Maine, even while I was stuck in landlocked Missouri. So it was with *The Paris Hours.* For the last few years I've had a lovely time strolling up and down the boulevards of Paris without ever leaving my desk. (Added bonus: no jet lag.)

It helps that I know the place well. I went to boarding school there when I was thirteen years old. Ten years later I returned, this time working as an attorney for an international law firm. When I sat down to write this book, it was a joy to revisit some of my old haunts.

But writing about Paris is not without its challenges. After all, there are already more books and movies set in the French capital than there are croissants in the city's boulangeries. The symbol of Paris is the most recognizable architectural structure on the planet. So how to tell a story that offered a fresh perspective?

First, I set the novel on the streets and in the parks where real Parisians live and work, away from all those famous tourist attractions. (In all the time I lived there, I never once visited the Eiffel Tower.) Second, I chose to set my story in 1927. Back then the city was in a postwar explosion of creative brilliance, populated by an army of geniuses whose artistic legacies survive to this day. Finally, and perhaps counterintuitively, I resisted the allure of all that celebrity. Some of those characters appear in the book, but by design they exist on the periphery of the novel, not at its heart. As a writer I am subject to my own preoccupations, and I am drawn to quieter stories. And so I redrew the focus away from all that dazzling genius. My four protagonists had their own tales to tell.

On the subject of dazzling genius, a brief word about the tune that appears at various points throughout the novel. *Passacaille* is the third movement of Maurice Ravel's Piano Trio, which is, for me, one of the most sublimely beautiful pieces of music ever written. Performed as intended, you will hear not only a piano, but also a cello and a violin. I reimagined the music as a solo piano piece, although I've never heard it played that way.

The character of Camille Clermont is based in large part upon Marcel Proust's real maid, Céleste Albaret—but this novel is not, and is not intended to be, an accurate representation of Céleste's life. While I have used some of her biographical details, I have also taken substantial liberties with ascertainable facts. For example, to the best of my knowledge Céleste's devotion to Marcel Proust was absolute and unwavering, both during his life and afterward. But when I read that she burned all of his notebooks at his request, the novelist in me immediately began to wonder what would have happened if she hadn't followed his orders to the letter. And, with that one small question, this journey began.

About the Author

A native of England, ALEX GEORGE read law at Oxford University and worked for eight years as a corporate lawyer in London and Paris. He has lived in the Midwest of the United States for the last sixteen years. He is the founder and director of the Unbound Book Festival and the owner of Skylark Bookshop, an independent bookstore in downtown Columbia, Missouri.